# THE ONE NIGHT STAND

L.H. STACEY

Boldwood

First published in Great Britain in 2026 by Boldwood Books Ltd.

Cover Design by Aaron Munday

Cover Images: Shutterstock

A CIP catalogue record for this book is available from the British Library.

Paperback ISBN 978-1-78513-869-0

Large Print ISBN 978-1-78513-870-6

Hardback ISBN 978-1-78513-868-3

Trade Paperback ISBN 978-1-80656-150-6

Ebook ISBN 978-1-78513-871-3

Kindle ISBN 978-1-78513-872-0

Audio CD ISBN 978-1-78513-863-8

MP3 CD ISBN 978-1-78513-864-5

Digital audio download ISBN 978-1-78513-867-6

This book is printed on certified sustainable paper. Boldwood Books is dedicated to putting sustainability at the heart of our business. For more information please visit https://www.boldwoodbooks.com/about-us/sustainability/

Boldwood Books Ltd, 23 Bowerdean Street, London, SW6 3TN

www.boldwoodbooks.com

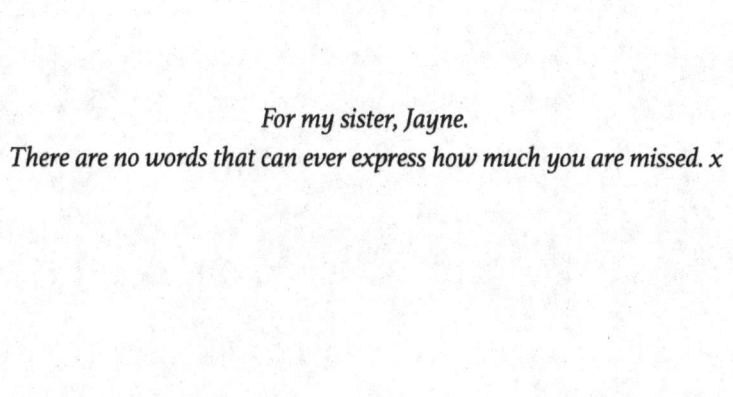

*For my sister, Jayne.*
*There are no words that can ever express how much you are missed. x*

# 1

## DAISY

*October*

'Sarah, listen to me.' Impatiently, Daisy Bailey moved to the edge of her seat and, conscious that the Uber driver was homing in on every word she said, she pressed her phone against her ear and stared out of the window, while travelling down what felt like every street in London. 'I arrived at the Leonardo earlier and...' She paused thoughtfully and turned her gaze to the roof of the car. Before making the call, she'd fully intended telling Sarah all about her day and how it had started. About the chance meeting she'd had and how she hoped the day would end. It was a feeling she hadn't felt for a very long time, and for just a few seconds she closed her eyes and took pleasure in the swarm of butterflies that fluttered in her stomach.

'And...?' Sarah questioned. 'You said that you'd arrived at the Leonardo earlier and... so... and what?'

Daisy sighed and caught the eye of the driver through the rear-view mirror. He was still listening. He too was waiting for a response, and nervously Daisy leaned forward to fiddle with the strap on her stilettos. They were high, bright red and she wished she'd worn something different. Something she could walk in.

'Yes, sorry. I was just going to say that the room is beautiful and that if I look very carefully, stand on one foot and lean to one side with my face pressed tightly against the window, I can just about see the Tower of London.' She tipped her head to one side and gave the driver a wry but mischievous smile knowing that he'd been waiting for her to say something a little more juicy, or something that was certainly a lot more interesting.

'Mmm, even for you, Daisy, that wasn't convincing,' Sarah threw back in response. 'So, you can either tell me what you're up to. Or, maybe, just maybe I'll catch the next train to London and let myself into this so-called hotel room.' She paused and giggled. 'And then, I'll see for myself what you're up to and who you've got secretly stowed under your bed.'

Unsure of how to answer, Daisy stared out of the window and up at the London Eye that stood impressively by the side of the Thames, illuminating the dark winter skyline. Intermittent flashing lights came from inside the large oval carriages, and she smiled at the thought of the constant stream of photographs that were being captured, creating lasting memories for all the people lucky enough to be standing inside.

'Sarah,' she finally answered, 'you're not coming to London. The last thing I need is you turning up. Besides, we have a business. It doesn't run itself, and when I'm away I need for you to be there. But as well as that, I do need a favour.' She paused as she nervously bit down on her lip.

'Go on...'

'I need to go off grid. It won't be for long. Just for an hour or two. So if Cole notices and he calls you, you haven't heard from me. I haven't called you and you have no idea where I've gone.'

'What makes you think Cole would believe me?' Sarah ques-

tioned with a loud laugh. In the background, Daisy could hear
the sound of a car door slamming. An engine was started, and a
familiar echo could be heard as the phone went from handset to
Bluetooth.

'Sarah, of course he'd believe you. You're the best actress in
the world and if anyone can fool Cole better than I can, it's you.' It
was true. Since Sarah had met Daisy's husband, Cole, twelve
years ago, she'd always been able to twist him around her finger,
and with Cole being an only child, he'd relished in the act of
finally becoming an older brother.

'No. I'm not having that. Cole knows we speak at least a
hundred times a day. He'd know I was lying. Besides, we always
tell each other everything. He isn't stupid, and without a doubt
he'd know I was covering for you.'

Closing her eyes against the bright city lights, Daisy considered what Sarah had said. It was true; she and Sarah had always
told each other everything... until now. With a sudden burst of
emotion filling her eyes, Daisy reached into her bag, pulled out a
tissue and dabbed carefully at her eye line. Every part of her
wanted to tell her sister what she was doing, but she couldn't.
This was something that Sarah would never condone, damn it; it
was something that Daisy wouldn't have condoned herself, not
until that morning. Now, because of what had happened, Daisy
knew that she couldn't share this secret, not even with her sister.

Holding her phone up in front of her face, Daisy swiped at the
screen, went into the Uber app and tapped to leave the driver a
generous tip.

'Why don't you phone Cole now, get it over with. After you've
spoken to him, it won't occur to him to call you later and then...
well then, you can go back to doing whatever it is you're up to.'
There was a pause, a beeping of a horn followed by the sound of
Sarah cursing. 'You damn idiot, it's a one-way street and you're

driving the wrong way down it so, that's right, turn the damn car round.'

'Do you know what,' Daisy said sarcastically, ignoring Sarah's all too common outburst, 'why didn't I think of that? But the truth is, Cole's been busy. He's always away on site, hardly ever comes home and, wherever he is, he barely ever has any signal. When I do get to speak to him, the noise in the background is loud and unbearable and I am not sitting in an Uber and screaming my head off just so Cole can hear me.' She tipped her head from side to side, thought about sending Cole a message instead.

'So, are you going to tell me what you're up to, or do I need to catch that train?'

Closing her eyes for a beat, Daisy took in a deep breath. 'I'm not up to anything,' she lied. 'I've been to a couple of business meetings today, the ones you'll have seen in the diary at work, but while I'm here I want to try and organise a surprise for Cole. Which is why I can't tell you what I'm up to.'

'Urgh, what is it with you two and all the surprises,' Sarah threw back. 'Actually, forget I said that.'

Tipping her head to one side, Daisy looked over the driver's shoulder. There was a queue of traffic ahead, no doubt caused by commuters trying to get in and out of the city.

'Sarah don't panic. I've known for a while he's up to something.' She paused, and rolled her jaw. 'When he is home, Cole's always trawling through stuff on the internet and I've overheard so many hushed phone calls, I've started walking down the garden just to get out of the way. I've started to relish the nights Cole is away because at least then I don't have to feel so damned awkward in my own house.'

It was true; Daisy had actually begun to prefer the nights when she could stay home alone, sit in the half-light and watch the sunsets. Being able to see the sea, the beach and the island of

Lindisfarne from her very own home had been her ultimate dream. A dream that had only become possible after her mother's death – a bittersweet gift bought with the inheritance she'd left behind. Now each time she walked through the door of her beloved home, she felt as though her mum were giving her the biggest and most protective hug.

The car came to a stop and as she pushed the door open, Daisy gave the driver a cursory nod, followed by what she hoped was a genuine smile. 'Sarah, I have to go. I just wanted one person in the world to know where I was, you know, just in case.'

'Just in case what? Are you in some sort of trouble?'

Lifting her oversized handbag on to her shoulder, Daisy took a step forward and with the phone still held in her hand she gasped in horror as her foot suddenly became cold and wet, as the sickening feeling of slime slopped around her ankle. 'Jesus Christ, what the hell?'

'What happened?' Sarah demanded.

'Uber driver, he just pulled up next to the biggest blocked drain in the world and I'm now ankle deep in... urgh... I don't want to think about it, it smells awful.' She paused, then cringed and hopped the short distance between the car and the pavement. 'And oh, for God's sake, my red suede stilettos are ruined. Absolutely ruined.' She lifted her foot in disgust and felt her bottom lip begin to tremble with emotion.

'You're wearing stilettos?'

'Thanks for that,' Daisy bellowed over her shoulder at the driver, and with the car door still wide open, she waved her phone in the air. 'I've a good mind to rescind your damn tip.' She took another step back and through fixed, narrowed eyes she glared with amusement while the driver had no choice but to walk around the car and through the water to close the door.

'Daisy, why the hell are you wearing stilettos? You hardly ever wear anything but trainers.'

'Can't a girl dress up?'

'Mmm not you. There's something wrong. You need to come home.'

Looking down at her foot, Daisy sighed. 'Look, I'm going to have to go. I'll call you later.'

After listening to the normal round of 'I love you's, and the reminder that Sarah was about to go out on a date, Daisy turned her phone to silent. She didn't want to be disturbed, and she pushed her phone into her jacket pocket and began to walk the short distance between the road and the bar. With every step, her shoe squelched and her repulsion grew until eventually she pulled a tissue out of her bag, knelt down, and dabbed angrily at her wet, smelly ankle.

'They're ruined,' she growled out loud as she swiped at the shoe and watched as small shreds of tissue bobbled on its surface. Frustrated that Sarah had been right, and that they most probably were the only decent pair of shoes she owned, she felt a single tear drop on to her cheek and a sob became caught in her throat. The good and productive day she'd been having had suddenly gone badly wrong; however, with a determination to turn it around, Daisy stood up straight, pushed her foot back into her shoe and cringed internally as the squelching continued.

It wouldn't have been so bad if the water hadn't smelt. If the odour hadn't lingered. And if she could walk in the shoes to begin with. 'I knew these shoes were a bad idea,' she grumbled under her breath as she wobbled precariously, and in an attempt to gain her composure, she stopped walking and leaned heavily against a shop window.

Looking through the window at the vast array of brightly coloured candles, she smiled appreciatively. They surrounded picture frames, ornaments and driftwood objects to create a striking display, and Daisy had to admit it was the type of shop she'd always liked and considered going inside just as she spotted a tall, oblong mirror. It was partly hidden by a large piece of driftwood, but Daisy homed in on the intricate mother-of-pearl edging that poked out from behind. It reminded her of a mirror her mum had once owned and as she moved closer to gain a better view, she caught sight of her reflection and the dress she was wearing. It had been the only dress she'd brought with her, one she'd thrown in her suitcase but hadn't really intended to wear, not in a city where everyone seemed to dress for comfort. And now she wished she'd worn something different. On reflection, the neckline was too low. It showed too much cleavage. The skirt was too short, and the frilly edge looked much too girly. Irritated by her own stupidity, Daisy pulled her phone from her pocket, looked at the screen and considered her options. She could go back to the hotel and rethink her outfit, which would have been a possibility if she'd brought an abundant amount of clothing with her. But other than the suit she'd worn for her meetings, her options were nothing more than a range of jeans and jumpers. No, this would have to do, and with a reluctant sigh and a newfound enthusiasm she set off to walk down a street that was busy with commuters.

But her enthusiasm waned when she rounded the corner to see that the nice quiet bar she'd been expecting to find was no longer there. In its place was a building covered in bright, luminous signage that shone out in the darkness. Daisy clutched her handbag tightly and stared up at the building as the door swung open, and the sound of loud music flooded outside.

It was a moment of panic that made her want to turn around and run. She flicked at the screen on her phone and was just about to cancel the meet-up when she spotted the message that had appeared on her screen.

TOM

I can't wait to see you x

Reading the words, Daisy couldn't help but acknowledge that her growing sense of terror was also mixed with excitement. Her mouth had gone dry. She could barely swallow, and she could feel the way her heart pounded with a ferocity she hadn't felt for too long. She felt a sudden urge to phone Sarah back and ask her advice, but she knew that she couldn't.

Even to Daisy, the chance meeting she'd had this morning on a crowded train with her ex-fiancé, Tom, sounded improbable. As she'd looked up from her laptop, he'd been there, sitting directly opposite. The initial shock and awkwardness between them had quickly turned into an easy flowing conversation. One that had resulted in both of them agreeing to meet. 'It's just a drink,' she kept telling herself, 'just a drink with an old friend.' She took in a deep breath, tried to imagine how Cole would feel if she told him what she was doing, but couldn't. Meeting Tom would be something he'd never understand, and even though she knew how much it would hurt him if he ever found out, she still really wanted to go – more than anything, she really wanted to know about all the things that had happened since they'd last been together, twelve years before.

'Just go inside,' she whispered. 'Say hi to Tom. I mean, what could it hurt?' The words were a challenge. A challenge she really shouldn't take. Deep down, Daisy couldn't even remember whether or not she'd told Tom that she was married. That she was still with the man who'd divided their relationship all those years before, following a moment's weakness on her part.

TOM

Hey, where are you?

The text from Tom appeared on her phone and broke into her thoughts. Nervously, she began to tap her stiletto-clad foot against the edge of the pavement. Bobbles of tissue still covered its surface, and with a lump rising and falling in her throat she blinked away the tears that were threatening to fall.

'He doesn't know that you're married,' she mouthed as she took a step backwards, bumped into a commuter who was busily looking down at his phone, and whispered a quickly mumbled apology. 'You should have told him. You should have got that in first before you agreed to meet him.' She swallowed hard and stared longingly at the door to the bar. As it opened and closed, she heard the small blasts of music and hesitantly bit down on her lip and pulled in a deep breath. Tom was in there. He was right here, in London. And right now he was waiting inside, which was why she'd already talked herself into walking straight past the crowd that had congregated in the doorway.

Walking across that threshold could easily change everything, and although her mind was conflicted with emotions, Daisy's stomach began to somersault with excitement at the thought of seeing Tom again. He'd been the first man she'd loved. The man she'd always thought she'd marry, and seeing him again that morning had brought back a rush of memories. Now, her eyes flicked between the bar and her phone, and she stared at the screen and at the question he'd asked, and for a few short moments she had no idea how she was going to answer.

# 2

## DAISY

'Excuse me—' she said as loudly as she could. 'Excuse me, if I could just...' Standing on her tiptoes, she began to inch forward. Her normal confident stride had become nothing more than a shuffle. Her voice was going unheard, and after getting into the main part of the bar she found herself surrounded by a mixture of darkness and strobe lights, which made her feel practically invisible.

'Seriously, I really need to get past you!' she yelled. 'If I could just—' Swallowing hard, Daisy quickly realised that if she was ever going to squeeze intimately past at least a hundred other people that she'd never previously met she had no choice but to push herself forward. Which she'd have felt much happier about if she'd been just a little bit taller, broader and wearing shoes she could walk in.

Standing shoulder to shoulder with so many strangers, Daisy began to regret coming into a bar like this one. She found herself recoiling nervously every time a pair of arms swooped towards her, especially when the continuous clink of glasses made her flinch. The glasses were much too close to her face and she found herself moving around the edge of the room where she felt more protected by the walls. Walking through a bar like this one was something she rarely ever did – even with Cole. It was a very different atmosphere to any of the bars they had in Northumberland, and with every step she took across the dark, sticky carpet, she felt the intensity build, the trembling increase and her curiosity grow.

'Keep going,' she whispered to herself. 'Just find Tom, say what you need to say and...' She paused momentarily and closed her eyes as she took long, slow breaths. 'And say what? Say that you shouldn't have come, say that you don't want to see him...' She opened her eyes and began to look from one face in the crowd to another. 'Well, that'd be a lie, wouldn't it, because you do want to see him.'

Once again, her conscience played with her mind. She'd once loved Tom with every single heartbeat. They'd grown up living on neighbouring streets and in their teenage years they'd been practically inseparable, until she'd met Cole and everything had changed.

'I'm looking for a house,' Cole had said as he'd walked into Harbour Estates and Lettings, a business that had been owned by her mother, where Daisy had worked every weekend. He'd sat down with a playful sparkle in his eye and had chatted about the kind of house he'd wanted to buy. He'd had a shortlist. The house had to have a cosy feeling, with a kitchen big enough to form a central hub. Being a builder by trade, he wanted the opportunity to extend in the hope that, sometime soon, he'd meet someone special. Being an only child, he'd grown up craving everything he'd missed – most of all, a big family of his own.

Daisy had found herself nodding in all the right places. Everything he wanted was what she'd wanted too, and she'd become enchanted by the way he'd spoken about the perfect family lifestyle he'd wanted to create. By the end of the afternoon, Daisy had agreed to show Cole around three different houses, where the initial light-hearted banter had turned into an intensity that had been almost palpable.

'If you were going to live in one of these houses,' he'd asked as they walked around the last of the three houses they'd looked at, 'if you were to choose, which one would it be? Because, do you know what, it's suddenly very important to me that you like it.'

'Oh, I'm not sure you should buy a house based on my decision,' Daisy had muttered, nervously. 'It all depends on what you want from the house, doesn't it? I mean, some people want a house that would suit them now, but others want a house that they could grow into and would suit them for years.' She'd tried to look everywhere else in the room but at him and she'd lifted a hand to the light switch. She'd had every intention of turning it on but as she went to flick the switch, she'd felt her hand connect with his. Almost immediately, their fingers had quickly become entwined and with a determination that was filled with sexual chemistry, he'd pulled her towards him.

'Right now,' he'd whispered breathlessly, 'I'm kind of thinking that the next decision you make will be the most important decision of your life...' Holding her tightly against his body, Cole had run a fingertip playfully across her shoulder until he came to the crook of her neck, where he rested his fingers just below her chin before saying, 'And I'm not talking about which house we might want to live in.'

The passion along with the gathering darkness had surrounded them both. The intensity of the moment had increased, and Cole had made her all the promises she'd wanted to hear. Becoming completely lost in the moment, Daisy had found herself struggling with her conscience. Thoughts of being with Cole had taken over her mind and even though after that day she barely ever saw him in person, she'd taken great pleasure in the constant stream of gifts that had arrived for her. Flowers had been delivered as a weekly treat. More often than not, there would be chocolates with them, interspersed with scented candles, and on a couple of occasions he'd sent the most beautiful handbags. The purchase of the house Daisy had liked the most had quickly gone through, and the moment he'd picked up the keys he'd invited her to join him for a dinner. An invitation she'd happily accepted.

Since the moment she'd met Cole, Daisy had found herself creating a distance between her and Tom. The guilt of kissing Cole had scalded her lips, and just a few days after the dinner invitation, Daisy had ended the relationship with Tom, in favour of Cole.

'Why did you come?' she whispered to herself again as she inched through the crowd, spotted a half empty beer bottle and, without thinking, picked it up, downed the contents and cringed as the sour taste hit the back of her throat. *What is it you want to know? Do you want to know if Tom still loves you? Do you have some unfinished business that you want to take care of? Or are you still trying to work out whether or not you made a mistake? Did you choose the wrong man? And if you had chosen Tom, would you now have that family you'd craved?* The thoughts spun around her mind and Daisy began to wonder what her life would have been like if only her head hadn't been turned and she and Tom had stayed together.

Turning to the bar, Daisy ran her eyes across the optics and wondered if she'd dare buy a drink. It was something she wouldn't have normally done. Her going into a bar was something that Cole wouldn't have liked but she needed the alcohol; she needed to numb her senses. And Cole wasn't there.

'Large neat Hendricks, please,' she shouted to the barman,

who picked up a glass to make her drink. With her eyes on him, she glanced up and into the mirrors that were positioned right behind the optics. Through them, she could just about see the crowd of people behind her, and she tried to scan the faces while looking for Tom. When the drink hit the counter in front of her, she immediately picked it up, lifted it up to her lips and inhaled. Her whole body buzzed with excitement. Then, in a single, swift movement, she drank the shot in one go. The alcohol ran down her throat, and as her heart raced she took pleasure in the burn that followed.

With the burning still there, Daisy paid for the drink and dodged to one side as a group of women all dressed in hen night T-shirts and bright pink fluffy boas danced their way past. It was a sight that made her laugh until a memory of her own hen night flashed through her mind. She'd been having fun with the girls, but Cole had turned up with a look of disappointment crossing his face and the dancing had stopped. But tonight Cole wasn't there, and with a newfound confidence from the alcohol, Daisy began to move rhythmically through the room to the sound of Gloria Gaynor's voice. It blasted out from the speakers making Daisy giggle as a few hundred people enthusiastically joined in with the chorus.

Holding on to a chipped dark wood table, Daisy slowly looked around the crowd, from one face to another, still looking for Tom, but each person blended with the next, and their faces swam in the strobe lights. With her phone held tightly in her hand, she tried to focus on the screen knowing that Tom was here somewhere in this bar and right now, right at that moment, she knew that he was probably watching her from afar, and in her frustration, Daisy began to tap out a message. Then watched the screen intently in the hope that the three small dots would appear to show that Tom would respond.

'I'm warning you, Tom. I will leave,' she said through gritted teeth and a little more loudly than she'd intended just as a hand dropped on to her shoulder, making her jump until the hand squeezed her gently in a way that created a tingling sensation that moved slowly through her.

'Hey, stop panicking. I'm right here.' Sidling up behind her, Tom leaned in so close she could feel his breath on her cheek. His whole body was pressed against her and with his fingers still massaging her shoulder, she suddenly found herself catching her breath. He was much too close. The temptation to turn and fall into his arms was too strong, and with a determined effort to move out of his grasp, she spun around and gave him a stern but welcoming smile.

'Well, you're lucky I'm still here.' Daisy folded her arms defensively across her body, and gave him a smile. 'I was just about to leave, and I would have but the hen party was keeping me amused.'

'I can barely hear you,' he said as he moved in closer, 'but here, I bought you a drink.' Holding a bottle of beer out towards her, Tom waved it back and forth like a slow-moving pendulum, and with deep, dark eyes that danced in the strobe lights, he returned her smile.

'Ah, okay then.' She laughed, grabbed at the bottle and lifted it straight to her lips. 'Then maybe, I'll forgive you...' She ran her eyes up and down his body nervously, until once again their gaze met. She felt as though she should say something funny to break the tension as a way of showing him that this was definitely not the first date of many. 'Do you know what, I'd say you're taller than I remember,' she finally said and nodded appreciatively. It was all she could think to say but the words had obviously amused him, and Daisy held her breath, waiting for the retort that she knew would come.

'Really?' he replied. 'So you think I've grown taller since this morning?' He sipped at his drink and in a friendly, familiar way he hooked his arm around the back of her neck, pulled her towards him and gently dropped a kiss on the top of her head. 'You are funny, Daisy, and my God, I've really missed that.'

Pulling away, Daisy drained the bottle before stepping to one side and allowing her gaze to take in the sight of Tom's well-cut jeans. They hugged him in all the right places, as did his white linen shirt, and as a surge in the crowd pushed her forward, she was pressed against him. She rested a hand against his chest to stop her from falling and beneath his shirt she felt a firm, well-toned body. For a moment, Daisy could easily imagine that the room had cleared, that they were no longer being tussled by the enthusiastic dancing of others – and that suddenly, they were both totally alone.

'Do you like what you see?' Tom asked, as he pulled her back into his hold. His expression had turned more serious, his eyes now intense and searching.

'Tom, I never stopped liking you.' Slowly she lifted her fingers up to his face and playfully ran them though his closely trimmed beard and then through his hair. 'Your hair,' she said, while staring at the grown-up version of the boy she'd known. 'I like it this way... I noticed how good it looked on the train but...' She paused as she looked into his eyes to see the way they danced magically.

Feeling the colour rise to her cheeks, Daisy looked over her shoulder. The silence she'd initially imagined had gone; now she felt acutely aware of the people around her. A group of women were dancing a little too closely, men jostled for position at the bar and everyone pushed past in an effort to find a small space for themselves on the dancefloor.

Without saying a word, Tom lifted a hand to her face. His

fingers gently traced her jawline, and slowly he manoeuvred them both into an area away from the others, where they could stand together without being jostled, and suddenly Daisy felt her breathing accelerate.

'And yes,' Tom said, 'Like it or not, I am going to kiss you.' Just as he had all those years before, he lowered his mouth and tenderly grazed her lips with his own. 'I've wanted to do this for a very long time.' A half-smile crossed his face. 'And I've waited, and I've waited and now...'

'Tom, please...' Lowering her eyes Daisy wanted to tell him to stop, that being here with him wasn't the best of ideas, but instead she found herself deepening the kiss and wanting him more until a shudder ran through her. It was a moment of bliss that turned into a breathless flash of panic as feelings of guilt outweighed the pleasure. All she could see was history repeating itself. And as usual, she was the cause. 'I'm so sorry,' she uttered, as her hand went up to her mouth. 'I shouldn't have come; I shouldn't have let you do that... My God, I shouldn't have kissed you.'

Pausing, Tom took a step backwards. He bowed his head apologetically and lifted his hands in the air. 'Daisy, I'm sorry, all right?' He pressed a hand angrily against the top of his head. 'Actually, do you know what, I don't know why I'm apologising. Because I'm not sorry. I've missed you; damn it, Daisy, I've missed *us*.' He looked up, and then more gently he lifted his fingers to touch her cheek and brushed away a curl that had escaped from the others. 'And half of me is sorry that I've obviously upset you but the other half...'

'It's been twelve years,' she whispered. 'Twelve years and...' Lifting her fingers to her mouth, Daisy traced the spot where Tom's lips had been. Looking up, she was surprised to see fear in his eyes. He looked terrified of what she'd say or do next, and, in her heart, she knew that whatever she did or didn't do would hurt him. She bit down on her lip and felt it quiver with emotion. 'We can't. You know that don't you...?' Alcohol had always made Daisy do unpredictable things and tonight was no exception. Hesitantly, she wondered whether or not she'd have allowed Tom to kiss her if she'd been totally sober.

'You're right. We shouldn't.' Once again, Tom moved forward. His mouth was hovering right above hers, his face so close that Daisy could feel his breath on her lips. The smell of his after-shave infiltrated her senses, and she couldn't help but take long, deep intakes of breaths. 'But I want to,' he added, tipping her chin upwards with a finger and smiling. 'I want to kiss you, over and over...' He dropped multiple light, tender kisses on to her lips in a playful manner.

Unable to pull away, Daisy studied Tom. His was a face she'd known so well, and she homed in on the tiny scar above his left eyebrow. An argument with a lamppost following a fair amount of alcohol had resulted in a night in the A & E department. With a half-smile, she lifted a hand and ran a finger across the line. 'This is another reason why we shouldn't drink. We become irresponsible and dangerous.'

'Which brings me to my next question.' He looked over his shoulder at the bar, where the crowd now stood three deep. 'Do you want another drink, because I think we need one, or...' He stared into her eyes in a way that pierced her soul and for a moment she wanted to run for the exit knowing that whatever she said next would determine the rest of the evening – and possibly her future.

'Have you really missed me?' she blurted out without thinking, then quickly added, 'No. Don't answer.' She held a finger up to his lips. 'Don't tell me, because...' She shook her head, felt his arms encircle her body. 'Because no matter how much I want to know, there's nothing I can do about it, Tom. I'm married. I married Cole, you do know that, don't you?'

'I don't care...' he quickly cut in as he lowered his mouth to meet hers, and within seconds the hustle and bustle of the bar disappeared, everything and everyone becoming distant. She felt as though they were the only ones in the room, and with her heart beating rapidly she welcomed his tongue as it teased and flicked against hers. It was a moment of pure pleasure that was accentuated by the feel of his body pressing against her. 'He took you away from me and now...' He suddenly dropped his arms, took a step back and held his arms outward as though in question. '...I want you back. You were mine first, Daisy. You were mine before you were his and I'm not going to lie, I don't feel any guilt for wanting you and what we once had.'

Confused by her own emotions, Daisy lifted a hand to her hair nervously. Tossing it backwards, she gave him a small smile. She had to admit that Tom had been on her mind for the past twelve years, too. In her eyes, he'd always been the one that got away, even though she had been the one to cast him aside. She knew that the right thing to do was consider her husband, be the wife she'd promised to be. The wife he *deserved*. After all, she'd married for life, hadn't she? There were no grey areas, and hadn't been, certainly not on her part. Not until today, when she found herself battling with her own wants and her needs, knowing that both territories were fraught with danger.

'*This*...' she finally breathed. 'Tom, I haven't seen you for years, we bump into each other on a train and now this... what is *this*?' She took a step backward, felt her back come into contact with a stone pillar. A narrow shelf ran around it, cluttered with precariously stacked glasses that wobbled at the impact. 'Because I'm totally confused.'

Tom leaned in and one by one, he moved the glasses from the

shelf and placed them on to a table. 'You don't want those hitting the floor now, do you?' he said as a hand dropped on to her hip. For a moment, he held it there, searched her eyes with his, and then as though it were the most natural thing in the world to do, he slid his hands upward until they were beneath her jacket where no one could see, and with a cheeky, seductive smile, he ran a thumb across each of her nipples, which caused an electric shock so powerful, and so violent, that she couldn't ignore it.

'Do you feel it?' he whispered into her ear. 'This is a need, Daisy. This is your body telling you what you want and that feeling isn't going away. We've waited a long time for this opportunity.' He took her hand in his, looked over his shoulder and discreetly moved her hand downward until it rested firmly against him. 'And this, do you feel it, Daisy? This is a man who wants you, more than anything in the world.'

With the intensity of her feelings overpowering her, Daisy tore her hand out of his. She couldn't help but wonder how a chance meeting on the train had led to this, to her contemplating having an affair with this man. Because, married or not, that's what this was, and even though it hadn't been planned, it was exactly what she wanted. Every part of her body ached for Tom. Every inch of her wanted to know if their lovemaking would be as intense as it had been. Whether she'd feel the same, or whether the guilt would circumvent her thoughts and make her change her mind.

'Hey,' Tom said, cutting through her thoughts. 'Look. Maybe I read this all wrong, but I thought... I thought meeting like this was what you wanted. It was what we both agreed to and when I suggested it earlier, you looked happy, and I was really excited...' Turning, he looked away into the crowd, to where he noticed a man who stood close by. He was watching what he and Daisy were doing, with his arms crossed in a defensive manner while impatiently rocking from foot to foot.

'Tom, I think we should...'

'You think we should what?' he asked, looking back in her direction.

Daisy could see the rise and fall of his shoulders, the confusion that had filled his eyes along with the palpable disappointment that showed on his face.

'You think we should get out of here, do you? And do what, go for a coffee?' he asked. 'Have a nice chat about our jobs, the latest book we read, or should we just chat about how you married the man who took you away from me and ruined my life?'

'Yes, no, I don't know,' she answered truthfully. 'I just...' She wanted to tell him how much she'd loved him, how often she'd thought about him. But she couldn't. She was here against her better judgement, and even though she wanted nothing more than to be alone with Tom and lie in his arms, unashamedly naked, the truth was, she was married. She had a husband and whatever she did next would cause one or all of them pain and heartache. Every action had a consequence; wasn't that what her mother had always said? And right now, Tom was fully expecting for her to reject him... again, which was why he'd turned so cold and defensive.

'Look, don't worry. I'm sorry; this is on me, not you. I shouldn't have...' He moved towards her, cupped her chin and placed a gentle kiss against her forehead. 'I shouldn't have kissed you, I shouldn't have presumed or said anything. I just... I got carried away. I thought...' Pausing, he bit down on his lip, his gaze fixing on hers. 'I guess that today, I saw it as fate, and I've missed you so much that I just wanted to relive the past, just for a few short hours.' He stopped short as the emotion caught in his throat. 'Do you know what? We should get out of here because I'm starving.' He laughed, took hold of her hand as though nothing had happened. 'We should calm things down and get some food and...' He looked down at her feet. 'And... I guess we should go and get you a new pair of shoes, something flat and more comfortable. You never did like heels, did you?' he rambled. 'And then if you fancy it, we'll go for a walk along the river... talk about all of those old times we had.'

'Tom...' Pausing, Daisy averted her eyes and looked down at the soggy red shoe on her foot. 'I'd like to walk along the river with you.' She held on to his hand, squeezed it lovingly. 'And I know what you hoped for; if I'm honest, it's something I've thought about so many times. But I'm married. Cole doesn't deserve this and what's more, I really want to *stay* married... which is why...' She paused thoughtfully, avoided his gaze. 'After tonight, I can't make any promises...'

Closing her eyes, Daisy once again felt Tom's lips press firmly against hers and with the alcohol now firmly in control of her senses, she allowed the kiss to deepen.

'I'm not asking for promises,' he finally said between kisses. 'If all we have is tonight... then I'm all in.' Running kisses down her neck, he lifted her hand to his mouth and dropped a single kiss against her wedding ring. 'And after tonight, I'll do whatever you ask. If you want me to walk away... I promise, I will.'

Feeling his lips tremble, every part of Daisy ached. She knew that what she was doing was wrong, and as Tom's arms wrapped tightly around her she pictured Cole's face and she tried to imagine how she might feel when she next saw him and told him she loved him, and whether or not he'd believe her. Or whether he'd see her for the adulterous liar she was.

# 3

## DAISY

*December 2024*

With her shopping bags held tightly in one of her hands, Daisy slammed the car door, clicked the key lock and walked slowly along the gravel driveway. Above her, she could hear the familiar sound of a seagull's 'keow'; it was loud and clear, and for a moment Daisy felt as though he were shouting at her and attracting her attention. In the distance, just a short way along the coast, she could hear the sound of waves crashing heavily against the rocky shoreline. They were the noises that always reminded her of home; sounds that made her senses come alive and, as always, the pleasure of simply being at this house overcame her, and she found herself inhaling the sea air and blinking away the tears of emotion.

Pushing the key into the door, Daisy swung it wide open, stepped inside, and because the shopping bag was still in her hand, she used her shoulder to close the door behind her with a sigh of relief. Getting home was always a happy moment which felt like receiving a warm, welcoming hug every single time she walked through the door. She dropped her bag on to the kitchen counter before glancing across the open plan lounge. At the back of the house was a patio door dressed with a grey voile curtain and black, cast iron decorative holdbacks. It was a feature of the house she'd instantly fallen in love with. Beyond it, she'd purposely not allowed the garden to overgrow, so that she could always see the oncoming sunset.

Pipistrelle was just one of the six properties that stood on an outcrop, along a coastal path above Budle Bay. The main part of the house looked out over the bay: a long, rugged coastline with views to die for.

Holding back the curtains, Daisy felt her excitement build. Once again, the sunset was promising a dramatic finale, and with high expectations of what might come she kicked off her shoes and stood, barefoot, on the cold, solid oak floor in an appreciative silence. It was a moment during every day that she always kept to herself, and she breathed in the quiet solitude, which she knew would end the moment Cole got home.

Until then, she had nothing else to do apart from stare at a darkening sky. It was interspersed with crimsons, yellows and deep shades of navy. Every night the sky blessed her with a different view. Each just as picture perfect as the one she'd seen the night before. A moment caught in time that always reminded her of something an artist might draw. Tonight, there were skeletal trees that bordered the frame. A sunset that looked as though it had been placed perfectly central on the canvas. Below it, the bay along with the infamous shape of Lindisfarne Castle that had been clearly etched into the winter skyline.

'If someone could paint me this exact picture, I'd definitely buy it,' she whispered with a smile as she cracked open the patio door, braved the cold winter breeze and focused on the sound of the sea as it rolled in against the shoreline. The only other noise that interrupted the repetitive, soothing motion was the sound of the clock in her hallway. A constant 'tick' that could be heard throughout the house. A sound that, in the growing darkness of the room, was a constant reminder that time was passing and that at any moment now, Cole would be home.

Leaning against the wall, Daisy steadied herself. Cole had been away for the past three days. It was something he did. His work away from home had always been a part of their lives, although Daisy couldn't help but always feel just a little apprehensive when he returned. In the two months since her trip to London, Cole had been away more than he'd been at home. Which even for Cole had been a little excessive. Part of her felt nervous and tense, and deep inside she wondered if he knew about her infidelity or if he'd spotted the guilt that had burned in her eyes and because of that, she'd found herself withdrawing. There had been so many times when she hadn't known what to say. The art of conversation between them had become stilted, and even though the chemistry hadn't completely disappeared, it had certainly dwindled. What Daisy had to work out was whether it had dwindled *before* she'd gone to London, or since she'd come back. She couldn't be sure, and it was just one of the thoughts that had continually gone through her mind since returning from London. Dwelling on the past and torturing herself over her actions was something she constantly did, even though she knew that, by doing so, she was creating a cavernous distance between her and Cole, and for the sake of their marriage, she had to stop.

'Okay, here's what you're going to do: you're going to make dinner. It'll just be the two of you,' she said out loud as she looked over her shoulder and scanned the room. Her plan was to make a nice Friday-night dinner, which was something they always did. It was the one night in the week that was always saved for each other. Like most Friday nights, she'd bought fresh flowers for the centre of the table and candles to light beside them, along with a couple of bottles of both red and white wine.

Feeling reluctant to turn on the lights, Daisy moved across the room in the semi-darkness, grabbed a tablecloth from the drawer and swished it across the table. Lovingly, she ran a hand across the material, closed her eyes for a moment and breathed in deeply as once again she felt the house surround her with the advice of her mother.

*You need to plan, baby girl. Decide on what you have to do to move on and then you need to do it.* That would have been exactly what she'd have said, if she'd been here. Words she'd said to her at least a hundred times in the past and Daisy looked up at a picture of her, her mother and Sarah that stood on the bookcase. It had been taken just a few weeks before their mother had died and was a picture where they were all smiling, pretending to be happy, even though all of them knew that their world was about to be viciously torn into shreds.

'Tonight,' she said out loud, 'tonight, you're going to stare into Cole's eyes and you're going to smile in all the right places.' She nodded, pulled open a drawer and took some cutlery out. 'For just a few hours, Cole has to see the woman he married, the woman he once loved and then...' She paused and swallowed as the nausea began and the acid rose in her throat. The guilt was becoming too much. It was tearing her apart, piece by piece. Which meant that, rightly or wrongly, she had no choice but to tell Cole what had happened.

'Daisy,' she whispered out loud in the same way her mother would have spoken, 'you're going to pull your big-girl pants on and tonight you're going to tell Cole the truth. If you want to move on, you have to tell him what happened in London.'

Closing her eyes for a blink, Daisy felt the tears form beneath her eyelids. 'You definitely want to move on,' she said anxiously. 'The question is, do you want to move on with Cole... or not?'

# 4

## DAISY

Sighing, Daisy turned back to the window, gave the sunset a final
look and, for just a second, she closed her eyes and committed
the image to memory.

If she went ahead with this, if she confessed about her night
with Tom, she couldn't predict how the evening would go or what
Cole's reaction would be. She shook her head sadly, because for
the first time in years, she feared how unpredictable and erratic
Cole's temper could be. Her confession could push him either
way and whether she liked it or not, their evening might not go
exactly to plan.

But the alternative was to keep living a lie that was slowly
tearing her marriage apart. The guilt had become too much for
Daisy and the only way she could think to put things right was to
be true to herself, to be honest to Cole, and to show some
remorse, in the hope that Cole would forgive her.

Reaching out into a darkness that had now completely taken
over the room, Daisy pushed her shopping bags across the
counter and turned on the soft, ambient lights that left the room
feeling relaxed and homely. The kitchen downlights lit up the

white glossy units. They made the black marble worktops sparkle and reflected in the double-fronted black and chrome American-style fridge that dominated the room.

Satisfied that, until Cole got home, she'd done as much as she could, Daisy returned to the hallway, which was long and narrow and painted in a soft dove grey. At the bottom of the corridor was the bedroom her father often occupied when he and his new girlfriend, Jenny, came to stay. There was a small but adequate cloakroom at the bottom of the stairs, and upstairs there were two double rooms, both with en suite, which included the bedroom that she and Cole shared.

Moving into Pipistrelle had been a bittersweet day. It was the house of her dreams, the house she'd always promised herself that she'd buy, but it was a property she'd only got because her mother had died. And even though it had everything she wanted, Cole had never really liked it. Her insisting on buying the house, with the money her mother had left her, had bruised his ego. He'd wanted to be the one to provide. After all, he was a builder. He ran his own construction company and had always said that one day, he'd build them a house of their own. But deep down, she'd hoped that he'd forget about moving or building and that one day, he'd grow to love this house just as much as she did. Or that had been the plan, until she'd been unfaithful, and now she knew that none of that was certain.

With a shrug, Daisy dropped her coat from her shoulders and hung it up. Then, poignantly, she lifted the coat back down and stared at the tall, oblong mirror that hung next to the coat rack. With a sigh she hooked her coat over her arm, lifted her fingers and ran them down the mother-of-pearl edging and smiled affectionately as she remembered the moment it had arrived, beautifully packaged and delivered to her at work. A gift from Tom that

came with an inscription that only one person in the world could
have written.

Take a good look in the mirror. *You're* the one that almost got
away!

At first, Daisy had hesitated about hanging it up. She knew
that Cole would ask questions, that he'd want to know where it
had come from, and she tried to think up a good explanation. 'I
saw it in an antique store,' she'd lied. 'I just fell in love with it...
and the inscription, wow, it really must have meant something to
someone, mustn't it?' It had been an explanation that Cole had
swallowed. He hadn't questioned it further. But now she looked at
it, she saw it through different eyes. The mirror was a symbol of
her infidelity, a constant reminder of what she'd done and, reluctantly, she considered taking it down, taking it to a charity shop
and giving someone else the intrigue over what the inscription
might mean. But for some unexplainable reason, she couldn't.

The telltale sound of a car's engine was followed by the slam
of a door and the crunch of feet. She looked through the window
to see that Cole was standing by the fence and he had his mobile
phone pressed against one ear; it was a call he obviously wanted
to finish before coming inside.

With the wait and anticipation becoming unbearable, Daisy
headed back into the kitchen. She picked up a bottle of red,
poured herself a glass and with her eyes momentarily closed, she
took a large mouthful. One sip turned into two and before she
realised it, the whole glass had gone.

While drumming her fingers impatiently against the worktop, Daisy held her breath as the front door opened and Cole
strode in wearing a pair of smart trousers, the Luca Faloni shirt
she'd bought for him the Christmas before, and his black

Moncrief overcoat. It was a coat that he normally only wore on special occasions and was a far cry from the clothes he'd normally wear for work. It was also more than obvious that he'd already showered, that he wasn't covered in the normal grime and dust that came off a building site, and if she wasn't mistaken, his short, manicured beard was glistening with freshly applied beard oil.

'I have a surprise for you!' she sang out as rhythmically as she could before she flicked back her hair, pointed to the table, and allowed her face to light up with a smile. 'I'm making you a special dinner, which I haven't started yet because I was waiting until you'd got home and showered, but...'

'Sorry, darling,' Cole chipped in, 'but the dinner will have to wait.' He flashed her a smile, brushed the lapel of his coat with his fingers. 'I have a surprise for you, too.'

'For me?' She laughed, poured him a glass of wine and carefully slid it across the kitchen counter towards him. Then, with a long, pointed finger, she waved it up and down at his outfit. 'Is there something I should know?' she questioned, 'You're all dressed up, but from what you told me, you should have been on site?' She gave him a searching smile, then without her eyes leaving his, she reached for her glass and refilled it.

'Hey, come on, not so fast.' Walking around the counter, Cole took the glass out of her hand. He placed his hands on her hips 'We're going out, in the car. So, we need to be sober.' He rocked against her in a sensual, well-practised manoeuvre and slowly lifted his hand and cupped her chin. 'As I said, tonight, I have a surprise for you, too.' Cole lowered his mouth and gently grazed her lips.

It was exactly the way Daisy had wanted the evening to go. A reminder for them both of who they were and what they'd once shared, and with the familiar undertones of vanilla and cardamon tantalising her senses, Daisy breathed in Cole's after-shave and pulled him in closer.

'Well, that was a nice welcome,' Daisy responded as the kiss came to an end. 'But seriously, it's Friday. I always cook on a Friday, and we never go out...' Playfully, she ran a finger up and down his body and squeezed her lip between her teeth. 'I was hoping for a quiet one. I haven't seen you for days and...' She paused, pointed hopefully to the food she'd laid out on the counter. 'I'm cooking sea bass, your favourite.' Once again, and with her act going to plan, she reached up and touched her lips to his. 'I thought it would be nice for us to spend the evening together.'

Moving away, Cole lifted his fingers to the lapels of his coat and with a hand on each he tweaked them playfully. 'Well, as you can see, I'm all ready to go out.' He paused, ran his gaze up and down the length of her body, 'And even though I'd really like to spend our evening here, together, this is important. Dinner can wait.' Lifting the glass of wine to his lips, Cole took a small sip. A genuine smile of appreciation formed on his lips and Daisy couldn't help but take in the square, symmetrical shape of his jawline, the way his sideburns came down to meet his beard, or the way his shoulders were pushed back proudly.

'Come on, you're looking really smug with yourself; tell me, what are you really up to?' she whispered as she picked up the fish and with a short, bladed knife, pierced the bag. She began to unwrap the fillets but stopped the moment Cole's hand covered hers. It was a firm, controlled action that made Daisy put the knife down, and with a sense of disappointment flooding her veins, she took a step back.

Cole on the other hand, took a step forward. He opened the fridge and with a single swoosh of his arm, he toppled each of the items off the chopping board. One by one they hit the chiller basket at speed, before he gave her a smug smile and closed the fridge door.

'They... can all stay in there until later. Maybe we'll cook them tomorrow,' he said firmly before turning and pulling her back into his arms. The mood had changed; Cole was more attentive, a little less arrogant and Daisy found herself closing the space between them as he ran his hands through her hair and began to tease her mouth with his. 'I have something to show you,' he said between kisses. 'Something important.'

'Isn't this important?' Daisy chipped in with a lustful smile as her hand landed playfully against his erection. For a split second, she caught her breath, wondered if she was doing the right thing and felt just a little uncertain. This was the night when she was supposed to be telling Cole the truth. Not a night for seduction. But her emotions were raging within her, and with her eyes dancing with his in the half-light, she tightened her hand in a small but significant way of telling him exactly what she expected. 'I mean, I did think about making dinner first, Cole, but,' she whispered, 'there are some things that a wife really needs to take care of.'

Cole lifted her to sit on the counter. Daisy forcibly pulled at his trousers, flicked open the button and with her toes she pushed them down to hang by his knees. The urgency, the passion, was turbulent; it was exactly what was needed. Each kiss became more desperate than the one before to the point Daisy felt her heartbeat accelerate. Her body ached; every touch felt like a new-found torture.

Nothing else mattered and ardently Daisy pulled at every item of clothing, until she lay there, naked. She hooked her legs around Cole's waist and with her eyes fixed on his, she sat up and pushed the Moncrief overcoat off his shoulders, smiling as her fingernails ran up and down the muscles that had been hidden beneath.

'You have no idea how much I want this,' she whispered as she caught his gaze and stared deep into his soul.

For a moment, as they stared into each other's eyes, she didn't trust herself to speak and bit down on her lip. The guilt was still present, and she couldn't be sure that right there, during this intimate moment, she wouldn't tell him what she'd done and how many regrets she'd had since, and as though Cole sensed her indecision, he took a step backward.

'Hey.' Cole laughed and with a smug look on his face, he pulled up his trousers. 'We need to slow down.' He searched her eyes again with his own and tipped his head to one side in a quizzical manner. It was as though he was studying her, trying to work something out. It was a look Daisy had seen before and meant Cole knew more than he was admitting. He'd purposely led her on only to slow things down, and with the humiliation spreading through her, she grabbed at her clothes.

'You bastard... there was no need for that...'

'Darling, I'm sorry,' Cole said with a disgruntled sigh as he picked his coat up off the floor. 'Trust me, this hurts me just as much as it hurts you.' He pushed his hand down his trousers and adjusted himself before zipping them up. 'But I need you to get your clothes on, because we are going to be late.' Pulling his phone out of his pocket, Cole tapped at the screen. 'Oh, and be quick, I've got people waiting.'

Arrogantly, he turned, strode down the hallway and with his phone held up to his ear, he swung open the door. 'I'm just going to make a quick call,' he shouted over his shoulder. 'So please, Daisy, be a good girl, pop upstairs and make a bit of an effort, which means getting changed, because right now '– he lifted a finger and waved it up and down in the air – 'turning up naked won't cut it.'

# 5

## TOM

As the bailiffs left, Tom slammed the front door, watched as it vibrated in its frame, and then slumped against it.

With disbelief and embarrassment flooding through him he lifted his hands up to cover his face. The slits in his fingers formed a barrier between himself and the reality of what had just happened, and with his fingers curling in and out of fists, he stood and punched at the light switch and took some relief from the immediate darkness.

Streetlights outside threw shards of light across the two-metre space at the bottom of the stairs. It was a part of the house that he hated the most and a door he only used when visitors arrived.

Narrowing his eyes, he looked through the small window panel of glass that went down one side of the door. It was long, narrow and frosted, which didn't help him to focus on the two burly bailiffs who stood arrogantly on the path outside.

'I can still see you, you pair of smug, ugly bastards...' Watching, Tom glared at the over-enthusiastic look on their faces and hated the confident stride and the way they walked away with his flat screen television held under one arm. Tom's eyes flashed across to the neighbours' windows, where the curtains were drawn, showing different shades of amber lighting. One or two houses stood in darkness, which meant that the occupants were either still at work or were standing with the lights off watching the circus unfold right outside their front windows. Tom reeled at the thought as he imagined them laughing and jeering while the two men marched out of his house and unceremoniously dropped his television into the boot of their car while patting each other on the back and shaking hands in a congratulatory manner.

'Oh, that's right, make a damn scene; make sure you get yourselves an audience.' Tom growled and turned the key in the lock. He had to do something to stop himself from rushing outside. His thoughts automatically flashed to the spade that stood right outside his back door. The perfect weapon should he choose to use it, but instead, he punched out with an anger he couldn't control, and with his breathing accelerated and his heartbeat quickened, he caught the architrave with his knuckles, screamed out in pain and he watched in horror as a small, tarnished picture fell to the floor.

'Tremendous,' he yelled out loud, 'that's all I need.' Crouching, Tom stared at the picture for a moment too long. The picture showed his wife, Grace, the summer before. She'd been lying on a sunbed, in a long hippie skirt that she insisted on wearing even though the weather had been boiling. The picture was just one of the items Grace had forgotten when she'd packed her things – a picture that had tortured his mind ever since.

'If you're going to compare every woman to her, then you're going to be a very lonely old man,' Grace had screamed following a brief unguarded moment when Tom had blurted out that his ex-girlfriend Daisy had once lived around the corner.

'So, that's why we've moved here, is it?' Grace had picked up one packing box after the other and, while not caring what the contents were, she launched them across the room in his direction. 'That's why you insisted buying this damned house, isn't it? What were you hoping for, another bloody reunion?' She'd glared directly at him with her face twisted with venom. 'Because it wouldn't be the first reunion you've had, now, would it?'

After picking up their son from his day crib, Grace had launched herself up the stairs, with Mason perched on her hip. 'So, shall we start with the pictures by the Thames, or would you rather we looked at those where you're lying in bed?' Throwing open the door they used as an office, Grace had pulled off her shoe and launched it across the room, at the computer.

'Grace, stop. I don't know what you think you know, but for God's sake, she doesn't live there any more,' he'd shouted out loud but closed his eyes as the words sunk in and the fear took over. 'As far as I know, she got married years ago. She moved away and I don't even know why I mentioned her,' he said, hedging his bets.

Tom hovered outside the door and through narrowed eyes peered into the office and directly at the screen on his desk, where he could see a clear image of him and Daisy, together in London. He could see the look, the smile, the way their faces had radiated with love.

'So, you've been through my things,' he began, his voice calm but cutting. 'You shouldn't have done that, Grace; you do know that don't you?'

'Really?' she questioned. 'Why is that, Tom? Because as far as I can see, I'm holding all the cards.' She'd hitched Mason forward, presenting their son to him. 'I'd say that you have a lot more to lose than I do. I hope a nice catch-up with your old flame was worth it?'

The sound of her voice had infiltrated his mind. A loud

humming noise had taken over his senses to a point where it had begun to haunt his dreams and he could no longer close his eyes without seeing her face full of tears, contorted and angry. All he'd been able to see was the way Grace had angrily packed. A bag had been followed by two large boxes, and he'd watched her, with anger coursing through him, as she'd moved slowly along the landing, with Mason still in her arms, dragging the suitcase behind her.

In the days that followed, Tom had tried to make sense of what had happened, but he couldn't. He'd felt sure that everyone knew, that the gossip would begin. That every time he walked down the street, the neighbours would point and laugh just like they'd been doing just now, and even though he'd kept his composure in public, privately the feeling of loss was immeasurable. Grace was gone and a darkness had surrounded both the house and his mind leaving him unable to work. His debts had spiralled out of control, added to the bills he already owed, and then the debt letters had begun to arrive.

With panic coursing through every sinew in his body, and with the bailiffs feet jammed in the doorway, Tom had had no choice but to let them in, and as he'd walked around the house behind them, he'd held on to his breath and had gasped with relief as they'd walked straight past his tool bag. Taking away his right to work as an electrician was one of his biggest fears. Working would be the only way he could get out of this mess and he'd felt sure that they couldn't take his tools. But with a quick scan of the room, he'd quickly spotted the things they could take and, surreptitiously, he'd kicked a laptop under the sofa. An Apple watch had been scooped up off a shelf and placed in his pocket and an iPad had been slipped down the side of a chair, behind one of the cushions.

The letter the bailiffs had left behind had been thrown on the sideboard. It had listed all the things Tom valued the most. Practically the entire contents of his office, apart from his tools and the oldest of laptops. Everything now owned by the courts, and his only chance of keeping them was to pay his debt in full.

Rushing up the stairs, Tom went into his office and stared at the huge monitor that dominated his desk. It was the same monitor that had been his downfall but still it was his prized possession. His link to the world. With it, he could watch the lives of other people... including that of Daisy.

'Now then, let me see what's happening.' His eyes quickly flicked across the screen as he wiggled the mouse. From up here, he could see that the bailiffs had gone, that the street was now empty. For now, the threat had gone and even though he still had a lot to do, he couldn't resist opening a browser and clicking into Daisy's social media accounts and scanning her content.

'You thought you were really clever, didn't you?' he said out loud as though Daisy were sitting there beside him. 'All that wine, you never could take your drink.' Laughing, he could still see her intoxicated face and the way she'd melted into his arms. While she was drowsy following their lovemaking he'd thrown her one or two leading questions and smiled as she'd openly told him all about the password she used.

'Come on, Tom, no one in the world would guess Pipistrelle. It's not a word anyone uses every day, is it? And if they did,' she'd giggled, 'they wouldn't know to replace all the e's with threes and all the i's with number ones, would they?'

Without realising what she'd done, Daisy had given him access and he'd quickly worked out that Facebook and LinkedIn were the accounts she used most. Her obsession with posting all about her day, along with her location, gave him quite a picture of where she was and what she was doing. But today there was nothing, and with his shoulders slumped with disappointment, Tom picked up his phone and tapped out a message.

TOM

I know I made a promise, but something's happened, and I really need to see you x

With the phone in his hand, Tom watched the screen and hoped for a response. He needed Daisy to care, for her to reply. But when the response didn't come, he felt a jab to his heart. Once again, Daisy had let him down and he had to remind himself that *she'd* left *him* standing on that platform in London. She'd gone back to her husband and right now, right at this moment in time, she could be laid in his arms, kissing him and making love to him.

'Come on, Daisy... don't do this to me again, answer the damn text,' he said angrily as he saw a picture flash up on his screen. It was a picture she'd only just posted. A picture that showed a sunset, a picket fence and, in the distance, the distinct shape of Lindisfarne Castle.

'So, you're at home, and you're taking pictures with your phone, which means that you must have seen my message.' He growled, threw his phone on to the desk and watched as it bounced along its surface. Jumping up, he began to pace back and forth along the landing. With his eyes closed, he thought of all the other things she might be doing alone, like cooking, reading a book or taking a bath... naked.

It prompted a memory back to their night in Daisy's London hotel room. He could still remember every detail about that night and the bath they'd taken together. In his mind, he could see every item of clothing as it hit the floor until she'd unashamedly stood before him, naked, and then, with a pointed toe, she'd tested the water before sliding in with a smile on her face. The bath, like in most hotel rooms, had been typically small, but even though there was barely any room for two, she'd looked at him with a look of invitation in her eye: one that told him undoubtedly that she wanted him, right there in the bath. With the heat of the water sloshing around them he hadn't thought twice about slipping into the tub and covering her body with his.

Smiling away the memory, Tom looked back at his screen. He tipped his head to one side and studied a map of Budle Bay for much longer than necessary. It was an area he used to know well, a beach he'd walked along a thousand times. One where, many years ago, he'd walked with Daisy, and after enlarging the map, he looked at each of the houses until he found the one called Pipistrelle and laughed out loud.

It was a house he knew, a house that he and Daisy had often pointed to as teenagers. A property they'd dreamed of buying. Where they'd planned to create a home that they'd fill with their children. But the thought that she'd bought it with him, Cole Bailey, set Tom's blood on fire. Angrier now, Tom looked up at his screen and with the bailiffs still in the forefront of his mind, he methodically began to grab at computer files and, one by one, he copied them and pasted them on to a hard drive.

'That should do it...' He gave a sigh of relief, reached up and stretched his arms above his head. Doing so, he caught sight of the trapdoor in the ceiling that led to the loft space. It was the perfect place to hide things that he didn't want the bailiffs to find and, arrogantly, he climbed up the ladder and hid the hard drive under the loft insulation. 'And now,' he whispered derisively, 'now, I have to make another plan, and one that involves earning some money.' He went back to his screen, clicked into a browser and looked up Cole Bailey. There before his eyes was the man that, through no fault of his own, he hated the most. The picture showed him standing beside a Ferrari wearing a posh overcoat, a pair of sunglasses in winter and a narcissistic gaze that fooled no one. The fact that he was standing there posing, while in the background Tom could see Daisy watching from a distance, proved that Cole Bailey thought nothing of anyone except for himself.

'And you...' Tom said with a conceited smile on his face, 'you, Cole Bailey. You are going to give me a job, and then I'm going to take your wife right from under your nose...'

# 6

# DAISY

'What the hell do you mean, this is our house?' Daisy looked anxiously at Cole and squinted through the darkness as they pulled up to a pair of eight-foot-high electric gates that towered above them. She fully expected Cole to laugh. For him to tell her that his words had been a joke, but he didn't. She watched nervously as the gates opened and then closed behind them with a thud, as Cole drove his Range Rover forward.

Turning to fix her gaze on the gates, she began to panic inside. The gates had suddenly created what felt like her prison, an entrapment she hadn't expected at the end of a short but fretful ride. With her eyes skipping frantically around her surroundings, she could feel every part of her body tremble with a growing anxiety.

The drive inland had taken just over half an hour. Country roads had turned into long, unadopted lanes and she'd watched anxiously as Cole had swerved the potholes. Deep, water-filled ditches ran along each side of the narrow, unnerving road. A lack of streetlights gave the lane an eerie feel and overgrown trees crowded the car, their long skeletal branches appearing to almost reach out towards them, like long spindly fingers.

The whole drive had been one that had made Daisy uneasy. Her anxiety had grown even more, and with her heart lurching into her mouth, she bit down on her lip as her phone flashed for the third or fourth time, its ringtone filling the car and Tom's name lighting up the screen. As quickly as she could, she grabbed at the phone and killed the call only to spot a message that must have pinged in earlier, unnoticed.

TOM

I know I made a promise, but something's happened, and I really need to see you x

Deleting the message as quickly as she could, Daisy chastised her own stupidity. Leaving Tom's name in her phone had been a ridiculous thing to do, although even if she only admitted it to herself, the sight of it made her stomach turn with excitement. Tom hadn't said that he *wanted* to see her; he'd said that he *needed* to see her. They were two different things and on the same evening when her own husband hadn't even been able spare her the five extra minutes it would have taken to make love to her, the message had given her a much-needed boost. Whereas Cole had humiliated her. He'd cut the act short. Only to bring her to a house where she didn't want to go to.

'Do you need to answer that?' Cole asked with an amatory smile before leaning in and dropping a light, apologetic kiss against her cheek. 'It's already rung three times, and I'd guess that means it's important?' Sitting back in his seat, he waved a hand in the air. 'Seriously, darling, I really don't mind if you want to answer it. I can just sit here and stare at the house.' His hand landed on her leg, where his fingers moved to the inside of her thigh. 'It's beautiful, isn't it?'

'Oh, I don't have to call her back...' Moving his hand away, Daisy replied, 'It's just one of the girls. She's going through a divorce and probably just needed a chat. I'll catch her later.' With nerves that were racing, she switched her phone off and dropped it back in her bag. 'Now then,' she said firmly as she turned to look at Cole, 'do you want to tell me what the hell's going on, because I'm sure you've just told me that this is our house.'

'I did say that, didn't I?' Taking her hand in his, Cole smiled. He patted her hand with his own, in a firm but controlling act. It was more than obvious he hadn't liked her moving his hand away earlier and he searched her eyes with his own. 'You know I once told you that I'd dreamed about building my own house, for us?' he said in a calm, loving voice and waited for her to nod in agreement. 'Well, Daisy, this is it.' Cole skimmed her chin with his fingers, pulled her towards him and placed another soft, tender kiss against her mouth. 'Don't you just love it?'

'You did what?' she interjected quickly, as though the tenderness of the kiss hadn't happened at all, and with the feeling of being dragged underwater she pulled herself backward. 'Cole this isn't a house; it's a bloody mansion. It's big enough to house at least four families.'

Leaning forward in his seat, Cole rested against the steering wheel and looked at the house as though he was seeing it for the very first time. 'It is big, isn't it?' He bit down on his lip, before tipping his head towards her. 'But that's what we want, Daisy, isn't it?' he questioned. 'You know that our families always want to come and stay, and if we get our wish, we could start a family and have a house full of kids. It's what we talked about for so many years and now we can do that.'

Slumping back in her seat, Daisy felt her mind blow up with questions that had no answers. Admittedly, having a family was something they had talked about. It was something she'd always desperately craved. But that had been years ago, when they'd first got married. Since then, it had been a subject that Cole had always pushed to one side with one excuse or another. The business needed attention; he had to work, put in the hours; he had to work away on site; and on and on. Eventually he'd convinced Daisy that the time just wasn't right for them and starting a family was something that they hadn't really spoken about since. As well as Cole being busy at work all the time, Daisy had also inherited her mother's business, Harbour Estates and Lettings, along with her sister, Sarah, who worked in the agency every Friday and Saturday. The rest of the week, Sarah worked for Cole. This meant that Daisy's time had become consumed by the business, which Monday through to Thursday she ran all alone, and so any thoughts of having a family had been pushed to one side.

Sighing, Cole sat back in his seat, closed his eyes and tapped his fingertips against the steering wheel. 'Jesus, Daisy, do you know how many hours have gone into this build? It's taken me months, and I really thought you'd like it. I really thought you'd be happy.' He paused dramatically, lifted his hands to cover his face, and rubbed at his eyes. 'I've had men working on this site for the last few months.' He turned to face her and switched on a questioning smile. With the moonlight catching his eyes, Daisy could see the undeniable excitement that lurked within. 'At one point, there were at least sixty men here. It's been crazy, and even though it isn't quite finished, I couldn't wait another minute. I just had to show you.'

Processing everything Cole had just said, Daisy looked up at a house that she already hated. It was huge and ostentatious, and it had been built without her knowledge. For a minute, she looked back at her husband and tried to work out how their lives had changed so much and when they'd both begun to keep secrets from each other. Maybe it was something Cole had always done. Maybe she didn't know him as well as she thought. The question was, did she know him at all? The idea that he'd built a house without telling her was infuriating. And as for not quite being finished, the only sign that Bailey Construction had been there at all was the half dozen bags of aggregate that stood to one side of the driveway.

'Darling, come on, this is a great house, you're going to love living here.' Shuffling in his seat, Cole gave the house an uncomfortable glance. Daisy saw a shift in his look, the impatient sigh and the raise of his eyebrow that told her he was expecting something to happen.

'This is a joke, right?' Picking up her bag, Daisy reached inside, took out her phone, switched it back on and nervously flicked at the screen. She was fully expecting to see another message from Tom or an indication that another voicemail had landed. Knowing that he was waiting for a response, she tried to work out why he'd called. He'd promised he'd wouldn't. *He shouldn't be calling.* The words went around her mind. She thought back to their time in London, to the pact they'd made and the promise she'd made to herself. She'd promised that she was going to give her marriage another chance, which was ironic when currently she wasn't even sure who she'd married.

'Honey, what makes you think that this is a joke?'

'Because, we have a house! Why the hell would you build us another, without mentioning it to me?' She laughed, hoped that the look on his face would change, that the way he'd fixed his jaw would turn into a smile. 'No one, absolutely no one, builds a house without telling their wife. It'd be ludicrous for anyone to do that.' Again she paused, hoped that he'd jump in and tell her the truth. 'Come on, Cole, whose house is this? Who really lives here?'

'Darling, come on, why do you find it so hard to believe I did this for us?' Puffing out his chest proudly Cole once again took hold of her hand. 'I know things have been a bit strained lately. You've been distant. Things haven't been right between us but that's going to change, and this... I just wanted to do something nice, something that would make us both happy.' He dropped her hand, pointed at the door. 'You always said you wanted a jet-black, shiny front door; can't you understand that I wanted to be the man who gave that to you?'

Stunned, Daisy's gaze went from Cole to the front door. In Daisy's opinion the door was wide enough, shiny enough and black enough not to have looked out of place on an official building. Or at least one of those big fancy houses that they'd walked past in London.

'Cole, for God's sake. Doing something nice for me is buying chocolate, or flowers, or taking me out for a meal that I didn't have to cook, but this...' Her hands went up in the air and then dropped as the desperation washed through her. 'This isn't just doing something nice... is it? This is monumental. It's you controlling where we live, without even asking.'

'It's a dream home,' he cut in. 'Think of the family we could have and the memories we could make. You could be proud of this house, Daisy, and we... we could both be happy here.' As he said the words, Daisy saw the irony. When she'd bought Pipistrelle, he hadn't had too much of a say. His only option had been whether or not he lived there with her. At the time, she'd been ecstatic that he'd agreed; however, today, after the humiliation he'd put her through earlier, she wasn't so sure.

Taking in a deep breath, Daisy was still waiting for the joke to be over, for the real owner of the house to step outside and for them to be welcomed in, but then she thought about the words Cole had used: 'we could both be happy here.' This insinuated that he wasn't happy living at Pipistrelle, which was something that, if she was honest, she'd known for a very long time.

Closing her eyes, Daisy went back over what he'd said and had to agree. She had been distancing herself from him since her trip to London. What she hadn't realised was that Cole had worked that out. That he wasn't happy either, and no matter how many times she blamed herself for the potential breakdown of her marriage, or for the fact that her husband was appearing to have a mid-life crisis, she couldn't negate the fact that this house looked practically finished. That a house like this didn't just happen, which meant that it must have been under construction for so much longer than Cole was admitting. It would have all begun before she'd met with Tom.

'Cole, seriously...' Daisy said as she casually rested a hand on his leg. 'We have a house. I love Pipistrelle. It has the best views in England and, personally, I don't need anything else or anything bigger.' She paused, saw the look of disappointment that crossed his face, the flicker of confusion that quickly followed, and despondently, Daisy sat back in her seat. She could feel her chest constrict. It was as though someone was squeezing her tightly, and with it, her breath began to dissipate, and she resigned herself to the fact that Cole was fully expecting her to love this house just as much as he did.

'Honey, this house is perfect too, please just give it a chance.' Once again, he leaned forward to rest against the steering wheel. 'I'll tell you what, just look at it. For me. Just give it a go and if you really hate it, I'll sell it, and we'll go back to Pipistrelle and we'll fit a couple of kids into the bedrooms we have.' He rolled his jaw dismissively. 'I can't be fairer than that, can I?'

Staring up at the house, Daisy had to agree that it was the kind of house she'd have drawn as a child; the only difference was that instead of the two windows she'd have drawn either side of the black glossy front door, this house had six. All of them were spaced widely apart, emphasising the size of the rooms inside. Above the front door there was one large arched window that broke into the roofline where a large piece of Yorkshire stone was set and the name 'The Willows' had been carved.

Leading up to the door, interspersed with bright, LED solar lights, were a dozen perfectly shaped bay trees, each in its own tall, grey concrete container. They reminded Daisy of a guard of honour outside a palace, except these trees led up to the house.

Three steps went up from the drive to the doorway and when Daisy looked more closely through one of the lower, downstairs windows, she could see a room that was brightly lit, with a snooker table all set up and ready to play. In the background, a fully lit bar complete with optics.

'That's the playroom,' Cole announced. 'Isn't it amazing? It has a full-length bar, and behind that is the entrance to the home theatre and the pool.' Once again, he gripped her hand and squeezed her fingers. 'Please give it a chance and at least try to love it, Daisy. Building a house of my own has always been important; you know that it's something I always said I'd do and now I have, I really want you to be happy here.'

Numb with shock, Daisy climbed out of the car and stood with her feet fixed to the floor. Biting down on her lip, she closed her eyes and tried to stop herself from saying something she knew she'd regret, and her bottom lip began to tremble with emotion.

The house was nothing like the one she had now. For a start it was inland. It was surrounded by a dark eeriness. A quietness that she knew she'd never like. From here, there was no sound of the sea. She couldn't hear the waves crashing up and on to the beach or the low-piercing 'keow' of the seagulls that flew overhead, searching for food. The silence was all but deafening. But above all of that, the thought that hurt the most was that she'd never get to sit and watch the sunset over the bay again. At least not from the inside of her own home, and the idea of that cut right through her.

'We don't need a damn playroom,' she finally whispered under her breath as she walked along the driveway and glanced at a cluster of dense trees which, even in the winter and void of leaves, were almost dense enough to block out almost every bit of the view or sunset that had ever surrounded the property. 'Cole, I'm still waiting for you to tell me that you didn't really build a house, not without telling me.' She lifted her hands to each side of her head and pressed as hard as she could on her temples. She wanted to squeeze every word he'd said out of her mind and return to an evening where she drank wine and made love to her husband.

Sidling up beside her, Cole ran his fingers down the arm of her jacket and took hold of her hand. 'Daisy, please, you have to understand. I know things have got a bit strained between us and I just wanted to put that right. I did this for us. Not just for me. *Us*. This is why I've been working away so much. I've been here. Making sure it was perfect.' He rolled his eyes up at the house, took in a deep breath. 'Admittedly, I should have asked you first, included you in the plans, let you pick out the furniture, but you're always busy with your own work and...' He paused and pulled in a deep breath. 'I wanted to create a fresh start, for both of us.'

'A fresh start?' she repeated. The words were more of a statement than a question, but the emotion spilled over, and Daisy held a hand to her mouth as a large sob fell out of her throat.

'How is this a fresh start, Cole, and who the hell picked out my curtains?'

'Hey, come on. It wasn't like that.'

Watching his mannerisms, Daisy could see that the man who was normally in charge of everything was fast losing control. His brow was furrowed. His jaw had become fixed and the excitement he'd had in his eyes just a few minutes before had gone. Her husband was crumbling in front of her eyes and there was nothing she could do to stop it. Building this house was something he shouldn't have done, not without talking to her about it first. But then hadn't she done things too? Kept her own secrets from him. Things she'd been about to own up to before his big revelation.

'Cole, you have to realise that this is a lot to take in. In my mind, I was waiting for you to come home after being away for three nights. We were going to have a lovely romantic meal and an evening at home, for just the two of us. And now I'm stood in a field that we apparently own, looking at a house that you built without telling me, and you don't even realise how ridiculous that sounds...'

Feeling her lip tremble again, Daisy choked back the tears. She didn't want to be here. She didn't want to look at this house. What she wanted was to go home and speak to her husband over dinner. But most of all, she wanted to clear her own conscience. It hadn't been a conversation she'd looked forward to, nor had she looked forward to the reaction he'd have possibly given. But she had to be true to herself and being honest about what had happened was something she'd needed to do. And now, she was here. Looking up at a house she already hated alongside a husband she didn't even recognise.

With her breath leaving her body all at once, Daisy gasped for air. She had to admit that, since the night she'd spent with Tom, she hadn't thought to question the fact that Cole had been away at least three or four nights each week. The times he hadn't been home had been her chance to breathe. She'd had the opportunity to battle with her guilt in a calm environment, where she'd felt both safe and secure – and no matter what, she couldn't move to this house with Cole, lose the bolthole that Pipistrelle gave her.

# 7

## DAISY

With her hand held up to her mouth and her stomach lurching, Daisy walked away from the car. She automatically headed back toward the gates, the need to escape high on her wish list, except she didn't exactly know where she was. With a reluctant sigh, she slowly spun on the spot and looked around in every direction.

'I don't like it,' she whispered under her breath. 'I don't like it at all.' She felt trapped, confined, and even though the garden was probably one of the biggest she'd ever seen in her life, it suddenly felt small and claustrophobic. Her mind felt restricted, and already she missed the view of the sea and the way the island of Lindisfarne called out to her from across the water, and suddenly she had the urge to stand in the middle of the driveway and scream out loud, just to see if anyone heard her.

'There are still a few bits to sort out in the garden.' Cole walked towards her and ran a hand nervously through his hair and then through his beard, as he gave her a hopeful but pensive smile. 'And the drive, as you can see, still needs laying. They're coming to drop the blocks early next week and the landscaping, well... that's a work in progress.'

With tears threatening to fall, Daisy looked back at the gates for a handle. She needed a way to unlock them, and right at that moment she didn't care how far away from the town they were, she still intended to leave. All she wanted was to go back home and if that meant that she'd have to walk all the way there, she would.

'Daisy, wait till you see the office. Seriously, you're going to love my new office, it's an absolute game changer, just wait and see.' Taking in a deep breath, Daisy could hear the excitement return to Cole's voice. He walked back towards her and ran his hand down each of her arms, before dipping his head and looking into her eyes. 'Hey, come on, come here, you're cold.'

'I don't like it, Cole, I don't feel safe.' Suddenly, Daisy began to shiver and with a determined effort she headed back to the car. 'Please, Cole, I want to go home.' She gave him an expectant smile and tried to think about what else she could say to get him back in the car. 'As you said, it's cold, and do you know what, we could still make that dinner; the fire was laid and ready to light, which means we could forget this happened and we could go home and get cosy.' She paused, sniffed. 'We could maybe finish what we started...'

Scowling, Cole followed, and with the familiarity they'd always had he spun her around, pulled her into his arms, wrapped his coat around her and snuggled her in. It was a moment of hope for Daisy. Cole had obviously heard her and was trying to look after her. While leaning into him, she breathed in deep and took in the musky aroma of his aftershave that stirred her senses. Automatically, she lifted her face to his, brushed his lips with her own and hoped that the kiss would win him over.

'I do love you, Cole,' she whispered. 'I really do and...' She stopped speaking mid-sentence as she saw a movement in the house. Daisy took a step back, grabbed at Cole's hand and ducked down, using the car to protect them. 'Cole, I think there's someone inside, I saw them. They're...' Her overactive imagination went from burglars to gunmen, her mind reeling with all that could happen.

But Cole stood upright. 'Darling, there's no one inside. Certainly no one that's going to hurt you.'

'But...' Daisy watched as he lifted a hand and waved in annoyance at the window. 'How do you know?'

'Because I do...' He laughed. 'I know exactly who is in the house and besides, this place is like Fort Knox. We've got more security than the Bank of England. When we have time, I'll take you over to the office and you can look at the twenty-four screens, from where I can see every part of this property, inside and out, all at once.'

'You have what?' Daisy looked through the darkness to where Cole pointed to a break in the trees and a building she'd thought might be a well-camouflaged garage. Tall laurels grew around its edges and the only thing that really gave it away was the narrow block footpath that went from the drive to the building. A row of solar lights at each side of the path led the way and now she looked more closely, there was a small sign by the side of the drive, with the words 'Bailey Construction' clearly written upon it. A painted arrow beneath the words was there to show anyone who needed to know which way they should go.

'I built it because I got sick of working away all the time, so...' He smiled, his face full of pride along with just a modicum of worry. 'This way, I can spend more time at home. We can have all the children we want and I can be close at hand to help you,' he rambled excitedly and pointed to another building that was also set back in the trees. 'That building's a gym, and behind that one there's an annexe that I built for Borys and his sister, Olena.'

Rubbing at her eyes, Daisy looked from one building to the

next while Cole tapped at an app on his phone. 'Give me a minute,' he said, 'and we can put the lights on.'

'Wow,' she finally gasped, 'you have it all worked out, don't you?' Daisy stepped on to the path and walked a little closer to the office. 'And while we're on the subject,' she asked with a growl, 'who the hell are Borys and Olena?'

'They're staff,' Cole replied in a matter-of-fact tone. 'You can't run a house like this on your own, and besides, they're good people, who are from Ukraine. They have nowhere else to be, and they're good at their jobs. Borys does all the gardening and the maintenance, and Olena looks after the house. She cleans and cooks, you'll barely even know they're here except for when you get home from work, when dinner will be served up for you.'

With his car keys still jingling around in one of his hands, Cole held the other towards her, but Daisy couldn't move. The last thing she wanted was staff and even though she knew how ungrateful that made her sound, she wanted nothing more than to go back home, cook her own food, and drink her own wine without having someone else to prepare it. It was just another sign that both she and Cole were on different pages, that she didn't really know him at all, and even though she'd been hoping to put their marriage back together, tonight's events had made her question everything.

Did she love Cole, or did she just love the security he gave her?

It was a question she had to answer, but her thoughts were interrupted as the front door flew open casting a bright light into the garden. With a look of disbelief, Daisy spotted both of Cole's parents, her own dad, his girlfriend, Jenny, and her sister, Sarah, who stood in the entrance.

It was a moment of uncertainty, a time when a sudden wall of noise came out of the house and hit her square in the face. Daisy found herself caught up in an explosion of clapping and cheering and she felt as though every member of her family suddenly wanted to hug her and congratulate them both. Apart from Cole's parents, who each picked up a glass of champagne and slunk off into the depths of the house without saying a word.

# 8

## DAISY

Turning her head against the white cotton pillows, Daisy furrowed her brow. Her first reaction was to panic, to wonder where she was and she found herself blinking repeatedly in a rushed attempt to pull herself out of the drowsy and semi-conscious state she'd been in.

Sitting up reluctantly, Daisy took in the room before flopping back against the pillows. Being here and sleeping in this house had been a mistake, and in an attempt to wake herself up, she stretched out her arms and tried to touch each side of the bed that she'd drunkenly crawled into the night before, after the copious amounts of wine she'd somehow managed to consume.

The night before, the bed had felt as though it had been moving beneath her, swaying like a boat on the waves. Worryingly, she'd hung on to the sides, just in case she'd fallen off. Whereas now, almost sober, she realised that the bed was not only big enough, but wide enough to sleep at least four people, side by side with room to turn over. Which begged the question, why was she alone?

Daisy listened as carefully as she could for Cole, but when it felt more than obvious that he wasn't nearby, she closed her eyes and tried to focus on the slightest of noises. It was something she always did at Pipistrelle. Most mornings she'd smile as she homed in on the sound of the sea. She could practically hear every single wave and had often counted them as they rolled in and out of the bay. But here, at The Willows, there was nothing. No sound. No atmosphere. No nothing. Angrily, Daisy leaned to one side and with her fist clenched as tightly as she could, she punched at the pillow.

'Cole!' she shouted, then waited. 'Cole... where are you?'

Knowing that if she agreed to this move, her life would change dramatically, she really needed to speak to her husband, and she wanted to speak to him alone, before the others got up. The last thing she needed was his mother, Teresa, joining in, or his dad, Patrick, airing his views. It was bad enough that the three of them were all in business together, and that any decision was made in triplicate. Whereas, this... this was her life, and she'd somehow gone from being at home and planning a dinner for two, to being totally derailed. Her whole life was now heading at speed in a different direction and, somehow, she had to find a way to hit the brakes on the rollercoaster she'd inadvertently climbed on to.

Leaning back, Daisy sighed. She knew that hitting the brakes wouldn't be easy. Not on a ride that Cole had initiated. He, along with their whole family, had planned this surprise. They'd all kept this from her, including Sarah, and without exception she felt betrayed by them all.

'So, why are you still here?' she asked herself. 'And why the hell did you drink so much? You know not to do that.' She thought about how easy it would have been to climb in the car and drive herself home, but she'd already had a glass of wine before Cole had got home. Which had been in the back of her mind and had stopped her from driving. Also, the idea of getting in the car and leaving wouldn't have been a great idea, not when she hadn't known exactly where she was or which lane she should turn down. Which all confirmed to her how trapped she'd felt, and a loud sob escaped from her throat.

She could still see the way her family had smiled, laughed and clapped with excitement as they'd burst through the door in a planned way. Only Teresa and Patrick had been reluctant to join in the fun, and the look, along with the unspoken words, his mother had given Cole hadn't got past Daisy. She'd realised that Teresa had been waiting for the argument to start between her son and his wife, for Daisy to kick back, which was exactly why she didn't.

'You can only try for so long,' Daisy whispered out loud. 'You do know that, don't you?'

With a sigh, Daisy wished she'd been true to herself rather than always trying to please others. Rather than stay and party in a house she didn't want or like, she should have called a taxi and gone home. She should have delivered the bombshell of a conversation she'd been planning, along with a profound apology, and then she should have awaited Cole's reaction.

'How can you tell him the truth now?' She rolled her eyes and after pulling in a long, deep breath, Daisy puffed up her cheeks and blew out slowly. 'So, what are you going to do?' she questioned as she thought about going back to Pipistrelle alone. It was her house, her home and one she didn't want to lose. Which left her with the question: what about Cole? Was this the end of their marriage? Was this where they both went their separate ways, with Cole living here in his big house with the office and all his fancy security?

Shuddering at the thought that Cole or one of his staff could be watching her right now, Daisy scanned the bedroom. Like the rest of the house, it was big and ostentatious. It was the kind of room that would have been suited to a posh hotel. Its walls had been painted in shades of beige and chocolate with the occasional gold leaf. An oversized pale cream rug lay beneath the bed and a matching cream sofa stood in front of a large picture window that was covered in shutters. With a memory of the night before, she could still see Cole standing before them, admiring the view and proudly giving her a quick demonstration.

'They're all automatic, voice controlled... Come on, Daisy, why don't you try it?' The excitement in his voice had been clear, but the alcohol had left her feeling drowsy. With all the fight having left her body some hours before, Daisy had simply collapsed on the bed, held on to the edge and tried to stop it from moving while Cole had his moment.

'At night, you can sit here, and you can see all the grounds. All five acres...' he'd said, as she'd drifted in and out of sleep. To her, nothing made sense. This house, and the way it had come about, didn't feel right and she knew, without a doubt, that Cole was hiding something.

Turning over, Daisy tried to think about how enthusiastic everyone else had been at the party. Clusters of balloons had been positioned in prominent places, champagne had been poured, and the music had played. In a kitchen that was bigger than the entire downstairs floor of Pipistrelle, there had been enough food to feed a small army, which hadn't made sense, until Cole had opened the back patio doors and at least fifty of his employees had entered. Even Teresa had lightened up and danced with her son. She'd laughed like a teenager and had given directions to the staff, who had all looked more than comfortable in her presence, which told Daisy that Teresa had been coming in and out of this house for a very long time and that if she were to lay a guess on who'd picked out the curtains, Teresa would be at the top of her list.

Sliding out of the bed, Daisy made her way into the dressing room. It stood to the right of the room and she cast her gaze across just one of the clothes rails. It was the only one with clothes hung on it, which either Cole or Sarah must have sneaked out of her wardrobe from home.

'Oh, so that's where they are...' she whispered as her fingers trailed across the rail and came to a stop when they rested against her favourite towelling dressing gown. It was old, over washed and faded, but nevertheless, it was an item she loved and, amid all her confusion, it left her with just a little bit of assurance. 'Well, at least he knew to bring you, didn't he?' she said before picking out a pair of jeans, and a soft woollen jumper.

After using the bathroom and getting dressed, Daisy pushed her shoulders back and headed towards the door that led to the landing. With her fingers grazing the doorknob, she hoped that, like in Narnia, she would step through it and automatically be transported back to the world she knew. But instead, she was faced with a large, sweeping marble staircase, its panels made of glass and chrome, all of which would need cleaning on a daily basis. At the bottom of the staircase, central to the entrance hall, she couldn't miss the deep, sunken wine cellar. It had a glass door above it and below she could clearly see a spiral staircase that was surrounded by a few hundred bottles of wine. The quantity of it was a sight that made her gasp in the knowledge that Cole had expensive taste and that the cost of that alone would be staggering.

'...it's not negotiable and I've told you to get rid of him.' Cole's voice came from downstairs and broke through the silence. It was more than obvious that he was taking a call from one of the sites and that one of his staff was about to be fired. 'Try the new guy but if he doesn't work, you'll need to call the agency and find a new sparky.'

It was a conversation she'd overheard at least a hundred times before but the mention of a sparky instantly reminded her of Tom. Of the message he'd sent, and the voicemail she still hadn't listened to. While perching on the marble staircase, she dragged her phone out of her pocket, clicked on the screen and once again she read the message he'd sent.

TOM

I know I made a promise, but something's happened, and I really need to see you x

For a moment, Daisy furrowed her brow and then clicked into her voicemail.

'It's me, it's Tom. I tried to message earlier but you didn't answer.' His voice was breathless and panicked. 'Anyhow, I've got myself into a bit of trouble. Debts I can't afford to pay and...' The line went silent, and Daisy pulled the phone away from her ear and looked at the handset. 'Anyhow, don't worry. I know you're not going to like this, but I didn't have a choice. I really need to earn some, and I spoke to Cole; I've got a job at Bailey Construction.'

For a moment, Daisy held on to the handrail. She felt as though the whole staircase had shifted beneath her and she closed her eyes and wondered if Tom was the sparky that Cole had mentioned. She felt the nausea begin. The thought that Tom had spoken to Cole was terrifying. It would have been a conversation that could have gone in so many directions and, with her fingertips tapping the marble steps, she wondered if Cole already knew the truth. If Tom had let slip who he was, how well he'd known Cole's wife. Or whether, obliviously, Cole had offered him a job. They were both scenarios she could comprehend, especially if Cole had found out about her secret before she'd had the chance to tell him. Was that why showing her the house had been so important?

With her foot hovering above the bottom step, Daisy hesitated before entering the kitchen where, just the night before, every worktop had been covered in carnage. But now, it was spotlessly clean. Soft LED lighting lit up the walkways, and a large island dominated one side of the space.

'Wow, someone's been busy,' she said as brightly as she could, and she trailed her fingertips across the top of the black marble worktop. 'I was fully expecting to have to get up and start cleaning.' She sauntered across the room to where Cole sat at a small oak table, surrounded by a large corner window.

'Darling, you're up and yes, Mum and Olena were stars, both up early and, between them, they got it all sorted.' Cole stood up and dropped a kiss on her cheek. 'But now you're up, we can make a few plans.'

Sliding into the chair beside him, with her head still feeling decidedly foggy, Daisy smiled and nodded, her gaze taking in the number of items that covered the table. To one side of her was a small bowl with six sections all filled with a different type of jam or honey, and in the middle, a round bowl, filled with butter. There were knives, forks, and spoons in all different sizes, which lay next to an array of flowery china crockery that she'd never previously seen.

Biting her tongue, Daisy shuffled around in her seat and blew out a long, slow breath. This room, this house, was where she was supposed to come to live. It was the house that Cole had asked her to love, yet right now she felt as though she were in the middle of a strange hotel.

'Where is everyone?' She looked over her shoulder, half

expecting to see Sarah bumble down the stairs and make an appearance. 'Are they still in bed, because I could do with a chat?' Cole had already mentioned his mum – with any luck, Teresa would have already taken herself home.

'Mum and Dad set off about half an hour ago and Sarah was up early and went to the gym.' He twisted in his seat, looked out of the window, 'And if I'm not mistaken, she's still in there, which means that we get to eat breakfast together.'

Daisy noticed the way Cole's eyes lit up as he spoke, and the way he nervously twisted his hands together told her he had a conversation of his own that he wanted to have. A conversation he'd obviously practised. 'As I said, Mum and Dad have already set off and they're going to make a start on the packing at Pipistrelle for us. I've ordered a removal van that will turn up around midday,' he said decisively, 'I've roped in some of the lads who were here last night and they're going to help load and unload. By tonight' – he lifted his arms, leaned back in his chair and hooked his fingers neatly behind his head in a pose – 'we'll be here. Starting a new life in this house. Isn't that incredible?'

'Wait a minute, they're doing what?' Daisy's voice quivered. Even though Cole had made it perfectly clear the night before that he had every intention of living in this house, he hadn't mentioned that he'd put Teresa in charge or that they'd be moving in so quickly. 'But I thought... I mean... what's the damn rush?' Moving to this house hadn't been on her agenda. She still hadn't decided whether she'd do it or not, and now with the extra pressure of Tom going to work for Cole, she knew that telling her husband about her affair had to come first, even though, by doing so, Tom could be out of a job before he'd begun.

In her mind, she'd been planning to drag the move out. She'd wanted to make it as difficult as possible. She'd actually hoped that once they got back to Pipistrelle, she'd be able to sit down with Cole and really talk, but once again he'd already moved the goalposts. The plan had already been put in motion, and with Cole determined to live in this house, by tonight, one of them was going to highly disappointed.

With her mind fixed firmly on her future self, Daisy knew she had to make a choice and quickly, and whatever that choice was, it had to be the right one for her and for her future.

'What do you mean, what's the damn rush?' Leaning forward, Cole ran his fingers along the line of her jaw, tipped her head upwards, and met her gaze with his own. 'It's what we discussed. You agreed that you'd at least give it a go... I think your exact words were "I'll give it three or four months and if I'm not entirely happy, I'll be back at Pipistrelle before spring is in the air."'

'Did I?' she questioned quickly and furrowed her brow, thoughtfully. 'Cole, I don't remember saying that.' She blinked repeatedly, gave her lip a worrying bite. All she remembered about the night before was small talk. She and Cole had barely had a minute together, with both of them being dragged in opposite directions for most of the night. The only time they'd had the chance to speak alone had been when they'd reached the bedroom and Cole had practically carried her upstairs.

'Seriously.' He laughed, pulled her towards him and placed a long lingering kiss against her lips. 'I guess you don't remember making love to me either?' He lifted a hand, fanned his face. 'Because, darling, you were unbelievably hot.'

Staring out of the window, Daisy felt confusion take over. She couldn't remember the lovemaking, nor could she remember a conversation that was likely to alter the course of her life, and now she was worried by her own ability to control her drinking. One glass had led to another and even though she hadn't thought she'd drank too much, she clearly must have. Which was worrying. She'd always known that drink made her act unpredictably –

after all, it had been a drink or two that had led to her adulterous affair with Tom. And now, when she thought about it, that whole evening had become clouded, too.

'I was drunk,' she said, and gave an incredulous gasp. 'You can't hold me to anything I said last night, Cole.' She shook her head, stood up and went to walk away but Cole grabbed at her hand and pulled her towards him. 'Please don't hold me to what I said, Cole. It wouldn't be fair. I really can't remember agreeing to making a move and what's more, I don't want to.'

Looking into his eyes, Daisy could see them begin to soften. But the moment was broken when a soft cough came from behind them, and with a roll of his jaw, Cole averted his eyes.

'I'm so sorry,' Olena said in a soft Ukrainian accent. 'I don't mean to intrude.' She looked down, avoided Daisy's stare and nervously held the plate out for Daisy to see. 'I brought your breakfast, and I was trying to wait for you to finish speaking but the food, it was going to go cold.'

Concerned about how long Olena had been standing there, Daisy jumped to one side and picked up the over-flowery teapot and began to pour the tea as the colour rose to her cheeks.

'Enjoy,' Olena said quietly as she inched forward. She had long blonde hair that was tied back from her face, high cheek-bones and a svelte figure that Daisy couldn't help but admire. Gracefully, Olena placed the plate on the table, and gave Daisy a hesitant smile before walking around the table's edge to remove the plate that Cole had been using. 'I'll take these away and sorry,' she mumbled, 'I didn't mean to disturb you.'

'Jesus Christ, Cole,' Daisy snapped the moment Olena disappeared out of sight. 'Is this my damn life now? I mean, what the hell is this?' Once again, she picked up the teapot and pointed to the china cup and saucer. 'Since when did we drink out of cups and saucers that looked as though they belonged in the sixties?

And as for her walking up behind us while we're having a moment...' She tipped her head, made sure that Olena still couldn't hear her. 'It just feels wrong.' She closed her eyes and tried to calm down. 'This is supposed to be our home, Cole, not a bloody restaurant where we have to mind our p's and q's and sit up to attention at the table...' She whispered the words dramatically, looked down at the plate of eggs and bacon and felt her stomach turn with nausea. 'I mean, isn't it bad enough that we have to say good morning to a practical stranger before we can eat?' Sighing, Daisy didn't really know what else she could say, and as she pushed the plate out of her way, she furrowed her brow in annoyance. 'I normally eat fruit and honey in a morning, not bacon and eggs, and I'm quite capable of laying and clearing my own table without having a housekeeper to do that for me.'

'Well, that's a shame, because you've got one,' Cole snapped back. 'You just need to learn how to manage her. You have to give her some boundaries. Borys has worked for me for almost a year, and she's his sister. She had nowhere to go. The war displaced her, and Borys asked me if she could stay in exchange for some work. He even offered to work extra hours to cover her costs, and I agreed and I'm not going back on my word.' Picking up his cup, Cole took a long slurp of his drink. 'Or would you like me to send her back to a warzone and a life of terror?'

With her face burning with the embarrassment of being chastised by her husband, Daisy slumped back into her chair. It wasn't often that Cole snapped, or lost his temper, not with her, and with her head still pounding from her hangover, she didn't like it at all.

Standing up to look out through the window, Cole studied the landscaped gardens that resembled a golf course. He placed his hands on his hips and Daisy held her breath, waited for him to make the speech that it looked like he was waiting to make. For a moment, she wondered if she should cut in before he could start, take her chance to wipe the slate clean and for her to finally tell him what had happened with Tom. But once again she knew the time wasn't right, worried about his reaction when he was already annoyed with her.

'I have some business to attend to on one of the sites,' Cole finally added. 'Now, can I trust you to be nice to the staff while I'm gone or are you going to sulk like a petulant toddler?' As he spoke, Cole turned and dropped a hand on her shoulder. 'Daisy, I love you more than words and I need you on side with this.' He held an arm out and pointed up to the ceiling where the chandeliers were hung. 'Because this is my dream, something I've wanted for a very long time, and I've worked so hard to make it all perfect for you. For us.'

Closing her eyes, Daisy knew he was right. Most people would give their right arm to live in this house. It was the perfect property. The problem was it was far too perfect. Everything was done, the furniture, the décor, even the ornaments had already been chosen by somebody else. Somebody had already made their stamp on this house, which made Daisy wonder what part of it was hers and whether or not she'd hold any influence.

Staring at her husband, Daisy knew that he couldn't have done this alone. That right now, he was a man she barely recognised. Gone was the loving, caring man who'd always taken her feelings into consideration. Now, he'd become the man who wanted her to leave her old home behind and, selfishly, he wanted her to live in this one.

'You have to make a choice?' she whispered to herself as she watched Cole walk away, out of the room. It was a choice between Cole and Pipistrelle – about whether she could she live without one or the other. Daisy just wasn't sure.

This house might be Cole's dream but buying Pipistrelle had

been one of hers. If she was totally honest, it had been a dream she'd had for a very long time and one she'd shared with Tom as a teenager. She could still vividly remember the days after school when they'd walked hand in hand along the bay. They'd chatted about the houses that stood there and each day, they'd picked a different house that they'd live in; they'd talked about how they'd make it their own and fill it with the family they'd create together.

But then Daisy had met and married Cole. She'd cast Tom aside and the dream was gone. Standing up and leaving her breakfast untouched, Daisy walked across the kitchen and into the hallway in search of Cole. She walked through the playroom where the snooker table stood with just one or two balls still remaining. It was more than obvious that someone had played a game last night without setting the balls back up, and slowly she ran her fingers across the green baize and grabbed at a ball, which she angrily rolled as hard as she could towards one of the pockets, laughing as it dropped over the edge and on to the floor.

'Cole!' she shouted out loud. The room had numerous doors and in her search for her husband she began opening one after the other. Behind one, she found a small home theatre; another room they didn't need. With an exasperated growl, she slammed the door, before pulling open another. Even though the anger was still spilling from her, she took a step back, looked around in astonishment and then smiled at the small but adequate swimming pool that stood right before her.

'Cole, where the hell are you?' Daisy sat down on the cream tile that bordered the water. She hung her feet over the edge and trailed her fingers in water that was much warmer than she'd expected. The atmosphere in the room was like that of a high-class spa – tranquil and private. Meditatively, she listened to piped music that filled the room and felt her body relax until Cole walked towards her. The sight of him wearing nothing more than a pair of swimming shorts, revealing his firm, contoured body, made her smile. She watched in admiration as he dived in. Impressively, the water barely splashed, and she laughed as just a few gentle ripples rolled towards her.

'Come on, you have to admit it, this is a great house, isn't it?' Cole yelled from the opposite side of the pool. He had a look of pride on his face, and with a mischievous grin, he leaned against the side with his arms spread outward. 'This is the first time I've ever got to enjoy a house that I actually built and, darling, I just can't tell you how good that feels.' He moved away from the side, leaned back in the water and for just a few minutes, he was floating, suspended in the water.

'I do love you, Cole,' she whispered and meant it. She did love her husband although, right now, she did feel just a little bit bullied and the only way she knew how to regain the control was to play him at his own game. 'And yes, you did do a good job with the house. It's amazing, it's just...' Leaning forward, she waited for him to swim towards her and, lovingly, Daisy took hold of his hands, pressed a kiss against his lips and ran her fingers across the wet, rough skin of his fingers. He'd spent years working hard and, genuinely, she did want him to have everything he wanted... except for this house. Especially if it meant trading this one for hers.

'Why don't you get in?' Cole suggested. 'The water's warm and relaxing and...' He smiled, splashed the water up and at her face and laughed when it dripped from her hair. He threw his head backward, pushed his hair away from his face and, jokingly, he lifted his eyebrows up and down. 'We could... you know... maybe finish what we started last night, right here in the pool?'

'Don't be crazy!' Daisy burst out laughing, looked over her shoulder and considered her options. 'We couldn't, could we?

Besides, according to you earlier, we made love last night right after I promised you that we'd move to this house.'

'I did say that didn't I?' He chuckled, and ducked his head under the water. 'But that was different and...' He tapped the water with a flat hand and pouted as he sloshed the water towards her. 'You said you didn't remember it, so in my book I'd say that means we still need to christen this house.'

'What, in here?' She shuffled away from the water, away from Cole's playful gaze. It was a look she'd seen before and she felt sure that, any moment now, he'd be dragging her forward. 'We can't, I didn't bring a swimming costume.' She looked anxiously over her shoulder, fully expecting Olena to be standing there. For her to be spying on them and watching from a distance.

'Baby, this is our home, you don't need a costume...' Cole answered before once again he patted the water, inviting her in. His seductive smile was followed by a cheeky but definite wink. 'It's twenty-nine degrees, absolutely perfect for skinny dipping.'

'Cole, no, we can't...' Automatically, her hand pointed at the door and windows where she could see Borys working outside. He was muscular, lean and easy on the eye, but the last thing she wanted was to give him a show. 'The staff, they're... well, they could be watching, they're everywhere.'

'Security, close the blinds,' Cole said out loud as a look of pride crossed his face and the blinds automatically turned to cover the windows. 'Security, lock the pool doors,' he added as he lifted his hands up in a told-you-so shrug, 'Darling, it doesn't get any easier than that, does it?'

Mesmerised, Daisy sat, mouth open. Her eyes flitted from Cole to the door, and nervously she looked up at a small red light that was lit above it. 'What's that?'

'That lets everyone else in the house know that the door is locked and we want some privacy. No one will disturb us, not now. And if you're wondering, the door can be opened manually from the inside and only with the keypad if you're on the outside. The code is my birthdate: zero five, zero two. It's the same for any door in the house including the gates. The only door that's different is the office. All you have to do if you want to get into most of the house is think of me and remember that number.'

'Why is the office different?'

'Because it is.'

'But...' Looking down, Daisy felt her shoulders lift and fall in a sigh, and for a moment she didn't trust herself to look into Cole's eyes. Her husband was definitely hiding something, but she didn't know what. 'Is there something in there that you don't want me to see?'

'Daisy, now you're being silly,' he said as he lifted both hands out of the water, and an array of droplets fell from them. 'It's a business, the office is separate and that's where I keep the safe. That's where the security on the house is. I'd be stupid to give everyone the number, wouldn't I?' Cole rolled his jaw, the tension surrounding him clear to see. 'Now come on, be a good girl, get in the pool.'

Sulking, Daisy took a step backward, shaking her head despondently. 'But then, I'm not just everyone, Cole. I'm your wife and this is the house you want me to live in,' she threw back as firmly as she could, before the emotion broke in her voice.

Sighing, Cole held out a hand. 'Okay, okay, the number is just the other way around: zero two, zero five, the normal code in reverse. But if you're going over there, I'd rather go with you. There's a lot of technology and I don't want you messing with it, not until I've explained it all.'

Nodding in agreeance, Daisy felt her anxiety level begin to calm down. Cole had given her the code, which must mean that there was nothing to hide, that her husband wasn't doing anything that he shouldn't, and a sense of relief caused her to tremble.

'Daisy, are you getting in or not, because,' he held up his hands, held them out palms forward. 'I'm beginning to shrivel.' He smiled cheekily and then he dropped a hand into the water and adjusted his shorts. 'And you don't want me all shrivelled, do you?'

Laughing, Daisy stepped awkwardly backward. She didn't really want to swim, but the idea of the lovemaking did appeal. She knew that during sex, she could ask him anything and get a positive answer. If she wanted Cole to call off the move, she had no choice but to at least meet him halfway – and at least now she knew how to get in and out of the gates. It was as though the prison door to this house had been left ajar, and now she had the permission to escape should she want to.

Sitting down on a lounger, Daisy considered her options but kept coming back to the same question. Did she want to save her marriage? Did she want to hold on to what she had with Cole or did she want to risk it all for a man she'd once dated? A man she really didn't know, not any more. But thoughts of Tom still played on her mind and it was more than obvious that Tom still thought about her too. Which meant making a choice – did she stay where she was and do all the things she'd always done, or did she take a giant leap into the unknown – and with her mind spinning like a vortex, she turned to her husband, kept her eyes fixed on his and she fondly watched the way he lifted a hand and beckoned her towards him.

'Come on, Daisy, make me a happy man, climb into the water?'

Slowly and sensually, Daisy stood up. She walked to the edge of the pool, crouched and pressed her lips against Cole's. The kisses were tender and slow at first, Cole's hands moving to each side of her face in a well-practised manoeuvre, and then, with a passion that felt unbridled yet familiar, she allowed him to take control, and right at that moment she chose her husband. It was the right choice to make. The one she should have made two months before, and whether she liked it or not, she had no choice but to forget about Tom.

9
_____

DAISY

'Fine, just throw them into the donate pile,' Daisy grumbled sarcastically to Sarah as she sat down on the floor and leaned heavily against the sofa. 'Seems like most other things have been put there.' She rolled her eyes angrily at Teresa, Cole's mother, as one box after the other was packed and hastily dropped into a pile.

Arriving back at Pipistrelle just two hours before, she'd felt happy and light-hearted. The lovemaking between her and Cole had been impulsive and explosive; the passion had been off the scale and her eagerness to repeat the experience was high on her list. But a couple of hours in the company of both Teresa and Patrick had brought her mood crashing to the floor, leaving her with a feeling of being both irritable and short-tempered.

An almighty storm had rolled in from the sea, and from where she sat she could see the rain hammering against the patio window with force, and a rumbling of thunder could be heard coming from somewhere beyond the castle in Bamburgh.

'These are only DVDs, and I've not watched any of them since we've been paying for Netflix,' she added. Picking up a marker pen she hesitated before scrawling a brief description on the side of the box. Giving her sister a forced half-smile, Daisy looked thoughtfully from one pile of boxes to the next. The earlier burst of energy and enthusiasm she'd had had quickly dissipated, and even though she'd tried to show willing, she knew that the deal she'd made with Cole wasn't really what she wanted. The realisation of what she'd agreed to had hit her. She felt bullied into a decision she hadn't wanted to make, and because of that she'd begun to fill small boxes with casual clothing and toiletries and took a small amount of pleasure in stacking the boxes up at the back of the lounge. 'These stay here,' she'd announced quite firmly, 'I might have agreed to go along with Cole's wishes, but I'm not quite prepared to empty the house completely.' She'd stared longingly at the boxes. 'Besides, I'll need changes of clothes etc., when I come down here to clean or do the gardening.' She knew that her words were no more than excuses; deep down, she simply didn't want to leave, and by leaving a small part of her life here, she'd be holding on to just a small part of her normality.

'Daisy, if it were me, most of this stuff would go in the bin.' Leaning back against the settee, Sarah pulled a face, looked down and began to study her nails. 'Because there's no reason to keep any of it. Not when you've got a house like The Willows, is there?'

'Well, gee thanks, sis, and which of your professional opinions is that?' Daisy snapped, angrily. 'As an estate agent, or as Cole's personal assistant?' As she said the words, she closed her eyes and wished wholeheartedly that she could take them back. It wasn't Sarah's fault that she worked for Cole, or that Sarah had only inherited half of her mother's shop. The result being she still worked both jobs, as well as having worked alongside Daisy for the whole of the morning. Blinking away tears, Daisy knew that her temper had frayed, that it had begun the moment they'd arrived home to find both of Cole's parents already in situ, packing and taking control of her home. Which had left Daisy feeling more than bereft. Every time a box was filled and put in a pile, she felt as though a piece of her heart was being torn out, and even though she'd found it difficult to hold her temper, she had. The last thing she wanted was to stir the cauldron. She'd always been convinced that his parents didn't like her. It was something that had never really been said, but over the years, it had become more than obvious, and while staring into the contents of one of the boxes, Daisy tried to imagine how Cole's life would be if only he'd met someone who they could have both approved of.

'Keep, donate or store?' Sarah asked again more sternly, seemingly ignoring Daisy's comment about her profession. She'd stood up and was currently waving a small clock around in the air. 'As an estate agent, even you would tell your clients to declutter, and put their crap in the bin and create a clear canvas. I've heard you tell them on so many occasions that they had to give prospective buyers the chance to imagine what their own possessions would look like in that space,' she added while she comically stepped back and forth between the two piles. 'And you have to admit, this clock is a bit ugly. So which pile would you like it to go in?'

Studying her sister through narrowed eyes, Daisy pulled in a breath and blew it out as slowly and calmly as she could, then smiled. 'That ugly piece of crap, as you call it, is the clock you bought us a couple of Christmases ago. So, you know...' She lifted a finger up to her chin as though she were thinking about the right answer. 'I'll let you choose the pile.'

Finding a modicum of amusement in the look that crossed Sarah's face, Daisy stood up and made her way along the hallway. She could hear laughing coming from the downstairs bedroom that her dad and Jenny were packing up. In direct contrast, Cole's dad marched up and down the stairs sternly. He was smartly dressed in shirt, trousers and a quarter-zip jumper and his glasses were perched on the top of his balding head. In his arms, he held a small laundry basket full of bedding and on top he'd placed a set of grey plastic bathroom scales. When he saw Daisy, he picked the scales up with a finger and thumb and waved them around in the air with a look of disgust.

'The layer of dust on these tells me that you don't use them very often.' Patrick curled his lip as he spoke. 'So, I'm guessing we can put them straight in the skip.' Without waiting for an answer, he tossed the scales on top of an ever-growing pile of things Cole's parents had designated as rubbish. Items that were obviously not quite up to their standards.

'This,' she whispered to Sarah as Patrick spun on his heel and left the room, 'is what I'm up against, all the damn time.' She felt her shoulders slump in despair, but defiantly she picked up the scales, carried them across the room and she dropped them on top of the pile that would stay at the house.

'Why would you even care what they think?' Sarah asked as she wandered into the hall to look in the mirror. 'You've got Cole, haven't you? You married him even though they were vehemently against it and, do you know what, I'd kill for that house he just built for you – and possibly your husband.' Sarah laughed. 'Okay, joke. But I mean, come on, that wine cellar and the games room are totally insane, and that gym! You should have come over there and joined me this morning, I had a great workout.' She lifted her hoodie to show off her stomach. 'You do know I'm planning on taking out an annual membership, don't you?'

'Sarah, use the gym whenever you want but you know how much I'd hate going in there, don't you?' Daisy replied as Patrick once again appeared in the doorway and dropped a small, wheeled suitcase on to the keep pile, before quickly disappearing back down the corridor. 'And what the hell am I going to do with a wine cellar?'

'You didn't seem to mind it last night.' Sarah laughed again. 'In fact, at one point, I thought you were going to go down there and sit on the floor and drink!'

'Mind? Did I have a damn choice? And as for going down there, it would have been the only way of escaping those two.' Daisy whispered as Patrick strode back into the room, a pile of clothes in his arms.

'Patrick, they're my clothes,' Daisy quickly said. 'I'd really like to keep those. And please, don't go into my bedroom. I'll sort that room for myself.' She gritted her teeth, caught Sarah's eye and gave her a smile that made the muscles in her cheeks contract. She tried to work out how many times she'd had to force her face into an upward direction during the last twelve hours. It was a thought that made her want to frown, just because she could. The other thing she wanted to do was to put all of her possessions back where they'd come from.

'Is it really so wrong,' Daisy whispered under her breath, 'that I just to want to stay here? I just want to lead a simple life and stay here in a house that reminds me so much of our mum.'

Dropping on to her knees to sit beside her sister, Daisy gave a cautious look over her shoulder at where Teresa had walked in and was now standing by the fridge. Her hair had been clipped back tightly to emphasise her perfect jawline, which, in Daisy's opinion just wasn't natural for a woman of her age. Surreptitiously, she found herself looking closely at Teresa's skin in the hope she'd spot the signs of a badly done facelift but frowned when she couldn't.

Sitting back, Daisy watched the way Teresa stood with her hands on her hips, giving the contents of the fridge yet another judgemental stare. She was lifting each of the items up in turn before slowly turning them around in her hand. 'The sell by dates, darling, you do check them, don't you?' she'd asked pointedly before curling a lip and deciding whether or not the item went in a box or a bin, and quite often without Daisy seeing.

'Is she the damn food police?' Sarah whispered with a giggle. 'It's bad enough that you're being all judgy today, without Cole's mum joining in.'

Daisy bit down on her lip. She'd given up hope that she'd ever fit into Cole's original family of three. His parents were a formidable force and with Cole being an only child, they'd very quickly tied him into the family firm, which was how and why he came to run Bailey Construction. Not being a part of the business was why Daisy had always felt like she was the extra cog that had somehow been dropped into the Bailey wheel. Even Sarah worked there three days a week, and because of this she'd quite often found it easier to bite her tongue and say nothing, rather than go to war with her husband or with his parents.

'Urgh,' Teresa shrieked, 'Daisy, is this fish?' She lifted a packet up to her nose and sniffed. 'It's in a drawer with the tomatoes. Why on earth is it in a drawer with all the other food?' She tutted loudly. 'You do know that you shouldn't do that, don't you? Didn't your mother teach you anything?' Holding the fish in one of her hands at arm's length, Teresa reached into the drawer with her other hand and pulled out the vine tomatoes, sneering with an air of contempt. 'You can't put the fish and vegetables in the same drawer, darling; you'll be giving everyone food poisoning.'

'I was...' Daisy was going to tell her how she'd bought the ingredients just the night before, how she'd been about to cook them before her son, in his wisdom, had thrown everything into the fridge and into the same drawer. But she didn't manage to finish the sentence before Teresa had dropped the thick, meaty fillets straight into the bin.

Standing up, Daisy marched out of the room. 'I can't sit here and listen to that,' she said over her shoulder as Sarah followed her. 'I need to get out of here because the smell of that fish suddenly makes me want to gag and I'm not having her saying anything more about the way I store my food.'

Swinging open the front door, Daisy went to step out but stopped abruptly. The rain was still falling, thunder still rumbled in the distance and, as though it were putting on one last show, a streak of lightning shot across the bay.

'Look, let's go upstairs,' Sarah took her arm and steered her down the corridor and straight up the stairs. 'We can start on your bedroom, before Patrick decides to go through your knickers.'

Smiling at the way her sister always knew what to say to lighten the mood, Daisy made her way to her bedroom and flopped on to the bed, in a dramatic, Scarlett O'Hara kind of a way. 'It's not that I'm not grateful...' she pleaded. 'I know Cole really wants this, but he's so out of order! I haven't had the time to prepare myself mentally for leaving, yet here we are...' She rolled on to her back and held her hands out in the air. 'And what's more, if I had the balls, I'd give him an ultimatum and hope that he'd choose to stay here, with me, in this house.' She paused, swallowed hard. Admitting to Sarah that things between her and Cole had been difficult for the past couple of months. She couldn't risk telling Sarah about her affair with Tom – not when Sarah had always idolised Cole. Within moments of them meeting, he'd quickly turned into the big brother that Sarah had never had – that's if big brothers happily gave you a job the minute you left school or forked out for a brand-new car for your twenty-first birthday. It was one of the traits that Daisy had always loved about Cole the most. Her husband was a successful businessman and with that success came pleasure and pain. Financially, Cole took care of everyone, including Daisy's father and especially Sarah. But the painful points were the hours he spent away from home, the times he'd worked the tools in all weathers and the pressure of ensuring the business was stable when times got tough.

Jumping up from the bed, Daisy knelt on the floor, picked up a flat-packed cardboard box that Teresa had left there and began to erect it.

'Look, you know I wouldn't leave Cole, not really, don't you?' she added. 'I just wish I could give him a bit of a shock, convince him to stay here, and then we wouldn't be doing this on a Saturday morning, but rather walking along the beach or into Bamburgh.' She paused just long enough to stare out of the upstairs patio window, with its small French balcony. It was the perfect place for two people to stand, breath in the air and take in the view. Or it would be, if the rain wasn't lashing down and blurring the beauty of the landscape and the rugged shoreline beyond. It was a view that, if she went ahead with this move, she wouldn't have for much longer. 'Sarah, what am I doing? I don't want to move and even though my mind is all over the place, I keep trying to think of a way I can stay, and right now I feel as though I've only got two choices. I can either go along with this... this farce and prove that us living in a house, decorated and finished by others, isn't realistic or I give him an ultimatum. We stay here together, or he goes and lives in his big flashy house all by himself?' Lifting her hands up to her hair, Daisy pushed it back and away from her face. 'Which would be difficult now, because apparently last night while under the influence of a bloody wine cellar – that I didn't know I needed – I've agreed to moving and giving it a try.' She shook her head and with the bile rising and falling in her throat, she pulled a tissue out of her pocket and held it cautiously up to her mouth. 'Which reminds me,' she said while blowing out slowly, 'I should really stop drinking; I've got the hangover from hell, that smell of fish turned my stomach and right now there's something in the room that's making me gag.'

'Are you sure you're not pregnant as well as being ungrateful?' Sarah threw across the room with a searching glare before speaking at speed. 'Cole thought he was doing a good thing, we all thought it was a great surprise, and you've got no idea just how difficult it all was to keep such a big secret. And with Cole's help, I had to pick out a kitchen. While Cole was away on site, I had to choose a colour palette for the home theatre. Which was really stressful. And all the time I was working on your house, my own job was going to the hills, and I had to spend hours and hours doing so much overtime.' Lifting Daisy's 'to be read' pile of books from under the bedside cabinet, Sarah slammed them into a box and quickly followed them with the contents of Daisy's bedside drawer. 'Eeew. What is all this stuff?'

Grabbing at the box, Daisy closed the lid and gave her sister an exasperated glare. 'Those are my personal things and why the hell are you emptying my drawers, you shouldn't be doing that, and as for the house, it should have been *me* picking out kitchen, not *you*.'

Sitting with her back against the bed, Daisy kept her eyes on the ceiling as the nausea worsened. Her hand went to her chest as the feeling of heartburn began, and for a few seconds she tried to relax and calm herself down. She was more than aware that Cole had been trying to do something amazing because everyone said so. But the fact that he'd kept a secret that big for so long just didn't sit well. Until she remembered that she too had kept a secret of her own and that secret was one that could quite easily blow their marriage apart.

Which begged the question: was she annoyed with Cole, or with herself? For the past few months, her guilt had been crippling her. She'd thought of nothing else but Tom since London and about how quickly and easily she'd fallen into his bed. It hadn't been something she'd ever thought she'd do, which had made her question her marriage to the point that she'd even considered what kind of a future she had and whether or not leaving Cole was the answer.

She'd even drawn up a list of pros and cons and on one side of that list she'd put that Cole was generous and loving. On the other side, she'd written the words 'occasionally cold and ruthless', which was true. Cole did have a dark side that, thankfully, he'd never used against her. He had however been known to cut someone dry without as much as a blink. He'd always been renowned for his temper on site and if he was riled, the men who worked for him had quickly learned to take a wide berth, none of them wanting to risk the consequences that might come.

'Wow, I think I've found what stinks: it's one of Cole's socks?' Sarah said as she pulled an odd sock out from under the bed. It was thick, woollen and had an overpoweringly strong smell of old, sweaty boots. 'It stinks awful,' she said as she playfully wafted it around in the air, right in front of Daisy's face.

'I'm going to be sick...'

Jumping up, Daisy ran into the en suite, slammed the door behind her, and with a lack of food in her stomach she began to heave. The smell of Cole's sock had finished her off. The sickness that had been lurking for the whole morning had suddenly taken over and with her head in her hands, Daisy knelt on the floor, right next to the toilet bowl, where she stayed, too afraid to move in case the sickness continued.

'Daisy...' Sarah's muffled voice came from the other side of the door. 'Daisy...'

Leaning against the radiator, Daisy felt her own forehead. She felt warm and clammy and with her head leaning forward until it almost touched her knees, she could hear Sarah's words spinning around in her mind. *You're not pregnant, are you?*

Kneeling up, Daisy ran the tap and splashed the cold water against her face. 'She's wrong. You can't be pregnant...' she whispered out loud, 'you just can't be...' She bit down heavily on her lip, tried to work out her dates and began to count on her fingers how many weeks it had been since she'd come back from London.

'Look, I'm sorry,' Sarah shouted, with her knuckles tapping relentlessly against the back of the bathroom door. 'I'll admit, you did look pale and wafting the sock at you was a step too far.' She paused, took a step back. 'Are you all right? Do you want some water?'

Shaking her head as though Sarah could see her, Daisy flushed the toilet. 'I'm fine,' she responded, 'I just... I just need a minute.'

Trembling with fear, Daisy closed her eyes. 'What should I do...?' she said out loud, as her eyes flashed open to rest on a small wicker basket. It was a decorative piece that she'd purposely placed on top of the bathroom cabinet to hold a selection of tampons and overnight towels. Her emergency supply, which she hadn't had to use for too long, and while she continued to calculate the weeks and months, she remembered the pregnancy tests she'd once bought following a false alarm that she'd hidden in there over a year before.

Sitting down on the edge of the shower cubicle, Daisy turned the pale blue box over and over, read the instructions and tried to convince herself that she didn't need to take it. Besides, the test was old. It might give a false reading.

Less than five minutes later, Daisy walked back into the bedroom, her tear-stained face enough to alert Sarah to the fact that something was wrong. 'You were right...' Daisy whispered. 'I did a test.' She held the small white stick up to show her sister. 'I did them both.'

Sitting upright with eyes as wide as saucers, Sarah held out her hand, swallowed hard, took the two tests from Daisy and stared at them both with interest. 'It says – oh my God, Daisy – they say you... you're pregnant?' Her eyes went from stick to stick, then to Daisy and then back to the sticks. 'I mean, this is fantastic and oh my God, I don't know what else to say but wow... Did you suspect anything? Does Cole know?'

Dropping to her knees beside her sister, Daisy felt the tears fall down her face as, lovingly, Sarah's arms immediately surrounded her. 'I only did the test because of what you said, so no, of course Cole doesn't know. Not unless he's good at telepathy.'

'Well then, that's the next job. You have to tell him.' Jumping up, Sarah began to dance around the room, excitedly. 'He's going to be stoked, and do you know what, I'm finally going to be an auntie. My sister is going to be a mummy and Cole, oh my God, he's going to make the very best kind of daddy, what do you think it will be, a girl or a boy?'

Pulling in a deep breath, Daisy pulled a tissue out of her pocket and dabbed at her eyes. The tests had both been positive. She was pregnant. The problem was, she couldn't join in with Sarah's excitement, not when she couldn't be sure whether Tom or Cole was the father.

The only thing that right now she *could* be sure of was that Cole – for all his good and bad points – had always given her security. He'd always supported her both mentally and financially in everything she'd ever wanted to do, and she knew that, without a doubt, her baby would have a good, grounded lifestyle. Whereas with Tom, she couldn't honestly say that.

Leaning back against the bed, Daisy stared out through the patio doors and towards the island of Lindisfarne that stood in the distance. Today, surrounded by rain clouds, it was hard to believe that as a sixteen-year-old girl, she'd walked along that beach, hand in hand with Tom. Back then, they'd had dreams and wishes, and at the time, she could have honestly said that Tom would have made a good, loving father. And even though he'd still been an apprentice electrician, he'd have done all he could to provide for them. But now, she barely knew him. The only thing she did know was what she'd seen in London during the one night they'd spent together. A time that now felt hazy. Like a diminishing dream that had disappeared the moment she'd woken.

'Sarah, I feel a bit confused, baffled and, I don't know... I need to tell you something. I don't know...' She gasped out loud as she cut the words short. She realised how close she'd come to blurting the truth but had stopped herself with just a second to spare and, horrified by her own actions, she clasped a hand across her mouth knowing that if she said it out loud, it would make it real. They would be the words she'd never get to take back. Which meant that, like it or not, she had to keep the truth to herself – and what's more, she had to put her one-night stand behind her.

'What are you saying?' Sarah asked quizzically as she sat back down, placed a hand on each of Daisy's shoulders and squeezed. 'Are you saying that you don't know what to do?' she questioned but continued without waiting for Daisy to answer. 'Well, that's perfectly understandable. But you do know what you want, don't you?' She raised her eyebrows comically in question. 'You need to go home, and you need to tell your husband that he's about to become a daddy!' She stopped and gave Daisy a wide, heartfelt smile.

Nodding, Daisy looked down at her hand, where her wedding ring encircled her finger. Sarah was right. She had no choice but to tell Cole about the baby, before it became obvious, and then, before she told anyone else, she had to convince herself that Cole was the father.

With the rain hitting the window and a flash of lightning streaking violently across a darkening sky, Tom dropped his tools, turned to the generator and hit the kill switch. The loud, overpowering noise stopped immediately and for the first time that day the building site went quiet, and Tom sighed a breath of relief.

Walking to the window, Tom moved the reels of wire off the sill before leaning forward and looking out. From the upstairs bedroom of the house he was working on, he could see the whole site. It was large and impressive and even though the weather was becoming worse by the minute, at least half a dozen men were still working outside. Their bright yellow high-vis jackets stood out against white aggregate that covered the paths and the road, with only the small patches of land in between that would one day be turned into gardens.

The house he'd been allocated to was just one of the twenty under construction, and from what the others had said earlier that day, this was on one of the smaller sites that Cole Bailey owned. Even though he hated the thought of working for the man Daisy had married, Tom had no choice, not with debt letters falling through the door at speed and bailiffs breathing down his neck. He shook his head and closed his eyes; he'd had no choice but to go back to work whether he'd wanted to or not.

Overnight, he'd panicked about what he was doing. The thought of coming face to face with Cole was disturbing. But Cole was the enemy, and he deserved to lose what was his, including Daisy. It was a plan he hadn't really thought through. But while he did, he had the opportunity to earn a good wage.

'You've just got to dig yourself out of the hole,' Tom said to himself in the knowledge that the hole was one he'd unwittingly created. A hole that the bailiffs had suddenly made deeper. Now Tom was worried about the repercussions that could easily follow. He thought about the spade he'd leaned up against the wall outside the kitchen, and the hole he'd intended to dig. 'Which is another thing you have to take care of.'

Unable to do anything about that now, Tom removed his hard hat, opened both windows and breathed in deeply. The smell of diesel caught the back of his throat and, after coughing sporadically, he leaned back on the sill, covered his mouth and took some enjoyment from the continuous banter he could hear being thrown back and forth outside.

'Hey, Jonno. Don't leave your snap tin down there, mate, young Davy over there, he'll go and eat it for you,' a man old enough to be Tom's father shouted to another before marching to the edge of the scaffolding and lowering a ladder. 'Little scavenger would take your last bloody crumb, wouldn't you, Davy?'

Davy, who Tom presumed was an apprentice, leaned heavily against one of the walls. He had his hoodie pulled up to cover his head while doing his best to shelter from the worst of the weather. Standing with his mobile phone held in one of his hands, he stared at the screen. 'Nah...' he finally replied without looking up, 'I wouldn't eat his snap, not if you paid me, I've seen the state of his bloody kitchen.' The retort was short and sharp but followed by laughter. One man walked across to him and enthusiastically patted Davy on the back; another tried to ruffle his hair through the hoodie.

'There you go, my boy, you're learning,' the older man threw back. 'I knew you'd learn how to throw a bit of banter at these buggers if you worked here long enough.'

In retort, Jonno climbed the ladder, walked across the scaffolding, picked the box up, curled a lip and threw it over his shoulder. 'Yeah, I've seen the state of my kitchen too and I'm not sure I want to eat from it most days.'

'Hey. While you lot are arguing about Jonno's snap and whether or not Davy might eat it,' Tom shouted in an attempt to join in with the banter, 'you might want to get your backsides off those poles.' He laughed but ducked as a roll of electrical tape was thrown at the window.

'Listen to this, the new boy giving out advice like your mother,' Jonno shouted across with a smile. 'He's up there, most probably wearing some curlers and a pinny. Aren't you, new boy?'

'Come on, new boy, show us your pinny?' One of the men, Monty, dressed from head to toe in high-vis shouted before he turned on his heel and gave him the finger.

'Hey, you can give me the bird all you like,' Tom continued while pointing up at the sky, 'but if that strikes, the last place you wanna be is up that scaffolding. Don't they teach you anything in college these days.'

'Sure, they do...' Monty shouted back. 'They teach us to mind our own damn business.' Standing on top of the scaffold, he faced Tom, rolled his jaw and placed his hands on his hips. Then, with an irritated nod, he dropped his tools, picked up the sandwich box that Jonno had tossed, pulled it open and took a bite from one of the sandwiches. 'Hey, Jonno, these are all right, apart from the tuna... they've gone a bit warm.'

Feeling suitably chastised, Tom closed the window and furrowed his brow. Infiltrating the ranks was going to be more difficult than he'd thought and he slumped against the wall, held his hands to his head and pulled at his hair. Once again, he felt alone and isolated.

Sitting down in the space he'd made on the floor, Tom listened to the scurrying of feet outside. There was a thud of boots on gravel as the men jumped down from the various heights and with a smug, self-righteous look on his face, he leaned back against the radiator, closed his eyes and gained a few moments of peace, followed by a spark of pleasure that the weather had worsened. The men had finally listened and had taken themselves inside to safety.

Shuffling, Tom pushed the offcuts of cable and discarded cardboard out of his away with his foot, then, leaning forward, he began to gather up the tools that were scattered around him. Yesterday, this house would have had twelve different trades working inside. It was a day when he'd wished he'd been here, because at least then he'd have got to know some of the others on site; would have perhaps felt more like part of a team. Whereas today he'd had far too much time to think about Daisy.

Resting his eyes, Tom listened to the sound of the storm. The commotion outside had all but gone and in a moment of reflection, he found himself remembering the way the bailiffs had marched in and out of his house. The stern manner they'd used. The demand for money that he just couldn't pay. Then, with a final smug smirk, they'd switched off his television, picked it up and promised that if he didn't pay, they'd come back for the rest.

It had been a moment of panic for Tom, followed by the humiliating call he'd made to Cole. He'd never wanted to ask

Daisy's husband for work but if Daisy had answered his multiple calls, he might not have had to, and with his fingers drumming against the floorboards, he thought about the pact that he and Daisy had made. Her words still as vivid as the day she'd said them.

'After tonight, we have to go back to our normal lives, we know that, right?' Daisy had declared while her eyes had flooded with tears. 'This, whatever this was, was just unfinished business. It was just something we both needed to do.' He'd seen it as her way of compartmentalising what she felt, a way of giving them both the permission they'd needed to walk away from the other and, after leaving London, to go back to living their normal lives, whatever that meant.

Pulling his phone out of his pocket, Tom stared at the screen. The picture he'd put there gave him a rush of adrenaline. It was of both him and Daisy looking excited and happy; Tower Bridge stood behind them, the illuminations bright and vivid. For just a few hours that night, he'd held on to the one person he loved the most. Nothing else had mattered and while they'd stood there, beside the bridge, they'd easily looked like the happily married couple that he'd wished they were.

With his skin prickling, Tom flicked at the screen and clicked into Daisy's social media. There were images that Sarah had taken of a party. Pictures of Daisy, stood beside Cole, the look in her eyes that of a frightened rabbit. It was a look that made Tom twitch, and with his jaw fixed angrily he flicked at the screen at speed to see a house from various angles, Daisy stood in the background on most of them. The caption above said:

New house for the Baileys!

Which meant Daisy was moving.

Trying to calm himself down, Tom quickly jumped up from the floor as he heard the sound of heavy boots walk across floorboards downstairs. It alerted him to the fact that someone was in the house, and with his breath held tight, he stood, and he waited.

'You up there, Tom?' a loud Scottish voice bellowed and made Tom cringe. Quickly he went over all the work he'd done and with a glance through the window he could see the other men, standing with their arms crossed, watching. They were staring across the road in his direction and obviously waiting for something to happen. 'Tom, where the hell are you?'

'Here... sorry, I was just concentrating on a fitting. You all right?' Tom brushed the dirt from his trousers. 'Just sorting out some of these components. There's a few left to do up here and then I need to go down and finish sorting the kitchen.' Tom could hear the echo of footsteps thudding on each of the stairs, and with a deep breath he picked up a light fitting and, with a screwdriver in his hand, he jumped on a ladder.

'Put your damned hard hat on,' Gary immediately growled as he stepped in through the doorway, and Tom felt himself tremble as Gary's shoulders scraped against each side of the architrave. 'Put it on, gather your tools and meet me in the cabin. The boss is on site. He needs a word.'

Sensing the tension in his words, Tom caught his breath. The boss meant Cole Bailey. The last person in the world he wanted to see. And him wanting a word, what did that mean? Was it a word about work, about the site, his qualifications, or was it a word about Daisy? Either way, it didn't sound good, and for a moment he stared at the hard hat, knowing that he was about to walk into a meeting with the enemy. A man whose reputation of being hard preceded him. And right now, Tom knew that he was on the back foot. Not only had he had no time to prepare for a face to face with Cole Bailey, but he still hadn't come up with a plan, which made him nervous.

Anxiously and with trepidation, he jumped down from the ladder and picked up his hard hat. Gary was right, the hat should have been on his head. While pushing it back on, Tom held his breath as he realised that Gary had avoided his eye, he hadn't looked at him once, and after kicking Tom's tools towards his tool bag, he'd taken to pacing aggressively back and forth on the landing. It was a telltale sign that Gary knew more than he'd said and that the meeting with Cole was going to be one that Tom wouldn't like.

# 11

---

## DAISY

With her low wedge heels clipping heavily against the marble floors, and her teeth clenched to a point that her jaw ached with tension, Daisy lifted her hands to her head and massaged her temples. The adrenaline she'd been running on since leaving the beach house had dissipated and a bout of exhaustion had taken its place.

The last half hour since arriving back at The Willows had been a battle of wills. Both Patrick and Teresa had gone into full organisational mode. Sarah had disappeared down the garden with her phone in her hand in search of Borys, and Cole, the only person that Daisy had really needed to be here, had messaged to say that he had to go to another site for an important meeting and wouldn't be back until late afternoon. In her disappointment, Daisy had sat on the bottom step of the staircase and, with tiredness enveloping her body, she'd closed her eyes, taken in a long, slow breath and felt her eyes grow heavy. For a few seconds, she felt her mind go into a trance-like state where the need for sleep quickly overwhelmed her, and even though the sound of Teresa's voice and the banging of boxes that came out of the van were irritating, they weren't enough to keep her awake.

'Mrs Bailey...' Olena's distant voice wormed its way into her consciousness and with a furrowed brow Daisy bit down on her lip and opened her eyes.

'Yes... what is it?'

'Are you okay, Mrs Bailey? You've gone very pale. Would you like me to get you a cold drink before I start cleaning the bedrooms?'

Nodding, Daisy lifted a hand to her brow. She felt warm and clammy, and she blew out slowly as she thought about the last few hours and how her life was about to change dramatically.

'Yes, I'd love one... Do you have any energy drinks?' Daisy asked. It felt like a ridiculous question in a house that was supposed to be hers. She'd always known what was in her own cupboards, but here she didn't know where anything was, and for the tenth time that day she felt like a visitor in her own home and watched despondently as Olena scurried off before returning quickly with a mixture of different coloured cans for Daisy to choose from.

Sipping at the drink, Daisy couldn't help but home in on the sound of Teresa's loud, piercing voice. She was standing on the threshold of the house like a formidable force and had been since the moment they'd arrived back here. She now leaned against the front door's architrave while peering over the top of a pair of reading glasses that were perched on the end of her nose. It was a look that reminded Daisy of a schoolteacher who was ready to pounce on a classroom full of very young and unsuspecting children, and once again she wished that Cole was here.

'Olena, do you know if Cole has mentioned anything about Christmas? Has he organised a tree?' Daisy asked as her gaze went to the double-height ceiling, the window that was positioned right above the front door and the six-globe light fitting that hung in a cluster from the ceiling above her. 'I guess that a huge hallway like this would need something grand, something showy, don't you think?' She hoped it would sound like a friendly conversation as a way of making up for the way she'd acted towards Olena that morning. It wasn't Olena's fault that the war had displaced her, or that she'd had to leave a home that presumably she might have loved just as much as Daisy loved Pipistrelle. With what she hoped looked like an affable smile she patted the step beside her, moved to one side and made room for Olena, who sat down beside her.

'White or green?'

'Pardon?'

'I can't decide which would be better, a white tree or green,' Daisy said as she waved a hand around in the hallway. 'I could put up a tree that once belonged to my mother; it has a branch or two missing but if we stand it creatively, we could hang some ornaments on it to hide the damage.'

'I think...' Olena whispered and shivered. She sat forward, flicked her long blonde hair over her shoulder and wrapped her arms around herself in a hug. 'Mrs Bailey, I think your mother's tree would be perfect.'

For a moment, Daisy and Olena sat together in a unified silence. Somehow, without saying too much, they'd managed to draw a line in the sand and for the first time since arriving at this house, Daisy felt some semblance of peace.

'Can I ask?' Olena finally said. 'Last night, you looked shocked and how do you say it... you were very surprised...' She held her hands out, palms up and furrowed her brow in question. 'I'm interested, how could you not know about the house?'

'You'll soon work it out, most of the time, I have no idea what my husband is up to,' Daisy answered and pointed to where

Teresa patrolled the threshold. 'And because he works with his parents, I prefer to keep it that way.' She smiled, sipped at her drink and kept an eye on what was happening outside.

Six men stood at the back of the van, with Teresa shouting out orders. All the men were young and muscular and all of them had been more than willing to oblige, especially at Pipistrelle when Daisy had insisted that the bulk of the furniture had been left behind and that most of the boxes that Patrick had put in a pile had been moved into the downstairs bedroom, where she'd happily left them.

'I've been told to bring this in here...' one of the men said as he went to walk past Teresa and into the hallway. He held out a box as though he were giving her a present and Daisy watched the way his eyes had darted around in all directions. He'd first homed in on the snooker table, possibly hoping to play. But then he'd spotted the wine cellar and couldn't help but stand above it, where he looked down with an intense look of envy.

'No, I've already told you, none of that's to come into the house,' Teresa said as three of the men headed towards her. They had their arms full of different sized boxes. Some that were heavier than others. 'You need to take that, that and that across to the storeroom. Patrick's across there, he'll show you where to put them.'

Standing up as Olena headed back into the kitchen, Daisy felt her head swim with a new bout of nausea; her legs became weak and, without wanting to draw attention to how she was feeling, she wandered into the playroom, where she sat on the window seat and, with her legs pulled up, she used her big woollen coat as a small but effective blanket. For just a few minutes she tried to relax but the continuous drone of Teresa's voice became more and more annoying, and with her mood becoming more volatile by the minute, Daisy found herself shuffling on the thick-padded window seat, where she unintentionally pressed her fingernails into the dark green fabric. With her blood feeling as though it were turning to lava, and with every ounce of self-control she had, Daisy pulled in a deep breath, grabbed at her phone and began to flick through her pictures, until she stopped on one that had been taken of her and Cole. They were sitting on a sunbed, with cocktails held in their hands, and they looked happy together, which made her wonder why she'd ever betrayed him with Tom. They had a good life, they were still relatively young, with their health and a pair of very successful businesses. They had seemingly had the perfect life. Or that's what she'd thought, until she'd bumped into Tom and, without giving it much thought, she'd willingly fallen into his arms. Worse than that, she'd fallen into his bed. An act that she'd now pushed so far out of her mind, she could barely remember. For a while afterwards she'd tried to work out whether or not someone could love two different people at the same time. Her mind kept flip-flopping between the idea of being with Cole, or going back to Pipistrelle and somehow turning her life around to be with Tom. But her thoughts became more and more confusing...

'All you've agreed,' she whispered to herself, 'was that you'd try. You didn't agree that you'd stay here forever.' She gave herself a small, decisive smile but then frowned with frustration. 'And now with the baby coming, surely Cole will agree that you'd be happier if you lived by the beach.'

Feeling determined to take back some control over her own life, Daisy got up and headed back to the stairs. She was about to walk up them when her mobile rang, the sound echoing around the room. In the hope that Cole was on his way home, she pulled the phone out of her pocket and stared at the screen and gasped as she once again saw Tom's name flash up on the screen.

'Aren't you going to answer that?' Sarah asked as she skipped past her and ran up the stairs in the direction of the room where she'd slept the night before. 'Might be important,' she added with an inquisitive smile.

With the phone held against her, Daisy realised that it was the sixth time that Tom had called. With a mixture of dread and guilt, she thought about the way the car had lit up like a disco the night before. The voicemail and message he'd left. She'd had every intention of calling him back but hadn't. Life had got in the way and now, she stood transfixed and unable to move.

'I thought it might be Cole, but it isn't,' she said with a nervous smile, 'it's just… it's just one of the girls.' She waved a hand as the phone went quiet. 'I'm sure she'll phone back later, tell me all about her divorce, how it's going and what she will and won't end up with.' She rolled her eyes and pushed the phone back into her pocket. 'I saw you talking to Borys earlier; he's a good-looking man, and I'm sure Cole mentioned the fact that he's single?' She deflected the conversation and instantly took note of the colour that had risen to Sarah's cheeks.

As the words left Daisy's mouth, she felt her stomach turn with hunger. It was much too long since she'd eaten, although after her earlier bout of nausea she hadn't had much of an appetite. Not until now. But with Tom on her mind, she pushed the thought of food to one side, giving preference to the idea of calling him back and hearing his voice.

Sitting down beside her, Sarah bumped her shoulder with her own and gave her a smile. 'Just ignore Teresa if she's driving you nuts. It'll all be sorted soon and then… well then, you'll have the time to rearrange the house however you want, won't you?' Sarah laughed, leaned against the glass banister and ran a hand through her hair. 'How about we go and unpack some of the things that've been taken upstairs?' she said casually, but then furrowed her brow as she looked down at her watch. 'Oh, damn it. Actually, no can do, I have somewhere to be and...' she winced. 'I'll catch you later. And don't forget, let me know what Cole says when you tell him.'

With tears threatening to fall, Daisy felt the nausea return; it came and went in waves and she pulled her jacket around her shoulders as she took deep breaths and headed out through the front door with the need to escape.

'Daisy... you don't want this, do you?' Teresa waved a personalised number plate around in the air. 'I mean... you've had it a while and not used it so it's not like you're that interested in it, are you?' The words were meant as a dig, a reminder that Teresa had thought her to be more than ungrateful for the things Cole bought.

'Yes, of course I want it,' Daisy shouted over her shoulder as she headed in between the trees and towards the office. 'Cole bought that for me; just because I didn't put it straight on a car, it doesn't mean I don't want it!'

'Take that away, will you? I'm sure that one day Daisy will get round to using it.'

Feeling berated, Daisy had to agree. She must *appear* ungrateful, but the truth was she needed the number plate just as much as she needed a new house to live in. In short, she'd never been interested in big fancy gifts. She already had everything she wanted and, if she was perfectly honest, there was nothing else she needed in life. Yet she still felt haunted by the look on Cole's face and the sparkle that had shone from his eyes when he'd spoken of the new car he'd planned to buy her. 'I spoke to a dealer; he has a convertible Jaguar E-Type coming in. It'd be a great car, a classic, and if you want it, I'm going to buy it for you,' he'd said lovingly. But Daisy had shaken her head with a smile, and even though she'd been grateful for his generosity, she'd refused the gift. Instead, she'd promised to get the plate attached to the small and inexpensive car she'd had for years, but she'd never got round to it.

She remembered reaching up to him afterwards and lovingly pulling him towards her as she pressed her mouth against his. 'Don't you understand, Cole? All I need in life is you.'

She could still hear the words as they'd slipped out of her mouth, the honesty she'd felt when she'd said them. But now the guilt was too much, especially now she had a baby growing inside her, and she couldn't help but wonder: if her love for Cole had been real, would that night with Tom have happened?

# 12

## DAISY

'Hey, where are you off to?' Sarah shouted as the flats of her trainers crunched their way across the driveway and, with keys in hand, she clicked at the fob as the bright amber lights flashed in response.

'I'm just going to grab some air, I just felt a bit... urgh.' Daisy paused, saw the look of concern on her sister's face. 'Don't panic, I'm fine. It's just been one hell of a morning.' She wished for a glass of water, for something to take away the strong metallic taste that was now in her mouth.

'Look, I'd stay but I'm in a bit of a hurry. I need to check in at the agency and Cole gave me Monday off, to help you catch up with any extra admin...' Pulling open the car door, Sarah dropped her handbag on the front seat, rummaged inside and retrieved her phone. 'Or I could call forward, delay things a little?'

'Don't be silly. I'm fine, and yes, check in at the agency. Make a note of the voicemails, and then you need to go and have a nice time without worrying about me. I'm pregnant, not dying.' Holding a hand up in the air, Daisy waved her fingers towards the car in a way that told Sarah to go. 'Seriously, thank you, you've helped me enough and I just kind of need to take a few minutes to myself, and get used to the idea of being pregnant, before the rest of the world finds out.' With acid suddenly hitting the back of her throat, Daisy spun on the spot and heaved in a place where the bushes were thick, green, and to her embarrassment, perfectly manicured. 'Which is really hard,' she said, 'when all I want to do is throw up.' Wiping her mouth on the back of her hand, Daisy stood up straight, closed her eyes for a blink and pulled in a deep breath.

'Shall I call Teresa, or get you some water?'

'No,' Daisy snapped, 'the last person in the world I want is Teresa.' Turning, Daisy sauntered slowly towards the office. The vast number of bushes and trees meant that the office had been practically hidden from view. Only a small part of it could be seen from the house, and as she rounded the corner the extent of it shocked her.

'Impressive, isn't it?' Walking along the path to stand beside her, Sarah pushed her phone into her pocket and shoulder-bumped her sister and practically bounced up and down on the spot. 'It's been quite a project.'

Nodding in agreeance, Daisy realised that she'd been expecting the office to look like nothing more than a well-built shed. Whereas in reality, it was a large, single storey building, with oak panelling, stone pillars and all painted in a colour to blend into the landscape. At least six windows went across the front, and there were areas of the building that had no windows at all. Daisy quickly worked out that if she pressed her head to one side against the window that she could look through, she could just see the rows upon rows of screens that were lined up on a wall.

'That must be the control room,' Daisy whispered as she blinked repeatedly and watched each of the screens as they flicked and changed, to show all the different rooms in the house. 'Now then, where's the screen that shows me the bedroom?'

Tapping her toes against the wall with anxiety, Daisy stared impatiently through the window. She wanted, no, she *needed* to know if Cole or anyone else could watch her at times when she was getting undressed, walking around naked or using the bathroom.

'Look, why don't you come back to the house,' Sarah suggested. 'I'll get Olena to make us a drink.' Pulling her phone out of her pocket, she began to tap on the screen. 'I can log into the office from here, put my meeting off and...' She reached out, placed a hand on Daisy's shoulder. 'And we can do something together, make a few plans.'

'Who watches these screens, you know, when Cole isn't here?' Daisy asked. She glanced back at the house, her mind spinning like a whirlwind as she thought about the pool, the wild unadulterated lovemaking.

'Come on, Daisy, you know that Cole has loads of staff,' Sarah chipped in. 'He normally always has someone sat there, apart from today of course, because most were at the party and those that weren't, well, they were working and now they're probably sleeping.'

Shaking her head, Daisy could feel her temperature rise. If Sarah was right, then at least today there wouldn't have been anyone watching the screens. But the thought that normally someone could be sitting there, watching them make love, was more than infuriating and certainly something she'd make sure would never happen again. With a sudden need to see more of the screens, Daisy brushed her sister's hand from her shoulder, marched towards the office door and pushed down on the handle.

'Damn it,' she yelled, 'why can't the door be open?' Once

again, the handle was slammed up and down as Daisy glanced over her shoulder, expectantly, in the hope that Sarah would open the door.

'Hey, don't look at me, I don't know the code. There's always someone here when I get to work.' She shuffled uncomfortably and held her hands up, palms out in submission. 'Honestly, I really don't know.'

'Do you know what, Cole did tell it me this morning, but...' She closed her eyes momentarily and felt the hot, scalding tears of frustration hit the back of her eyelids. 'I can't remember which way the number went.'

Placing a hand over Daisy's, Sarah gave her a pensive smile. 'Just don't get it wrong, or the whole place will lock down.' She paused, and glanced down as her phone vibrated. 'Look, why don't you give Cole a call, get him to come. I'm sure he'd tell you the code again, and while he's here, he could show you round the office.' As she spoke, her concentration dwindled as she looked at her phone. 'He's worked so hard to make this special, Daisy, he'd be so chuffed to show you around it.'

'But Cole isn't here,' Daisy snapped. Once again, she pressed a hand against the window, used it as a shield for her eyes, and with her gaze once again fixed on the screens, Daisy watched as she caught sight of Olena on one of them, stealthily tiptoeing behind Teresa, who was still standing in the front doorway. She made her way up the stairs and then, for a few minutes, the view changed. It cut to the kitchen, then back to the pool room before returning to the vast, open hallway, where Olena descended the stairs, one of Cole's rucksacks held in her hand. 'What is she doing?'

'Who are you talking about?' Moving back to stand beside Daisy, Sarah mimicked the way her sister stood with her face pressed up against the window.

'Olena. I really want to like her, but there's something...' Taking a breath, Daisy held a hand to her mouth. The taste of bile still more than evident. 'There's something I can't put my finger on.'

'To be fair to her, she's always busy. Her and Borys never seem to stop, so you might want to try and get used to them.'

'I get that, but can't any of the rooms be sacred? She really doesn't need to go in the bedrooms, does she?'

'Why not? You don't seem to mind the cleaners on holiday and she's only in there to clean and change the bedding...' Sarah said, sounding genuinely puzzled.

Sarah was right. But here, it felt different.

'It just doesn't feel right, nor do the cameras,' she finally added. 'You, Cole and his parents might love the security following you around, but I don't, and I need private spaces.' Pausing, Daisy looked from her sister's shocked face to the house. It didn't surprise her that Sarah had quickly fallen in love with this lifestyle.

Shaking her head, Daisy frowned. She still couldn't understand what Olena had been up to. Why she hadn't simply walked past Teresa, or what she'd needed with an old rucksack.

## 13

### DAISY

Willing herself to manage it without falling and with her hand gripping the handrail as hard as she could, Daisy made her way up the stairs and reached the confines of her bedroom, where she pulled open the door and slammed it behind her.

Inside, she could feel her breath accelerating. Her heart pounded hard in her chest, and with her mind spinning in panic, she leaned against the door, closed her eyes, bit down on her lip, and trembled with a sudden influx of emotion.

Her mind was tormented with not knowing who the father of her child was, and the sudden realisation of what was about to happen hit her. The thought that the baby could be Tom's and not Cole's was devastating. Not that she hadn't once loved Tom; she had, but if Tom were the father, she'd be igniting the touch-paper that would quite easily blow the world she knew apart. It would be the deciding factor for what she did next, and no matter how hard she tried, she couldn't possibly expect Cole to understand this one.

Frantically, she tried to remember the times that she and Cole had been together, but she knew that those times had been few.

Cole had been working away. And with her head held in her hands, Daisy slid down the door until she was sitting on the floor and tried to remember if, other than this morning, she and Cole had made love since London. But as far as she was aware, she'd managed to avoid his advances on one or two occasions, which meant that there had been very little interaction between them.

Which left Tom. She still hadn't responded to his message or voicemail. She still wasn't sure why he'd called. What she did know was that he'd gone to work for Bailey Construction and, whether she liked the idea or not, she needed to speak to him and had to find out what he was up to. The night she'd spent with him had become too much of a blur. Nothing made sense and even though she'd been happy to see him, the sexual attraction had been off of the scale. The questions she had about that night were ones that only Tom could answer. The drinks, how strong they had been, and whether they'd used protection on the night in question. All of which she couldn't ask without telling him about the pregnancy, which caused her a problem.

Daisy flicked through her phone until she came to Tom's name, and with a deep breath, she lifted the phone to her ear. But just as quickly as it had begun to ring, she cancelled the call.

'Cameras...' she whispered. Cole had told her that she'd always feel safe, that he'd installed cameras all over the house, and while closing her eyes, she tried to visualise the screens she'd seen in the office. She felt sure that none of them had showed the bedroom. But what if she just hadn't seen them. What's more, if Cole had come back. If he were sitting in his office, right at this moment, he could be watching every move that she made and listening to every word she might say.

Searching the room, Daisy wondered if Cole would have really stooped so low that he'd have put cameras up in the bedrooms. It was a chance she just couldn't take. She couldn't possibly let Cole find out about Tom in this way, and after picking herself up from the floor, she headed into the en suite, and looked at the white appliances that were all set against a marble floor and walls. Every part of it was smooth and clean and, in her opinion, there was nowhere left for a camera to hide.

'Not even Cole would be that voyeuristic, would he?' She shook her head and then, with her mind spinning with confusion, she switched on the shower. It was something she'd once seen in a film, a way of masking the noise, and with her stomach turning in a constant somersault, she flicked at the screen of her phone and, once again, she clicked on Tom's name.

# 14

## TOM

With dark clouds circling above him, Tom slowed his pace as he tentatively pushed the cemetery gate open. It was heavy and it was wide, and Tom peered through the dark green metal bars, which stood in front of a sea of gravestones that all fanned out in the distance. Every grave was two-foot high by one-foot wide. A jet-black marble reminder of a life that had been lost. A name upon it to tell the world who it was that had been laid to rest. A place where people came for a self-gratifying experience in the hope that the person who'd been buried there might actually know they'd cared, and Tom was no different.

Walking slowly and solemnly, while dragging long deep breaths of air into his body, Tom kept his head down while he navigated the path he'd walked at least a hundred times before. It was the same path he always took while visiting the grave of his mother. Although each time he did, it felt as though the path had been extended. Today, he felt as though he'd gone out for a hill walk and, in its place, he'd found an arduous mountain. Which wasn't surprising after the morning he'd had to endure.

If working at a new site – and on a Saturday – hadn't been bad enough, Gary's tone of voice had set him on edge. The comment 'he needs a word' had totally derailed him. The fact that Cole was on site had made his heart rate quicken. His palms had turned hot and clammy, and his chest had been tightened with the anxiety as Gary had marched him in an undignified way across to his locker. He'd been made to open it in front of the others, where he'd immediately spotted the laser – a key piece of site equipment that he shouldn't have had – and with Tom's mouth drying to a point where he could barely swallow, he'd turned around to face Cole Bailey.

'You do know that I didn't put that in there, don't you?' He'd looked into Cole's eyes in the hope he'd believe him. But the moment he'd said the words, he felt his throat close. 'I've been stitched up, one of them...' He looked out of the portacabin door to see where Monty, Jonno and three of the others all stood with their arms crossed looking like a lynch mob ready to pounce.

'Okay, we have two choices,' Cole had said firmly when he'd walked back into the portacabin that had been turned into a makeshift office. 'I want you and that rust bucket of a car off of my land.' He'd sat there, a smug look on his face, and just like the lynch mob, his arms were crossed defensively. 'Or we can involve the police. Things could get messy and you, my friend... you'll never work in Northumberland again. And before you ask, I'm not paying you, not for today.' He uncrossed his arms, picked up his pen and tapped it aggressively against his notepad and, rather than look Tom in the eye, he averted his gaze and stared down at the desk.

Trembling with emotion, Tom had considered grabbing the pad, taking it from him, reading the notes and then ramming the pad as far down Cole's smug, egotistical throat as he could. But he hadn't. He'd simply stood there, staring directly at the man who'd taken Daisy from him. And even though the rage had torn through him, he wouldn't beg for his job. His pride wouldn't let him. Instead, he did the walk of shame and made his way past all the other men who worked on site in a final act of humiliation.

A part of Tom wanted to lay bets on which member of the workforce had nailed him. It was definitely one of them, he just didn't know who, which made his blood rise to a boil. But the more he thought about it, he realised that, even though they had no reason to hate him, none of the men had wanted him there... Apart from Cole, who'd given him the job, only to humiliate him at the first opportunity, which was why Tom had followed him here, to where he now stood in the graveyard.

Following in his rust bucket of a car, as Cole had called it, Tom had watched the way Cole Bailey had pulled up, jumped out of his car and, with a determined walk, he'd entered the ten-acre plot. And now, although Tom had no wish to do anything more than put the record straight, he had every intention of finding him.

With footsteps approaching, Tom heard the gentle sobs of both a man and a woman who looked to be in their mid-twenties. He stood to one side respectfully, but watched the way they held on to each other with a fierce determination not to let go. Tears streamed down the young woman's face, and the man helplessly searched the sky with his gaze in an unsuccessful attempt to keep a stiff upper lip. As they walked past, the man gave Tom a nod, a knowing, silent communication shared between the two men. Tom couldn't help but feel as though their world was falling apart, just like his.

Casting his mind over what had gone wrong, Tom instinctively wanted to blame all of his issues on Grace. She was going to abandon him too. She'd been planning on taking herself and their baby, Mason, away. Except, she hadn't been the first woman to leave him. It had been a pattern that had happened right throughout his lifetime. At some point, everyone he'd loved or cared for had left. First his mother, then Daisy, and finally Grace. When all he'd really wanted was someone who would stand by him, someone who'd wanted to hold him as though their lives had depended on the outcome.

Which was why meeting up with Daisy in London had been so very intense. It was a meeting that hadn't happened by chance, but one that he'd engineered following a random night out in a bar. He and Grace had been arguing; her hippie ways and lifestyle weren't always what he agreed with, especially when it came to their son, which was why he'd been sitting in a bar, alone, listening in on a conversation between two people. They'd obviously been there on a date and even though he hadn't intended to listen, he'd homed in on a voice that he'd immediately recognised and, after carefully looking over his shoulder so as not to be seen, Tom had spotted Daisy's sister, Sarah. Surreptitiously, he'd moved across the banquette, to listen more closely. 'I know...' she'd said, 'I have to look after the office next weekend, while my sister gets to go into London. It feels so unfair...'

It had been a comment that Tom had held on to. The thought that Daisy would be going to London was a thought that he didn't want to let go of but had, until he spotted a post on Daisy's social media:

I'm off to London on Friday. A whole weekend to meet up with clients. *Happy face*

Quite a few of their mutual friends had posted their comments. One read:

Oh, I wish I were coming.

Another read:

Oh, you're not going in rush hour are you. It was a #bigmistake the last time I did that.

Daisy had replied simply:

Not a chance, I'm catching the 9.30 a.m. to Kings Cross, most of commuters should have hopefully gone by then! *Smiley face*

Without hesitation, Tom had bought a ticket and had made a plan to 'accidentally' bump into Daisy. Now, with thoughts of that weekend still spinning around in his mind, he found himself smiling at the numerous memories that they'd packed in to such a short time. With his phone in one hand, Tom went to the pictures of London. While he'd been there, he'd been happy. A few stolen moments with the one woman he'd always considered his own. The woman he should never have lost. But he had lost her and now, so many years later, Daisy was married to the man who'd just found a way to sack him. With tears of anger and frustration flooding his eyes, Tom looked at the pictures knowing that, for just one more night, he'd had the woman he'd loved in his arms, which would have made him happy, if it hadn't all been a lie.

Angrily, he pressed her number on his phone and listened to the ringtone until his call went to voicemail for the fifth or sixth time in the last few hours.

'I'm sorry, I can't take your call right now but...'

Closing his eyes, Tom ended the call and waited. He wanted Daisy to phone him back. For her to care enough to do so, but when she didn't, he went to his messages and hesitantly, he tapped out the words.

TOM

> Daisy. Life or death. Please call me. x

'Life or death' were the words they'd agreed to only use at a time of crisis. But right now, it was all he could do to get her to call him. Because God only knew that nothing else had worked. He'd lost count of the messages he'd sent, the calls he'd made and the apologies that followed. In London, he'd had every intention of walking away, of being respectful to Daisy and to her marriage. But his debts had grown, the bailiffs had arrived and Cole had sacked him through no fault of his own. And now his plans to take Cole down and steal Daisy from under his nose had been foiled.

Closing his eyes, Tom pressed send. In his opinion, it was life or death. He wanted to tell her what kind of a scumbag she'd married. He could still see the way Cole had refused to look at him, the way he'd made a pretence that he'd call the police. His methods brutal and humiliating, and even though Tom had been innocent, he hadn't wanted to risk the police snooping around in his house. It was bad enough with the bailiffs.

Now, with his phone still in his hand, Tom continued to walk through the cemetery, looking for Cole. The path was wide enough for a car and Tom felt confident that he could see far enough ahead that he'd be able to spot Cole first if he walked towards him. But just to be sure, he checked the people who sat at the graves and, carefully, he looked along every row. He was determined to speak to Cole alone – man to man – now that Cole didn't have the advantage of the other men listening.

Tom continued along the path until he reached an old, skeletal oak tree. Underneath its branches there was a long wooden bench with a large brass plaque screwed on to the backrest that was now tarnished and dirty. But it wasn't the plaque that caught Tom's attention; it was the sight of his mother's grave that stood just a few rows behind. With his strides suddenly becoming shorter and a lot more hesitant, he slowly counted the next five rows, until he came to stand by her headstone.

Sitting down on the grass next to the grave was something he'd always done, but today, he pulled a face as the moisture seeped through his jeans. The past three days of weather had been more than changeable and the thunderstorm they'd had that morning had left the ground sodden.

With a deep intake of breath, Tom shuffled on the spot and avoided looking at the words on the headstone. Instead, he watched the other mourners around him. One or two were laughing and sharing jokes but most were solemn. A few of them carried flowers and water containers, and others, like him, simply sat by the graves and busied themselves with cleaning the stones with their fingers.

With his throat tightening, Tom finally ran his gaze across the words and caught sight of his mother's picture. It had been mounted on a small oval disc carefully set into one of the corners. The picture had been a favourite of Tom's, taken on a day when they'd all gone to the seaside and his mum had been standing next to the sea wall, eating a huge ice-cream that dripped down her fingers. She wore a large floppy hat on her head and had the biggest smile on her face, which had depicted her character perfectly.

'Hey, Mum, it's me, Tom. I...' He looked around the neighbouring graves mournfully. Some of them were the graves of children, covered in flowers, small toys and pictures. Whereas his mum's grave had nothing more than a single white stone that

Tom had placed there a few weeks after her death. It was a stone Tom had chosen because of its cloud-like shape. In a moment's weakness, he'd painted it in rainbow colours, with the words 'When the rain stops, I'll look for you in the rainbows.' It had been something he'd always promised he'd do, but the words, like the rainbow, had long since disappeared, leaving the stone to look just a little odd and nothing like the cloud he'd originally imagined.

'I'm so sorry...' Tom blinked repeatedly as he reached across to the grave next door. With a quick glance over his shoulder, he lifted a few of the violas out of the neighbouring vase and placed them on his mum's grave. 'I didn't bring flowers. In fact, it's not that I didn't bring them, I didn't really know I was coming...' Tom closed his eyes as a loud, audible sob left his throat. 'Mum. I lost my job, and on the first day I had it...' Tom swallowed hard, unsure what else he could say, and feeling lost and alone, he picked up his phone and looked at the screen. It had been a good few minutes since he'd messaged Daisy, but still there was still no reply, which broke him. Then he felt the first drops of rain fall from the sky; another storm was threatening to break, and he suddenly heard the scurrying footsteps as the other mourners quickly made for their cars.

Exhausted, Tom couldn't find the energy to move and, without thought, he lay dejected on the cold, sodden floor and let the rain fall. With an intense fatigue taking over his body, Tom found himself drifting in and out of sleep. It was the first time he'd slept in a number of days and even though the rain continued to fall, Tom felt as though he'd lost too much and no longer cared whether he lived or he died. But as the cold seeped into his bones, his body shivered relentlessly. One loud sob after another left his throat, and once he felt as though he could cry no more, he pushed himself up from the ground and took a swipe at his eyes with the back of his hand. With his head still lowered, his mind still tired from his slumber, Tom suddenly heard two voices behind him.

'You have to tell her what the hell's happening; you can't just allow her to get caught up in your mess,' a woman's voice yelled out in alarm. Her tone was angry, distressed and troubled enough to make Tom lean to one side and listen more carefully. 'It's gone too damned far and it isn't worth it.'

Pulling his hood up, Tom bowed his head and watched as the woman tried to storm past him. But then she stopped, waited, and only when the man caught up with her did Tom realise who they both were. Cole Bailey was still dressed in the same pair of jeans and the oversized hoodie he'd worn that morning but now, rather than him dishing out a berating across a table, he was the one receiving the angst. It was something he obviously wasn't used to, and in response, he glared furiously at Daisy's sister, Sarah.

'Come on.' Cole lifted his hands and pressed them down almost aggressively onto Sarah's shoulders. 'Sarah don't be stupid, we can't tell her, not now. We're so close to pulling this off.'

'Stupid, am I?' she shouted, 'Well, do you know what, Cole, I must be because I found myself lying to my sister. She was on her way to the office, she wanted me to let her in and stupidly, because I didn't know what else to do, I refused her the number. I told her I didn't know it and now, if she sees me walking in, she'll know I was lying.'

Pulling an arm free of his grasp, Sarah swung it outward, and caught the side of his face in a slap. 'Now I'm warning you: you sort it out or I will tell her, and if I tell her, I'm going to tell her to run for the damned hills.' She paused, took in a deep breath. 'Because I'm telling you now, the moment she realises what kind of an arrogant, lying bastard you are, she's going to divorce you.'

'She wouldn't.'

'You just watch her.' Taking a step back, Sarah looked down at the ground. 'Cole, you've got so much more than Daisy to lose.' She closed her eyes and shook her head, then hurriedly, she turned her back and walked away.

'Sarah...'

'I shouldn't have said that.'

'Sarah...?' This time, Cole's use of her name had lost its aggression. In its place was a worried tone, a man desperate to find the truth. 'Please... there's something you're not telling me. So please, what the hell are you talking about? What more do I have to lose?'

'Cole, go home and speak to your wife.'

Confused by what was happening, Tom listened intently. He hadn't seen Sarah, not properly for a number of years. Even in the pub on the night he'd listened in to her conversation, she'd had her back to him. If she'd seen him, he'd felt sure that she'd have easily recognised him. So instead, he'd stayed where he was, rooted to the spot. Hidden from view. Which was what he needed to do right now. After the morning they'd had, it wouldn't take Cole much to recognise him now, which was why he stealthily turned his back, lifted his phone and flicked on the camera. Then he reversed the screen and used it to watch what was happening behind him.

Sarah was no longer the young, gangly teenager he'd once teased. She'd grown into a stunning young woman, with perfect curves, in all the right places. But the words that were falling from her mouth had left Tom feeling shocked and concerned and a million different questions ran through his mind.

Tom moved positions and even though both Sarah and Cole had moved further away, he tried to get them both in the picture. Sarah had moved in closer towards Cole, her mouth just millimetres from his. With his breath held in anticipation, Tom thought they might kiss, and he allowed his finger to hover right over his screen, hoping to snap the perfect picture. One that he could use as evidence against Cole. It would be a way of bribing him, a way to get his job back and, if that failed, it was a picture he could use as leverage with Daisy.

Disappointed that he hadn't quite got the picture he wanted, Tom smiled in amusement at the image he'd snapped. It was close enough, damning enough and ironically, just as he studied the frame, Daisy's name flashed up on the screen. She'd finally called him, which meant that she cared. It was a moment he wouldn't have thought could get better until, with the phone still flashing silently, he watched the way Sarah lifted her knee, caught Cole square in the crotch and then, with a laugh that echoed around the graveyard, she took a step back.

'...because, you bastard, your wife is pregnant.'

# 15

## DAISY

After navigating the lane that led between the new house and Bamburgh, Daisy pulled her car into the car park that stood opposite the castle and circled until she found a spare space.

It was only just after six, but following the rain they'd had earlier, the weather had turned cold. The pavements were slippery and the gritters were out in force, doing the best they could to make the roads safe. Despite the cold, crowds of people were gathered outside the two most popular pubs, surrounding tables from which they served cardboard cups full of hot Christmas toddies, along with a Christmas punch that was non-alcoholic. But the favourite beverage that everyone always bought was the hot chocolate that came with or without a large splash of brandy.

'You must be downright bloody stupid...' Daisy grumbled to herself under her breath as she reached forward, turned the heater down and tapped her foot against the accelerator as she listened to the rhythm of the engine.

There was still at least thirty minutes to go before she'd arranged to meet Tom, and with her gaze moving between the clock and the imposing walls of Bamburgh Castle, she thought about the phone call she'd made.

'Tom,' she'd said quickly, 'I can't talk for long, what's wrong, are you okay?'

'Daisy,' he'd said, 'thank God you called, you have no idea how much I need to talk to you. Do you remember our pact? This is life or death.'

They were words that told Daisy that Tom really was in trouble. The playful laughter in his voice had gone, and in its place, she'd heard a devastating tremor, one she'd only ever previously heard when his mother had died. Her mind had flashed back to the agreement they'd made, a promise that had passed between them while they'd stood on a cold, windy platform in London. 'If it's life or death, we'll be there. We'll always show up. Promise.' They'd sealed the deal with a long, tender kiss and as the kiss had ended, Daisy had closed her eyes, turned and walked away from him.

'Okay, meet me tonight. I'll be in the village around six o'clock,' she'd said that afternoon while standing in the en suite, with the shower blasting out beside her. 'There's a big Christmas thing going on by the pubs, I'll be somewhere in the crowd, come and find me, but you have to make it look as though we're meeting by chance.' As soon as she'd finished the call, she'd put down the phone, switched off the shower and sighed. She'd called Tom to say that she'd thought she might be pregnant, to get his feelings on the matter and to see if he openly offered any thoughts on the evening they'd had. Half of her had hoped he'd jump in and tell her how crazy she sounded, that protection had been carefully used. But instead, he'd pulled out the life-or-death card, and without any further thought for her own predicament, she'd hidden her phone in her pocket before walking back into the bedroom and dramatically throwing herself on to the bed, just in case Cole had been watching.

And now, with her heart lurching out of her chest, Daisy realised what she'd agreed to. Meeting in a public place was a risk, one she shouldn't be doing, especially after the day she'd already had. The nausea had now gone but her legs still felt weak, and her breasts felt as though they were about to explode. To top the evening off, Cole had invited both Teresa and Patrick to dinner, which meant that, whatever happened with Tom tonight, she had to be home by eight, paint on a smile, eat a meal that could turn her stomach at any moment and pretend to the two people that she probably disliked the most in the world that everything was fine.

On the plus side, she didn't have to cook. Olena had already been to the shops; the food would have been stored in the correct compartment in the fridge, and Teresa would have no reason to criticise.

'Just pretend to bump into him,' she said to herself as she paid for the parking. 'You'll have at least a hundred witnesses.' She smiled, and tried to summon up her best acting skills. She just wasn't good at lying, which was why, since London, she'd had an apprehension building up in her chest like a pressure cooker waiting to blow, and she wished she'd had her moment with Cole and the chance to wipe the slate clean. Because now telling him she was pregnant would come as a shock, and if he found out she'd met Tom, she'd be making things worse. One chance meeting could possibly be forgiven, but multiple meets would be seen as nothing less than a torrid affair.

As she rounded the corner, she caught sight of the huge, towering Christmas tree that stood on the edge of Front Street. The sound of 'Jingle Bells' drifted towards her and, without effort, she found herself smiling pleasantly at the small crowd of children who stood around the tree. They were all wearing matching coats, hats and scarfs and, as she grew closer, Daisy could see how red the children's noses were and how cold they looked. Their lips were as red as cherries and each of them had their eyes so wide open that Daisy could see the reflection of the tree lights dancing within them. For just a few moments, her own anxiety drifted away.

The children had all shuffled together in a messy line, each of them gripping their hymn sheets tightly, and some were stood on their tiptoes, desperate to spot a parent within the crowd. In response, Daisy spotted at least a dozen men or women waving and beaming with pride as they watched their children, clapping profusely as the song came to an end.

The air was filled with the smell of baked potatoes, alcohol and the distinct aroma of pipe smoke. Behind her, an elderly man leaned against one of the trees, his pipe held tightly between his lips. A look of love and joy crossed his face as he concentrated on the songs the children sang. He looked kind, but lonely, and Daisy gave him a hesitant smile.

'It's my granddaughter,' he said gently. 'Her mother won't let me see her. But every year I come here and I break the rules.' He held a finger up to his lips. As he spoke, the sadness showed in his face, the longing deep in his eyes. Daisy saw one of the children waving at him and automatically, with her hand on her stomach, she looked from the child to the old man, and her heart broke for them both. It was more than obvious that the two of them had a deep love for each other and Daisy vowed that, where her baby was concerned, she'd always consider its family, even if that meant calling a truce with both Patrick and Teresa.

After bidding the man goodbye, Daisy moved nimbly between family groups and parents, all trying frantically to keep hold of their other children. A young girl of around three or four jumped up into her father's arms and tugged off her woollen hat to show eyes that were full of mischief.

'Daddy, Mummy says we're going to have some hot chocolate.' She placed a hand on each side of his face and stared straight into his eyes as she spoke. 'She says we can have extra cream and lots of marshmallows.' She emphasised the words 'lots of marshmallows', then leaned into her father and buried her face in the nape of his neck. It was a precious sight that made Daisy melt, and for a moment she wanted to reach out and tell the father to hold on tight to these memories because in the blink of an eye his little girl would be all grown up and this magical time would be over. But of course, she didn't. Instead, she held out a hand, rested it against one of the trees and took long, deep inward breaths.

With her eyes peeled for Tom, she watched another woman walk past. Behind her there was a chain of nine children ranging from three to six, Daisy guessed. 'Murdoch, hold your sister's hand,' the woman shouted as she continually counted heads and made sure the chain wasn't broken. 'Serves me right,' she said as she walked past Daisy. 'You'd think I'd have stopped after the first set of triplets, wouldn't you, but oh no... not me, and two sets later, I'm already pregnant again.' She patted a stomach that was hidden beneath a navy-blue coat. 'I think I'm going to buy a new telly, start watching that instead or get him snipped. Now then, who said that they wanted hot chocolate?' she shouted, as her voice was met by an accumulative squeal.

Smiling thoughtfully, Daisy felt her hand touch her own stomach. She'd often wondered what it would be like to become a mother. How it would feel to carry a baby inside her and, probably most difficult of all, how she'd manage to nurture that child through its lifetime. What she hadn't counted on was having that baby with doubt hanging over who the father might be. And while staring at the Christmas tree, she could imagine a pendulum swinging. One minute, it swung in Cole's direction, the next in Tom's. If the baby were Cole's, it would stop her life from imploding. She'd get to carry on with the life she had now and possibly convince Cole to move back to live by the beach. But with the dalliance she'd had with Tom, her dream of having a big family and living by the beach had become marred by jeopardy. No matter whose this baby was, the joy of it was tainted by the one-night stand she'd had and the mistakes she'd made.

After queuing for a drink, Daisy made her way back across the road and into the crowd that stood on a grassed area beneath the trees. The children had stopped singing and an adult choir had taken their place. Searching the crowd, Daisy noticed a woman. She was chatting to the old man from earlier, with her hands moving around in an animated way. Her face was a mixing pot of emotions, and for a few seconds Daisy watched carefully in the hope that she wasn't annoyed and that, just for once, the man would get his wish to meet his grandchild.

From somewhere behind them, Daisy heard the sound of multiple whoops that came from the crowd and turned quickly to see a brightly lit sleigh that was being pulled by four enormous reindeer.

'Tink, look, it's Santa,' a mother called down to a young child who stood by her side. As the child looked up, Daisy noticed her eyes were filled with tears. 'He found us, Tink, I told you he'd find us, didn't I?'

'But Mummy, I don't want Santa, I want my daddy,' the child replied. 'Please Mummy...'

They were words that made Daisy stop in her tracks. She knew there wasn't much she could do, but for a few moments she stood and watched as the woman knelt down in front of the girl, her eyes also glimmering with unshed tears. 'I know you do, baby... but do you see that really bright star that's right up there?'

It was more than obvious what the woman was going to say and Daisy found herself turning away to give them both some privacy.

'It should be magical, shouldn't it?' Tom asked as he wandered up to stand beside Daisy. He too had a cup of hot chocolate, and while keeping his eyes on the sleigh he lifted off the lid and blew on the hot liquid inside. 'And maybe I'm crazy, but I always had an idealistic belief about what it would be like, you know, when we got to our age and had a few children, all of our own.'

Feeling the edge to his voice, Daisy pretended to smile as though she'd only just recognised him. Then, just like he had, she lifted her cup to her mouth and, with steam blowing upward and into her face, she blew at the drink.

'What did you think it would be like, Tom?' She pressed her lips tightly together as she listened to him speak, more or less knowing what he might say.

'I thought we'd have had a couple of kids running up and down the bay by now, and on a night like tonight, we'd have come into town as a family.' He pointed across the road. 'We'd have stood by that tree, and proudly watched as they sang their carols.' He paused, sipped at the drink. 'Or I'd have sat the youngest toddler on my shoulders and you'd be looking after the baby. We'd go from stall to stall, then from pub to pub and we'd buy them all the things they didn't need... and we'd make it magical.'

Opening her eyes, Daisy looked around the square as her imaginary pendulum swung heavily back in Tom's direction. She could imagine the life Tom spoke of and the children they might have had. It was a feeling that left her warm and happy until she thought about the devastation she'd have to cause to get to that point. Confusion set in and she felt as though someone had suddenly stood on her shoulders.

Distracting herself, she pointed to the crowd. 'It all looks so easy, the way people muddle through, even when times are not as magical as they might seem.' With a knowing look, she could see the young girl whose only wish had been to see her father. She was now sitting on her mother's knee, sobbing as her mother pointed up at the stars.

It was a stark realisation that nothing was perfect. That everyone, no matter how young or old, had a story and she began to berate herself for the things she'd done. For the way she'd allowed her own story to turn into one where the control had become dissipated into a million tiny pieces.

'What's your story, Tom?' she asked, knowing that every minute she spent here, where everyone could see her talking with him, was a minute too long. 'You said it was life and death, that you really needed to see me...' She looked nervously over her shoulder at where the old man was now hugging the woman. The young girl who'd been singing beside the tree had run up to join them, a look of delight on her face, and Daisy found herself feeling happy that the family had been reunited.

'Your husband sacked me,' Tom suddenly threw in. 'And I can't afford to lose my job so I'm begging you, Daisy. You have to do something.'

'What happened, why did he do that?' she shouted over the sound of the carols. The sound of 'We Wish You a Merry Christmas' reverberating loud and clear.

'Today was my first day, and before I knew it, the bastard had set me up. He marched me to my locker and opened it up and, Daisy, I swear to God, I hadn't put the laser in there. Jesus Christ, I'd barely had time to hang my coat up or change my high-vis.' While he spoke, Tom stood rigid and with his jaw fixed, he stared at the tree. 'Your husband made me look like a thief, in front of the whole damn site. But I'm telling you, it was a set-up...' He glanced away quickly but Daisy could still hear the unmistakable crack in his voice, the emotion that was unbelievably close to boiling over. 'I've got bailiffs banging on my door demanding money on a daily basis. My TV has already been taken, and I have threats hanging over me that they'll be back for more. And your husband has made sure that no one will ever employ me.' He paused for a moment before looking away from Daisy again. 'So, I need you to speak to him. I need that job back.'

'Tom, I can't... I mean, what the hell would I say?' With the cup of hot chocolate held up in front of her mouth, Daisy closed her eyes for a blink, thought back to the telephone conversation she'd overheard that morning. The harsh way she'd heard Cole say, '...it's not negotiable and I've told you to get rid of him.' At the time she'd known that Cole was in a bad mood, that he'd been intent on firing someone. What she hadn't known was which employee he'd meant, because in the same breath he'd also spoken about a sparky that he'd just employed, which had left her confused.

'Tom, I don't know what you want me to do. I never get involved with Bailey Construction, it's Cole's company, not mine, and if I suddenly started questioning him, or telling him what to do, he'd see straight through me.' She took another sip of her drink without blowing and felt the scorch of the fluid as it hit her lips. 'I'm so sorry, but surely you can get a job somewhere else,' she whispered apologetically.

Daisy's thoughts went between Tom and Cole; both of them were important to her. She'd loved them both. Correction: she *still* loved them but in very different ways. But right now, she could see the pain in Tom's face, the disappointment in his eyes and the way his shoulders had slumped heavily forward. Tenderly, she reached out and, even though she knew it was dangerous, she took his hand in hers. 'I'm so sorry, Tom, but where Cole is concerned, it's difficult, you do know that, don't you?'

'So, you're not going to help me?'

Daisy dropped Tom's hand and turned to see the way his eyes had totally changed. The sparkle she'd always known had gone. The laughter within his voice had completely disappeared and in its place, there was a stern roughness that, even masked by the overriding sound of Christmas carols, she didn't really like.

'Daisy, Cole... he isn't what he seems. I saw him...' Tom shifted heavily from foot to foot and looked down thoughtfully.

But Daisy wasn't impressed. 'No. Just don't!' she yelled. 'I know that leaving you for Cole was wrong. I know you got hurt and I know that you came here today because you're angry with him but please, don't start throwing accusations around that you just can't prove.'

Her mood had turned from emotional to angry. It was more than obvious that Tom was about to say something about Cole that she wouldn't have liked.

Turning, Tom suddenly placed a hand on each of her shoulders and pulled her roughly towards him. He spun her around, backed her up to lean against a tree in what might have looked like a romantic embrace. 'Daisy, Cole, he's up to no good and other than the fact that he just sacked me, there's something about him I don't like.' He ran his fingers through her hair, searched her eyes with his own. 'You're not going to like this, but today he was in the cemetery, I saw him, and if I'm honest, he made my blood boil. The thought that you go home to a man like him, night after night, drives me insane.' He closed his eyes, as though feeling his pain. 'Daisy, leave him. Me and you, we could be together, we could start again, because do you know what, there's still time for us to do that.' His voice softened and he nodded emphatically. 'I'd work hard, I'd find another job and, if you want me to, I'd buy you another house. One that stands on the beach and I... I'd never cheat on you, not ever.'

Anxious that they were causing a scene, Daisy did her best to wriggle out of the grasp that Tom still had on one of her shoulders. His fingers were pressing into her skin like a claw, and in an attempt to calm herself, she tried to bite down on her lip as she noticed the way people had turned to stare at them.

'You need to get off me, right now,' she demanded. 'You're causing a scene and... and I'm not even sure what it is you're saying.'

'Daisy, think about London, about that night we shared. It was perfect. If you'd loved Cole, it wouldn't have happened, which is why I think you're confused. You have no idea what you do and don't want – that's why you're still married to him instead of being with me.'

'Tom, you're being stupid,' she growled aggressively. 'I'm not leaving Cole. I've told you, I married him and I'm going to stay married to him. Now please,' she yanked her shoulder away from his hand, 'get your damned hands off of me.' As the words left her mouth, she wanted to take them back. But being pregnant had changed her mindset and now she realised how wrong she'd been to meet with Tom in the first place, and anxiously she began to look around her in the hope that an escape route would appear and that she'd be able to use it without drawing any more attention than they already had.

Rummaging around in his pocket, Tom dragged his phone out and flicked at the screen. 'Well, I've got news for you, Mrs Bailey. This is the husband you plan to stay married to...' He hesitated for a moment too long and Daisy went to push her way past causing Tom to make a grab for her wrist.

Losing hold of her cardboard cup, Daisy felt the splash of the hot chocolate as it hit her jeans and soaked straight through them. The burn of the hot liquid made her squeal, and as her hand came up, she went to push Tom away, but the ground under her feet was uneven and with an agonising crunch, she landed heavily against the tree. A pain shot through her arm, her shoulder and her back and, before she knew it, she was lying on her back, on the cold, damp ground. With her pride as bruised as her arm, she went to stand, but her energy failed her and through the corner of her eye she saw the elderly man rush forward to take hold of her hand.

'Oh dear, deary me, are you all right, my lovely?' he questioned in a broad Northumberland accent. 'That was a really nasty fall. Now, come on, keep hold of my hand, and let me help you get up...'

Smiling gratefully, and even though every part of her body ached from the impact, Daisy gripped his hand tightly. Tentatively, she stood up to brush the dirt, twigs and leaves away from her clothes. Her cheeks burned with embarrassment, as she now had half the village watching her every move. Her eyes scanned the crowd as she searched for Tom, but she was met with nothing but the eyes of strangers, and she quickly concluded that Tom was gone.

# 16

# DAISY

'Please, take a seat,' Sarah said as she ushered the two elderly people, a man and a woman, across the office at Harbour Estates & Lettings. It was a wet Monday morning, and they both shook their umbrellas in the doorway and pulled at coats that were still damp from the earlier downpour. Respectfully, the man took off his flat cap and folded it up and into his pocket.

'We'd like to move house,' the elderly gentleman said determinedly. 'The one we have... well, it's all a bit much for us now, isn't it dear?' He leaned in lovingly towards his wife and gave her a tender smile.

'Well, you've come to the right place,' Sarah said jovially. 'Now, let me put the kettle on and get some coffee organised, you both look perished with the cold.'

From the opposite side of the room, Daisy watched how lively her sister had suddenly become. It was quite different from the Sarah she'd picked up outside her house early that morning. That Sarah had been quiet, an introverted version of her normal self. It had been a mood Daisy had expected. Sarah preferred working with Cole to working at the agency. But after Cole had dropped the whole house move on them both at the weekend, the agency had been unexpectedly closed and he'd insisted on Sarah giving Daisy a hand with the backlog.

'I'm just tired and hungover,' Sarah had said sorrowfully when she'd dropped into the passenger seat of Daisy's car. 'I'm planning a quiet day. I'm going to hide in the back office, and I'll get some of that paperwork done.' She'd nodded into the folds of her coat and pulled it up to surround her face.

The talk of Sarah having a hangover was never something that Daisy allowed herself to worry about. For her sister, having a hangover was a necessary requirement that followed the weekend. But the thought of Sarah turning up on a Monday morning and volunteering to do paperwork was just a little more than concerning. It was something she never usually did.

'I'm Mr William Baxter,' the old man replied, as Sarah jotted his name on an A4 white notepad. 'And this is my wife, Willamina.' He laughed, riotously, 'That's right. We have similar names, and we've been laughing about it for the past fifty-four years.' He turned, patted his wife's hand benevolently. 'Haven't we, my dear?'

Dropping her pen on the desk, Sarah gave them a warm, wistful smile. For a split second, she'd glanced across at Daisy and caught her eye as though she'd been about to say something meaningful but hadn't. Instead, she stood up, walked to the kettle and proceeded to pour the boiling water into two ceramic mugs.

'We've lived in the village for the past thirty years,' Mr Baxter continued. 'And even though we don't really want to move' – he paused thoughtfully – 'it's all getting a bit much. We don't drive any more and with us not having a shop that we can easily walk to, or even a pub' – he stopped, nodded, sniffed back his emotion – 'it's time we moved on.'

Listening intently, Daisy went to stand up but winced with the pain. The fall, along with the house move, had taken its toll. Right now, she felt as though she had pain in muscles that she'd never previously felt. Her arm was bruised, her hip was tender and, in an attempt to hide her injuries from Cole, she'd spent the whole of Sunday in one of the snug rooms pretending to read. Today, she'd dressed quickly in an oversized lambswool sweater that was long in the sleeve and hung over her hands.

'On a clear day we can see Lindisfarne from our house, can't we, darling?' Mr Baxter continued. 'We can sit on the patio at the back and watch the sunsets; they're to die for.'

Closing her eyes for a beat, Daisy could immediately imagine the sunsets and surmised that the couple most probably lived in one of the cottages that stood close to the beach just down from her own property. She knew that all of the cottages but two were rentals because she managed them on behalf of an investor. The two properties she knew of stood right at the end of the row and Daisy tried to remember if she'd ever noticed the couple before, but couldn't.

Not having spent enough time at the beach was just another regret she knew she'd now have to live with. In the time she'd lived there, she should have walked down there more, paddled in the water, and taken advantage of all she'd had, while she'd had it. And now, life had changed. She didn't live there any more and, with a hand resting anxiously against her stomach, she did all she could to push the thought of a pregnancy out of her mind.

Staring across the room, she saw the lines of worry that fanned out from the corners of the man's mouth and his eyes. She could see the deep, meaningful love and respect that he gave to his wife. That, and the years they'd spent together, was much to be admired. But Daisy couldn't help but wonder if they'd all been happy years. Had one of them ever strayed? Or had either of them wished for a different love to the one they'd had? These were the types of questions that had crossed Daisy's mind every day since she'd spent the night in London with Tom. She'd allowed herself to indulge in unfinished business and it was a night that, for as long as she lived, she'd never forget. The passion and the excitement had been completely addictive. But her moment of joy had been followed by a deep-seated heartache.

'This can't be the end,' Tom had said to her with a gentle parting kiss as they'd stood together on the platform, 'it just can't be.' He'd held her tight, showered the nook of her neck with kisses. 'Unless it's life or death – then we'd be there for each other, wouldn't we?'

As he'd said the words, Daisy had hesitated for just a moment too long, before nodding intently. She'd felt the tears spring into her eyes, and following the parting kiss, she'd been tempted to keep the affair going and to take the consequences that she knew would come. But deep down, she couldn't. She loved Cole, loved the security that being married to him gave her and, what's more, he'd done nothing to deserve her betrayal. She'd felt a moment of deep and utter longing for both men that she loved, and with her heart tearing in two, she'd made her decision and torn herself out of Tom's arms and walked away, without looking back.

'Daisy, please...'

She'd heard him shout out but, deep down, she'd known that the weekend had to come to an end. That she had no choice but to separate her love for Tom from her love for Cole. On the other side of the platform barrier, she'd once again become Mrs Bailey – loyal wife. It had been a promise she'd kept, until Tom had produced his life-or-death card, only to leave her with a million different questions. She still wasn't sure what Tom had really wanted her to do, what he'd meant when he'd said, 'I'd never cheat on you, not ever.' It had been quite a statement, and then he'd made out that he'd had a photograph, one that she'd needed to see but, conveniently it had been a picture he'd never shown. Which made her wonder if he'd had one at all or whether it had been nothing more than a ruse to thread strings of doubt through her mind.

'I love the island. It's one of my favourite places,' Sarah said as she took in a deep breath and closed her eyes. 'I'd love to live there,' she said, dreamily. 'My sister lives on the bay and it's always so magical, and the island, it takes on a different atmosphere when the tide surrounds it, doesn't it?'

Bringing herself back to the present, Daisy smiled at the way Sarah had dropped into her normal sales patter with ease. It was a pitch she'd perfected over the years, as was the way she perched on the edge of the desk. Today she was dressed in the smart, tailored suit that she normally only wore to impress important clients, as were the shoes, one of which currently hung precariously from the toes on her foot. A bright red mark showed on the back of her heel and, occasionally during the morning, Daisy had noticed the way Sarah had slipped them off and kicked them under the table while she'd spent a good hour on her phone, flicking at the screen and sending messages. It made Daisy wonder what Sarah was up to, and why she'd come to work so dressed up when she was only planning to file paperwork.

Turning to her monitor, Daisy studied her spreadsheets. There were another two properties that had come up for sale, which she hadn't previously seen, and she clicked on her mouse and printed out the details. The weeks leading up to Christmas were always slow and challenging and because of the excitement most people had around Christmas, no one ever wanted to buy, sell or rent during the winter months. Most of the clear, Perspex document holders that she'd hung around the walls to showcase the properties available were currently empty, and Daisy took the files off the printer before standing up and sliding the pictures into one of the displays in the window.

'I'd love to live in a house that overlooked the beach,' she heard Sarah say, '...you love living on the bay, don't you, Daisy?'

Smiling, Daisy picked up her camera and playfully waved it around in the air. 'I've always loved living there but my husband, he built a new house which means that, like it or not, we've just moved out and if I'm honest, I'm totally devastated at the thought of selling. I'm probably going to go over there and photograph it later,' she said in a voice that was more than emotional. The thought of anyone else living in her house was still too much to handle and her plan to go over there and take some pictures was nothing more than a ruse. A way for her to escape her reality, and spend some time back at the house where she intended to unpack some of the boxes she'd stashed in the spare bedroom.

Daisy gave a sigh as she turned her attention back to her work. She needed to go over the details of the house she'd been to that morning. It had been a small terraced house in the centre of Seahouses, walking distance from the shops and on a street where they'd previously sold quite a few of the neighbouring properties. Daisy had been excited to see it, but when she'd arrived, the disappointment had been huge. The house was dirty, chaotic and a strong smell of urine had met her as soon as the door had opened. A young woman covered in tattoos had ushered her in and they'd walked past a row of dirty litter trays lined up in the hallway that had made Daisy want to gag.

Now, back at the office, she was struggling to rid her nostrils of the smell or write a detailed outline. Coming up with something to enhance the sale wasn't going to be easy, knowing that any potential buyers would be put off the moment the door was opened. Flicking back through the images she'd taken, she knew immediately that there was little to salvage.

She began to click through her files and found herself looking for a leaflet on how to prepare a property for viewings and tried to decide whether or not she should send it to the vendor. Whether they'd take the hint and clean the place up. But Daisy had seen one too many houses that looked the same and she'd quickly come to realise that people rarely changed. With a sigh, she knew that the chance of selling a property like that, with only two weeks to go before Christmas, was impossible.

'You wouldn't mind doing that, would you Daisy?'

The clicking of the keyboard and the mention of her name brought Daisy's attention back into the room. She cocked her head to one side and listened to what Sarah was saying. Automatically, she pulled in a slow, deep breath and forced a smile on her face.

'And what wouldn't Daisy mind?' she said with a laugh. Purposely, she turned to Mr Baxter and gave him a wink. 'Because if it means going out in the cold and the rain anytime soon, the answer is no.' It was true, Daisy didn't want to leave the warmth of the office. She'd been out all morning. Her feet were like ice blocks. What she really wanted was to go home – and by home, she meant Pipistrelle. But instead, she'd be going back to The Willows, where tonight she needed to speak to Cole. Without mentioning Tom, she needed to try and find out what had happened at the building site, and whether Cole had any idea who he was. Then, she had to tell him the truth. He had to know who Tom was. He had to know about the one-night stand and about the pregnancy. Only then would she be able to move on with her life, even if that was a life without either Cole or Tom in it.

'Your sister says that you might pop in and do me a quick valuation,' Mr Baxter said with a smile. 'To be honest, the sooner the better for us.'

'Okay, but if you want me to come today, we need to hurry. That downpour isn't going to wait, not for anyone.' She pointed out of the window to a sky that had turned grey and dismal. Even more rain clouds had formed, and the Northumberland coastline had taken on a dark and moody atmosphere.

Leaving Sarah to organise the finer details, Daisy picked up her phone and scrolled through her messages. She'd hoped that Tom would have apologised, or that he'd have at least asked if she was okay but instead, the only message she'd received from him had been cold, and intimidating.

TOM

I will prove what he's up to and I will find a way to be a part of your life.

His message had riled her, and she was both scared and nervous about what he might do, which confirmed to her that speaking to Cole was the right thing to do. The Tom she'd known before would have walked away with dignity, but this Tom was different. He'd grown and changed, and she thought back to the aggression he'd shown towards her even though half of the village had been watching.

Daisy thought about listening to the voicemail he'd left her again. Maybe by listening to it she could convince herself that Tom was still the kind, loving man she'd once known. The sound of his voice reminded her of the joy she'd felt in London, the laughter they'd shared as they'd roamed the city hand in hand. It had been an adventure that had been followed by a whole night of lovemaking. A night that had passed in a haze, before the heartbreaking moment when their weekend had come to an end, and she'd forced herself to leave the city without him.

They were all feelings she'd thought that she could success-fully compartmentalise but even weeks later she was still struggling. As she looked up from her computer, she suddenly saw Tom walking past the window. He didn't smile, or wave at her, but just walked into the cafe on the opposite side of the road and, nervously, Daisy moved to peer through the small space between the literature holders that hung in the window. It was a position where she felt sure he wouldn't be able to see her, not even if he were watching. The thought that he was sitting just across the road was daunting, but it was a feeling she also didn't understand. Tom had never seriously hurt her. The fall had been an accident and, rather than draw any more attention to them, he'd simply left. Hadn't he? Daisy's mind went back to the look in his eye as he'd grabbed hold of her shoulders. The way he'd grabbed her wrist as she'd tried to walk away from him. And now, just a couple of days later, he was sending threatening messages and had gone to sit in a cafe, right opposite the agency.

'It's not a problem at all; Daisy will be over at two,' Sarah had shouted as Mr and Mrs Baxter said their goodbyes. Daisy had painted a smile on her face but felt her shoulders drop with annoyance.

'Thanks for that, Sarah,' she said abruptly. 'You've been in a mood all day, you've spent more time on your phone than doing any work and now you've just organised my diary without even asking...' Pulling in a long, hard breath, Daisy crossed her arms and kept one eye on the window.

'Look, I'm sorry, all right, but I thought you'd be happy, business is business.'

Daisy pushed her shoulders back and placed a hand in the small of her back. The pain she felt there was getting worse and the paracetamol she'd taken a couple of hours before hadn't worked. 'Do you want to tell me what's wrong? It feels like you've been moody since you went out on Saturday.'

'No, there's nothing to talk about...'

Abandoning her position beside the window, Daisy walked across to where Sarah stood and immediately noticed the tears in her eyes. 'Hey, what's wrong? Why wouldn't you want to talk? It's what we do, isn't it?' She shoulder-bumped her sister and gave her a kind smile. 'And you know I'm a good listener.'

'No, Daisy... that's what we used to do,' Sarah quickly spat back, her voice sharp and full of venom. 'But then... you went to London, disappeared for two whole days, and you still haven't told me why. Which means that you were probably doing something you shouldn't. And that big surprise you were talking about doing for Cole, well, that didn't materialise, did it?' She perched her bottom on the edge of Daisy's desk and once again began to scroll through her phone. 'Plus, who are you to talk about being moody? You haven't exactly been the life and soul just lately, have you?' she said, pulling a face at her sister. 'So, it's up to you, do we go back to telling each other everything, or do we keep a few secrets?'

'Sarah, that's not fair...' Closing her eyes, Daisy moved back to her position in the window. She didn't like the direction the conversation had taken and needed to do something to change the subject and take the focus off London.

'Why isn't it fair?' Sarah snapped back without hesitation. 'You were obviously up to something.'

'Are you seeing someone?' Daisy questioned. It was all she could think to say while her eyes were still fixed on the cafe opposite and she tried to decide whether or not Tom would have gone there just to annoy her. 'Sooner or later, I will get it out of you, you do know that don't you?'

'There's nothing to tell.'

'Of course there is,' she said, diverting attention. 'You got all dressed up for today and in clothes you only wear when you're trying to impress, which tells me that you're up to something.'

Laughing, Sarah tipped her head to one side. Her cheeks flooded with colour, and she jumped down from the desk. 'You're quite the detective, aren't you?'

'So, who is he?'

'Just someone. You know what I'm like, I go on dates for fun.' Sarah winked, smiled and her face lit up with an obvious memory until it clouded over, and with what could have been the flick of a light switch, her eyes became vexed and filled with angst. 'There's one man I like, someone I've known for a very long time, and do you know what, if I wanted to, I could make a move on him, but there's something holding me back... So, you know...'

Picking up her coffee, Daisy thought about the kinds of men Sarah had dated in the past. There had only ever been two kinds: the ones who'd been just a bit more than a casual fling, and the others who hadn't got past the first date. Most of them had fallen into the latter category.

'Your turn...' Sarah threw back, and smiled smugly at Daisy, who still had her eyes on the window. 'Spill the beans.'

Closing her eyes, Daisy battled with her conscience. She'd come close to telling Sarah the truth about Tom on a number of occasions. She'd always prided herself as a role model for her younger sister and had taken great pleasure in the fact that Sarah had often said how much she wanted a life just like hers. *'You have the perfect life, Daisy, the perfect house, husband and everything you could ever wish for.'* It was true, Daisy did appear to have the perfect life, but even though she appeared to have everything she needed, she wasn't sure it was all that she wanted. If she was truly happy, she wouldn't have strayed, she wouldn't have fallen into Tom's bed so easily, would she? Which brought her back to her trip to London. Did she tell Sarah the truth before she told Cole? It was a thought and something she'd almost always do, but for some reason it didn't seem right. Telling Sarah would alter everything. She'd then have no choice as to whether or not she did tell Cole in the future. But if she didn't tell Sarah, it would soon become obvious that she'd lied to her, and she'd have broken her trust, which was something she'd never get back. But it had to be done.

'Sarah, you're not going to like what I'm going to say...' Pressing her lips tightly together, she glanced up as Tom bounded out of the coffee shop. He was wearing a pair of snug fitting jeans and an open waxed jacket, giving her a view of the open-neck shirt he wore beneath. With a determined and calculating smirk, he stopped, stood, and he stared. Directly at her.

With her heart plummeting deep in her chest, Daisy felt her legs weaken. At that moment, she had no idea what Tom was about to do, and she convinced herself that he was about to walk across the road and in through the door. That he was about to say something to her, in front of Sarah, and Daisy knew that once he had, it wouldn't take a genius to put two and two together. London, secrets, Tom, and a suspected pregnancy, all formed a picture that Daisy wouldn't be proud of.

'Sarah, you're right. I do have something to tell you, but you're not going to like it,' she said in a voice that tremored. 'It was a big, fat, stupid mistake. I was reckless and I absolutely know that I shouldn't have done it. Because, you were right, I did do something I shouldn't have.' Blurting out the words at speed, Daisy felt her heart accelerate. Tom was still standing there, staring while rolling his jaw. In a bold move, Daisy moved further into the window and into a place where she knew Tom could see her and lifted her hands and shoulders in a questioning shrug.

'What the hell are you talking about and who are you looking at?' Joining her in the window, Daisy heard the audible gasp that came from Sarah, and the rattle of the literature holders as she moved in to take a closer look.

'Sarah,' she began but paused, closed her eyes and with her chest constricting and the air squeezing out of her lungs, she took a step backwards. 'And I know what you're going to say, I know that Cole gives me everything I need and that I should be more grateful...'

With her mind on Cole, she suddenly realised what this admission could do to her marriage. That once she'd said it, she couldn't take it back, and that even though she trusted Sarah with her life, she still felt nervous about admitting the truth.

'Sarah. You have to understand. It was unfinished business. It was something I had to get out of my system and now, I...' Again she paused. She couldn't say she regretted her actions, because to say that would be telling another lie. With the room spinning around her, Daisy felt her heart lurch as she heard the front door slam and she spun around expecting to see Tom standing there, ready to argue.

But instead, the office was empty... and Sarah was gone.

# 17

## TOM

With the sky turning a dark and gloomy shade of grey and the clouds accumulating to look like large boulders rolling in from somewhere beyond the harbour wall, Tom gave Daisy a final look before he checked the time on his phone, called in at the florist to collect his order, and scurried as quickly as he could back to the car park.

His free hour of parking was running out fast and with a deluge looking as though it was about to fall from the sky, he pulled open the passenger door of his car. With the aroma of lilies, roses and carnations drifting towards him, he carefully placed the bouquet of flowers on the passenger seat, and he clipped the seat belt around them.

'You all right there?' A man dressed in an overcoat, football scarf and thick woollen gloves asked as he walked past in the car park. 'Nice flowers, mate, who's the lucky lady then?' He laughed at his own question, lifted a hand in the air and, without waiting for an answer, walked to the pay meter.

Feeling satisfied that the flowers had been carefully stowed. Tom glared in the man's direction. He hadn't needed or wanted a stranger's opinion and with an exaggerated growl, he pulled off his jacket, and threw it into the back seat of the car. Arrogantly, he slid into the driver's seat, checked the clock on his dashboard and sighed dramatically. He was later than he'd hoped. His unplanned diversion to the coffee shop had meant that he'd turned up at the florist almost half an hour later than he'd originally intended. The florist had thought him a no-show and the twenty-pound bouquet of flowers he'd originally ordered had already been sold.

'I'm so sorry, Mr Burgess, I didn't think you were coming and someone popped in who needed a bouquet, so I let them go,' the florist had said apologetically. 'And I don't have any others ready, apart from these. Will these be all right? I'll do them for thirty.' She'd smiled, no doubt jubilant at the extra value sale that Tom had reluctantly agreed to. It was another hit on his finances that he couldn't afford, but with everything else against him, he'd dropped his credit card down on the table and watched as she'd happily taken his money.

Dramatically, Tom hit out at the steering wheel with the heel of his hand, and with his stomach turning with hunger, he expelled a breath and looked up to see Sarah standing on the edge of the pavement, with her hands on her hips and a look of impatience crossing her face. Sarah lifted herself up on to her toes occasionally whilst obviously searching the car park for someone. Without fully knowing why, Tom found himself trying to fold his body downward into his seat.

Hidden by the other cars that were parked either side of his, Tom kept one eye on Sarah. She had a fixed, expectant look on her face and her hand went up to hold back her hair as it billowed in the breeze. She was wearing a smart tailored suit that showed off each and every one of her perfect curves, which Tom had to agree, he more than approved of. The fact that he found

Sarah sexually attractive was a shock to his system, and after just a few minutes he had no choice but to sit up in his seat, adjust his jeans and make himself feel just a little more comfortable.

'You wouldn't, would you?' His gaze scanned up and down her body and he thought back to all the times he'd teased her as a young and impressionable teenager. The times she'd curled up on the sofa, with her head on his lap following a teenage heart-break were too many to count. They were memories that were a long way in the past, but now he gave her an appreciative nod. 'You've grown up a bit, I'll give you that much,' he said smugly. 'It's just a shame you've turned out to be a deceitful, manipulative witch.'

He allowed his mind to recall what had happened back in the cemetery. He could still feel his skin prickle when he'd spotted Sarah with Cole. The information he'd gleaned there had been liquid gold, and in his eyes, it was more than obvious that Sarah was so much closer to Cole than Daisy knew – why else would she be meeting him in a cemetery on a dull winter's day? And why would Sarah be telling Cole that Daisy was pregnant?

There was only one reason Tom could think for Daisy to have kept it a secret from her husband, and with his confidence return-ing, Tom considered opening the door and shouting Sarah over. He could pretend he'd been there by chance and once she looked to be comfortable in his company, he could lead the conversation in the direction of Daisy and dig for the truth about Sarah and Cole.

But then, with a disgruntled sigh, he thought about Daisy. They'd spent two amazing days in London, or so he'd thought. In his mind they'd been rebuilding bridges and putting the past where it belonged. He'd even begun to allow himself to imagine the life he could have with Daisy in it and, for a brief time as he'd held her in his arms while she slept, he could almost see the family they were about to create. But the weekend had ended. Daisy had climbed on a train, and for the second time in his life, she'd cast him aside. He'd done his best to walk away, to go back to the life he had with Grace and with Mason. He'd planned to leave thoughts of Daisy alone, but now Grace was gone, Mason too, and things had changed.

'You should have expected it, you fool,' he grumbled under his breath. 'She told you she was married. It was more than obvious she had nothing to offer and you... you should have known what she'd do.' He furrowed his brow at the thought of Daisy going home to another man who she'd kiss in the same way she'd kissed him. It was an image he didn't need in his mind, especially when her marriage wasn't as perfect as she thought. Because if it was perfect, she wouldn't be hiding a pregnancy. She wouldn't have gone out in the dark, to meet up with a man who she'd recently spent a night with, and she definitely wouldn't have turned up when he'd sent the life-or-death message.

With his gaze still on Sarah, he remembered the way Daisy had lain in his arms; influenced by the drink he'd given her, she'd chatted to him about anything and everything, which was when she'd brought Sarah up in conversation.

'Our Sarah, she's always on one of those dating apps...' Daisy had scowled. Her disapproval had been obvious, and she'd leaned against the pillows, sipped at the wine, and tipped her glass dangerously towards him as she'd spoken, the deep, red fluid almost pouring out. 'And get this, her code name or whatever you call it, is "Executive Lady 1999", which is ironic, because she's far from being an executive and she wasn't born in 1999, she was born in 1998, but apparently "Executive Lady 1998" had already been taken...' While rambling on, she'd lifted her phone in the air and flicked through the pictures on Sarah's profile.

At the time, Tom hadn't thought much of it. He'd been more

interested in spending time with Daisy than talking about Sarah. But now, while watching the younger, attractive sister, he could recall the photos and the site that Daisy had mentioned.

Picking up his phone, Tom logged into the app and created a profile for himself with a similar ambiguous name. 'Confident Sparky'. It was enough to say who he was without giving out detail. That, along with a distant photograph he'd had taken a year or so before, and a single paragraph, completed his profile and with a satisfied sigh, he began to scroll. The site suggested the profiles of lots of other women he could date, but Tom couldn't tear his mind away from the thought of sending Sarah a brief but titillating message.

The sound of raindrops began to hit his windscreen with force, and he quickly looked up to see that Sarah had gone. He looked down at his screen and debated sending her a message. It would be quite easy to write something funny in the hope she'd respond. But he had much more going on in his life than finding a date because dates cost money. And the thought of taking a woman back to his house wasn't something he'd ever want to do. He'd only moved in a few months before and the house still had a lot of jobs he had to complete and he couldn't face the embarrassment of a woman asking him where the television had gone, or why a whole pile of boxes still needed unpacking. Besides, no matter who he dated, he knew that he'd always compare them to Daisy.

'But Sarah *is* comparable. She's the closest alternative you'd ever be able to get,' he mumbled to himself, and with her image still showing up on his phone, he ran his gaze up from her stilettos until he met with her face. 'She'd certainly be a challenge, and you did tell Daisy that you'd find a way to be a part of her life.' He smiled sardonically. He could just imagine the way Daisy would react, especially if he and Sarah became a thing and he had to attend a family event. The thought of walking into Daisy's house, arm in arm with her sister, was an event he already looked forward to, and not all because of Daisy. He couldn't wait to see the priceless look on Cole's face either.

Smiling mischievously, Tom gave the screen a determined flick and swiped right on her profile. He found himself watching and waiting for just a few minutes until her response bounced back, which didn't take very long.

> Hi, I'm Sarah. I have to say, your profile looks intriguing. I'm going to take it that you're a man of very few words. Lol. xx
> PS: We live quite close and there's not too many singles in our neck of the woods. So, it's good to meet you. Xx

Tom smiled... this was going to be fun.

# 18

## DAISY

With the rain hammering against the shop window, Daisy rushed to the door and hurriedly searched the street for any sign that Sarah was heading back to the agency.

'Come on, where are you? And where did you go in such a hurry?' she yelled as a rumble of thunder was quickly followed by a crackling burst of lightning. It shot across the harbour, making Daisy jump backward.

With the dramatic change in the weather, the streets had emptied. Even the die-hard locals who were rarely fazed by the Northumberland weather, had all disappeared.

Pulling her phone out of her pocket, Daisy flicked at the screen. After what she'd just confessed out loud, she couldn't help but worry about where Sarah had gone. Especially when she'd spotted Tom standing outside the cafe, staring. Daisy tried to work out whether Sarah had seen him or not.

'Why did you panic?' she whispered out loud. 'You were doing so well until...' Her hand went to her stomach and then to her back. The nagging pain was still there and, with her hand massaging her back, she leaned against the door, still hopeful that at any moment, Sarah would run back through it.

She had expected her sister to scream and shout, yes, but what she hadn't expected was for Sarah to run. After taking a quick glance at Sarah's desk, she saw she'd left her own set of keys behind, which meant Daisy was now standing in an office that she couldn't lock up because Sarah wouldn't be able to get back in.

Shivering relentlessly, she walked to the radiator and leaned against it, enjoying the feel of the warmth on her hands. Even though Sarah was her main concern, as she stared out through the window, she realised a part of her was still looking for Tom. With a nervous twist to her stomach, she knew he could easily be out there in one of the shops. Watching. Waiting. Looking for his opportunity to speak to her again, and for a second she considered locking the door to keep him out.

With a determination to get on with some work, Daisy began to rummage through her case that Cole had thoughtfully bought for her. Pulling the case open, Daisy smiled fondly. Just by buying her the case, it had shown her what a caring and loving husband Cole could be and, once again, the self-reproach got worse. He hadn't deserved what she'd done to him or to their marriage. He was a good man, honest and trustworthy, although, since Saturday, Tom's words had spun around in her mind: Tom knew something she didn't. He'd been about to show her a picture that could have explained but he'd disappeared before he could show her. Which had sent her mind spiralling around in every direction. Was Cole having an affair, or was he doing something illegal? After all, building a house like theirs cost money. A lot of money. But the idea that Cole was up to something so bad, as Tom had implied, just didn't sit right.

Balancing her phone under her chin, she took in a deep breath and tapped at the screen to call Cole.

'Morning,' Cole said just a little too cheerfully. 'Actually, it's afternoon. What are you up to?'

She laughed and tapped the pen on her notepad. 'I'm just packing my case. I'm off to do a quick valuation. You know one of those quick valuations that will probably take the best part of two or three hours. Sarah kindly dropped it into my diary without even asking, so I'm furious.'

'Hey, don't be too hard on her. Business is business.'

'Strangely,' Daisy said, 'they're the exact words Sarah used; you two are rubbing off on each other.' She looked up at the clock and, dismissively, she shrugged off the sudden thought about Cole and Sarah that flashed into her mind. They were close. They did think and speak the same language, and the comment Tom had made about always being faithful was making her feel paranoid. But it was a thought she didn't have the time to go into. It was almost two o'clock, which meant that if she didn't leave soon, she'd be late. 'Anyhow, the appointment is down in the bay, so while I'm there, I'm going to check on the house and then I thought about popping in on Dad, and check that he's okay.' Biting down on her lip, Daisy held her breath as she heard the exasperated sigh that came from the other end of the phone. The silence that followed, even though it only lasted a few short seconds, felt like a lifetime.

'Is something wrong, Cole?'

'Yeah. No, I don't know,' Cole pondered, 'My parents, they were going to stay for dinner and I kind of hoped you'd be home.'

'Again?' Looking down at the doodle, Daisy saw the way she'd written the word 'Tom'. It was right there on the pad, written in bubbles. A small love heart had been drawn next to his name, and she gave herself a silent berating. She was giving far too much thought to Tom and not enough to her husband. If she wanted her marriage to last, she had to put Cole first. 'Look. I'm sorry,' she heard herself saying. 'Do you want me to bring food, cook something nice? Once your parents have gone home, we could go and relax in the hot tub, or...' She let the words hang in the air before she continued. 'Or did I hear you mention a steam room?'

With a mischievous chuckle, Cole grunted his approval. 'You certainly did hear me talk of a steam room and a hot tub, and... I can make sure both are warmed up ready if you fancy it.' His voice drifted off dreamily. 'In fact, do you want me to put my parents off tonight and then you and me can...'

'No,' she suddenly snapped back as she straightened, felt the repeated nagging ache that came from her hip and thought about all the bruises that still covered her body. She had no feasible way of explaining them, not now, not two days after the event when they were turning a gross shade of yellow. 'You can't do that to your parents and, to be fair, I did promise Dad so, if it's okay with you, why don't you have dinner with your parents, and we'll catch up a little later, okay?'

Closing her eyes as the phone was put down, Daisy felt another wave of regret wash through her. It was as though one lie had led to another and now, even if she wanted to, she couldn't spend any intimate time with Cole because of the fall she'd had and all the questions that would undoubtedly follow.

Right now, she'd go to see Mr and Mrs Baxter, she'd do their valuation and afterwards, she'd go back to Pipistrelle and spend an hour or two there. If she was lucky, the storm would clear away, and she'd be there in time to watch the sunset. It was a thought that brought a smile to her face and, with one eye still on the door looking for Sarah, she picked up her tape measure and dropped it in the top of her bag, just in case, once out on site, her laser failed.

Once organised, Daisy groaned at the weight of the case, dropped it back on the floor and glanced through the window to see that the rain had slowed.

'Sorry... I had to dash out.' Sarah laughed as she flounced through the door, with damp, windswept hair. An umbrella that had obviously been borrowed was dropped in the doorway. 'I spotted someone. You know what it's like, I needed to speak to them and then there was the rain, so we ended up...' She lifted her hands in the air and with a radiant smile she turned to her desk, pulled her phone out of her pocket and clicked on the screen. 'We sat in his car and I borrowed his umbrella to walk back with, which means I'll have to see him again, just to return it.' Laughing at her own words, Sarah stood up, picked up the kettle and set it to boil. 'Now then, do you want a drink, it's cold out there, I'm absolutely freezing.'

Sitting down in her seat, Daisy caught her breath. She was desperate to ask Sarah how much of her earlier confession she'd heard. How much she knew. But from the way Sarah was acting, Daisy presumed that her sister hadn't heard anything at all. Otherwise, Sarah would have definitely had something to say and, with the fear of making things worse, Daisy had no intention of restirring the pot.

'Oh, actually, have you seen the time,' Sarah suddenly blurted out as she poured the hot water into her cup. 'You should probably get going... Mr and Mrs Baxter were expecting you by two and by the looks of it' – she laughed – 'you're going to be late.'

# 19

## DAISY

Pulling off the main road, Daisy followed the curve in the road. She automatically went to veer to the right and towards the house where she'd lived but slowed the car just before turning. Pulling up in front of a metal five-bar gate that blocked the road, Daisy stared at a lane that she'd driven down at least a thousand times before. But today, it felt unfamiliar and suddenly she felt as though she shouldn't be there at all.

'Let's get the valuation done,' she whispered with her hand resting lovingly against her stomach, 'then, we can pop to the house and maybe me and you, we could do one of my favourite things and we could sit down and watch the weather as it rolls into the bay.' Climbing out of the car to open the gate, Daisy realised that she'd subconsciously begun to talk to the baby. In her mind now, there was no doubt that the test had been correct, that she was definitely pregnant, and that somehow, she'd find a way to bring this baby into the world, with or without a father figure in it.

Standing in front of the gate, Daisy rested a hand on top and looked at the cottages that stood in the distance. She stared at the rugged coastline, the sandy beach and the island of Lindisfarne in the distance. To her, this view depicted everything needed to feel at home.

After double checking the cottage's name on her phone, she'd worked out that she was going to the one on the end. It was one of the two properties that were still privately owned, and she'd already realised how quickly and easily she could sell it. All it would take would be a phone call. She had an investor who currently owned and rented just about all the other cottages in this row. It would gain her a fast commission without doing much work, and her visit today would be nothing more than a mere formality.

If the properties had been closer, she'd have risked leaving the car behind and walking the length of the lane, but with her case being so heavy, she got back in her car and made her way down the lane, trying to avoid the sheep that grazed in the field. Daisy leaned back in her seat and stared across the fields towards the castle in Bamburgh. It was a twelfth-century fortress that stood high up on a volcanic outcrop, practically etching itself into the skyline. Above it, the sky still looked moody and unpredictable. Pale grey went to a dark navy blue, interspersed with a vivid streak of crimson, which was a sure sign that the storm they'd had earlier was still hanging around, or that a second wave was looming offshore, and biding its time before hitting the coastline.

Yawning, Daisy realised that it had already been a very long day. She was tired and stressed and now she wished she'd asked Sarah again about what she'd heard. Her disappearance had been odd and for Sarah to leave without saying where she was going, or taking her keys, was normally unheard of.

Without warning Daisy's stomach began to grumble. She'd missed both breakfast and lunch, and with the afternoon passing so quickly, she realised that it was now getting close to dinner time. She began to rummage around in her bag and felt a surge of relief as her fingers unearthed a small chocolate-covered biscuit. The packet was sealed, but she tore it open, used her hand to catch the crumbs and ate what she could of the biscuit.

Winding down the window, Daisy held her hands out and dusted them off. She couldn't help but automatically pull in a long, deep breath. The air was crisp, earthy and sweet. It had the smell of imminent rain and with that in mind, she considered what she still had to do. She could go to the house and do a fast valuation, follow it with a call to the investor, and have the house sold in moments. After which, she could easily be back at Pipistrelle in time to watch the sunset, weather permitting.

Closing her eyes for a blink, Daisy felt her phone vibrate with a message, and even though she normally received quite a few each day, she pulled the phone from her pocket with a new-found sense of apprehension and a small part of her already sensing who would have sent it.

TOM

Daisy. I need to speak to you, urgently. Life or death.

Once again, Tom had pulled the life-or-death card, which after what he'd done two nights before, really annoyed her. Part of her had always loved him, but now she wanted to hate him. He'd walked away when she'd fallen. He'd left her sitting on the cold, sodden ground bruised and humiliated. An act that had since weighed heavily, and even though she wanted to forgive him, a small part of her knew that it was time to break free of his hold.

DAISY

Tom. Sorry. Not a good time. I'm working!

Sitting for just a few minutes, Daisy watched her screen. She looked for the familiar three dots that would indicate a response but when no further message came through, she pulled her notepad out of her bag. Whether she liked it or not, she had a job to do. The quick sale was not guaranteed, which meant that she couldn't cut corners, and with one eye still on the phone, she climbed out of the car.

Picking up her camera, Daisy looked through the viewfinder. Getting a picture of the island while it looked so moody was imperative. It was always a great selling point, but the sea fret was coming in fast and with the need to get the job done, she shot multiple pictures.

Satisfied that she had a good shot, Daisy jumped in the car, just as her phone bleeped with another new message from Tom.

TOM

I know that you're pregnant!

# 20

## TOM

With darkness pulling in and the rain once again coming down to lash against the windscreen, Tom went through the large, metal gates of Seacroft Park.

With a stifled yawn, he sat back in the driver's seat, pushed his shoulders back and stretched. The weekend had taken its toll, the minimal sleep he'd had since Friday wasn't the best combination with driving. Coupled with the fact that Daisy had kept a secret from him which had really annoyed him.

What he really wanted to do was recline his seat, close his eyes and sleep, but the nervous anticipation of walking inside, along with the bright lights and commotion that he could see going on through the downstairs windows, kept him transfixed. The building was made from a series of modern architectural blocks, creating small distinctive apartments at ground-floor level that each had their own tiny individual lawned garden. Some, but not all, had their own front door with a shiny brass knocker and a post box with a surname written on it. From what Tom could see, the nicer apartments had a patio chair and table outside, not that anyone would sit outside in the winter but even so, it was still a luxury that only a few could afford.

Glancing up, Tom stared despondently at the windows upstairs, of which most were shrouded in darkness. The residents who didn't have the opportunities and comfort of those downstairs tended to go to bed early and Tom was never sure whether or not that was down to choice or whether the carers simply worked on a rota and those upstairs were put to bed first.

Resigning himself to going inside, Tom climbed out of the car. He picked up the bouquet wrapped in cellophane and cradled it in his arms, in the same way he'd once cradled his newborn son.

'Mr Burgess. It's been a few days,' a young woman dressed in a nurse's smock top and black nylon leggings muttered sarcastically. Her hair was tied up in a bun, and her make-up was minimal, just a little gloss on her lips. She stood behind a reception desk that was long, dark, and built from old-fashioned mahogany. Beside it, stood a tall glass-fronted cupboard which contained at least a hundred books, along with multiple ring binders. The whole room was surround by high-backed chairs, which Tom had quickly come to realise were never really used because no one was ever encouraged to sit in them. Instead, the residents always sat in a room at the back of the house. A room where the visitors were taken.

Tom rested a hand on the visitors' book and added his name to the list before striding as quickly as he could to walk past the desk and towards the door that led to the large, sweeping staircase.

'Mr Burgess.' A soft voice came from behind him, and the woman spoke in a tone that made him stop and prepare himself for what she'd say next. 'Mr Burgess, sorry to bother you but if you could pop into the office after your visit, Matron would like a quick word.'

And there it was: the dreaded summons to the office that he got each time he came to visit. The awkward conversation and totally untenable explanation he'd find himself giving about the unpaid fees. With each visit came a new demand for money and a list of requests that would have to be quickly adhered to. There was one battle after another and as Tom took in the expensive wallpaper and the heavy luxurious curtains that covered the windows, he tried to imagine a world where he didn't have the anger or the resentment he continually felt.

'Sure,' Tom responded with a pensive smile as he climbed swiftly upward. 'I needed to speak to you too about something, but first...' He pointed to a long-panelled corridor that bore the scuffs marks of being persistently banged into by wheelchairs or the residents' walking sticks. As though on cue, Tom reached the top and stood to one side as an elderly man shuffled right past him. He wore clothes that were stained with the remnants of food, his pale blue cardigan hanging loosely from his thin shoulders with its buttons fastened haphazardly. His frail, twisted fingers were curled tightly around the hard plastic handles of a walking frame. Under his breath, Tom could hear him cursing and with tired, narrowed eyes he watched and waited for the man to trip at the top of the stairs, for his life to be extinguished in a single step, or not. He knew from experience that things didn't always go to plan, that a trip and a fall could quite easily result in a death, which was why he stepped forward, and protectively he placed his arm across the top of the stairs and steered the man in the opposite direction.

'Oh, no you don't. That's not the way your night should end,' Tom said as two carers, both dressed in scrubs ran towards him.

'For God's sake, Frank, how the hell did he get out?' One of the men rested a hand against the old man's arm, eased him to one side of the corridor. 'Where are you off to, Harold?'

'Get off me, I'm hungry...' he cursed angrily and threw Tom a look. 'I was going for a sandwich...' He picked up his walking frame and held it out in Tom's direction before being manoeuvred by the carers into the stairlift. His seat belt was tightened and with Harold's walking frame hooked over his arm, the carer walked down the stair beside him. 'One minute he's sleeping, the next he's escaping, aren't you Harold,' he said, cheerfully. 'Anyone would think you didn't like it upstairs.'

Scoffing at the thought, Tom closed his eyes as Harold reached the bottom and climbed out of the stairlift. It was a sight that once again made his stomach twist with anxiety as he turned and made his way down the corridor, each step taking him closer to the rooms where the smells got worse, and he couldn't help but hold a hand over his mouth. Somewhere in the distance he could hear the sound of a woman wailing loudly. With his heart rate racing, he took in a long, deep breath as he looked over his shoulder and back at the staircase. All he wanted was to leave, to get back in his car, go back to Bamburgh and salvage whatever part of his life he could.

Out of habit, Tom tapped twice on the door of room thirty-six before pushing it open and gasping as he saw that the single divan bed had gone. In its place there was a large hospital bed covered in white cotton sheets, which could only mean one thing, and without trying to hide the smile that covered his face, he stepped into the room, spotted the care assistant who was cleaning the bathroom and put on the act that had become well practised.

'Grace, now then, what's all this...?' He dropped the bouquet on a table and walked across to the bed that dwarfed his wife. In it, her small twenty-five-year-old body looked frail and vulnerable. Her arms had lost their shape, her hair hung around her shoulders and the eyes that had always sparkled with laughter and joy had lost their colour. They'd now become sunken and narrowed with the severity of the injuries she'd suffered.

'I'm sorry I've not been for a few days, my love. I've been... well, I've been working.' He walked around the bed, straightening the sheets and, hesitantly, with one eye on the care assistant, he dropped a kiss against Grace's forehead but couldn't help himself from recoiling as the smell of his wife hit the back of his nostrils. Instinctively, and even though it was cold outside, he pushed open the window and leaned towards it.

'I brought you some flowers,' he finally said, as he retrieved the bouquet from the table. 'They were the best in the shop. Nothing more than you deserve.' Moving back to stand by the window, he held the flowers out to be seen and wafted them around in the air before standing up on his tiptoes to look through the window. He'd long since worked out that if he stood up on his toes, he could just about see the sea but only if he ignored the rooftops, the tall chimneys that dominated the skyline and the smog that continually puthered around them.

With deep inhalations of breath, he took a moment to think about the introduction of the hospital bed to the room. It meant Grace's condition must have taken a turn for the worse. That her time was close. With a malicious smirk, he bit down on his lip as he turned back to the bed. Her deterioration was obvious, which meant that soon his nightmare would end. The constant debt he was incurring wouldn't have to be paid because Grace's insurance would eventually cover the bills. And soon, he'd be able to breath without the constant fear of the bailiffs' return.

Moving to the side of the bed he grabbed at a small chair that had a thin vinyl seat pad. It definitely hadn't been built for comfort, which was probably as well because, right now, Tom had no intention of staying for long. But just for a while he had to keep up the pretence. Since the accident at the top of their stairs,

Grace had had no mental capacity to speak, and for a while, he'd just had to sit there and make sure that she couldn't. The last thing he needed was for the authorities to start asking questions.

Taking hold of her hand, Tom studied his wife. Grace no longer had access to the outside world and, by all accounts, was now a prisoner within this one room. The only way she ever left was if she was taken out in a wheelchair. It would be balanced at the top landing and, like Harold, she'd be lifted into the stairlift. It had been an act that had made her scream and shout, which hadn't been surprising after the fall she'd had, and the misery she'd had to endure, since the day it had happened.

'You shouldn't have done it, should you?' he whispered, with a growl. 'Because of you, we both lost Mason, didn't we?'

'Noooooo...' Grace yelled out. Her tone long and animalistic, almost painful to hear. 'Mmmmm... noooooo...'

'Shush.' Holding the sheets up to cover her mouth, Tom sneered and pressed them against her just hard enough that they brought a look of fear to her eyes. But not enough that the pressure might bruise her. 'You brought this on yourself, didn't you?' He lifted his hand for a moment, waved his finger wand-like around in the air. 'You deserve to be here. Don't you?' Once again, the sheet was pressed against her until Tom saw the slight nod of her head. 'Good girl. That's right, losing Mason was your fault. Which is why you had to come here. To this hell hole, where you don't even deserve to look out of a window.' He laughed. 'All those hippie friends of yours, that commune they live in. Where are they, Grace? Did you think they'd come for you? Care for you. Well, they didn't, did they?' Standing up, Tom thought about the free spirit his wife had once been. The way she'd first walked past him, young and naïve, wearing a long, boho-style skirt, a plain white tee and a pale denim jacket. As she'd turned to catch his eye, the sun had caught her face. It had lit up her eyes in a radiant way, a look he'd initially loved, and for a while, she'd been his distraction. He'd slowly encouraged her to leave her commune, and she had, until the night their son was born. 'I need to give birth my way,' she'd uttered dismissively as she'd climbed into a van, 'with my people.' During the next forty-eight hours Tom hadn't known whether Grace would ever come back. Whether she'd integrate back into her community, with the people she classed as her own. But then, as though nothing dramatic had happened, she'd walked in with their baby, Mason, held in her arms.

'Well, I made sure you wouldn't ever leave me again and go back to them, didn't I?' he whispered, as he walked back to the window and thought about the way he'd convinced her to move to the house near Bamburgh, a whole fifty miles from the people she knew. It was far enough away that being unable to drive, she hadn't gone back there. Which had been exactly what Tom had wanted.

Turning back to her, Tom noticed that her eyes had closed. The pained expression had gone, and her wrinkled brow had relaxed. For a moment, Tom found himself holding his breath and listening intently to the slow, laboured noise that came from her mouth. It was more of a crackle than a snore and he nodded slowly in acceptance that for the next few hours Grace would sleep. Tom closed his eyes, leaned forward, and rested his head against the white cotton sheets. Tiredness overcame him and he drifted into a deep sleep where he could see Daisy smiling, the way she'd laughed effortlessly with him and the way she'd danced her way through London. In his dream she had been a woman who had loved him with every beat of her heart. He dreamed of the type of life he'd always wished for. But then, as though someone had viciously torn the dream away from him, his vison of the future had changed, and he'd recalled the way

Daisy had looked today. The horror and fear she'd portrayed on her face as she'd stood in the window with her hands held out, palms upward in question.

'M... Ma...'

The sound from Grace was enough to drag him out of his sleep. A deep-seated moaning sound as Grace did her best to say her son's name. It was something she often did and was the only noise that had ever really come from her since the day she'd fallen. Tom saw the panic that crossed her face that was followed by a devastating scream that came out of her small, ravaged body.

'Come on, there's no need for all of that, is there?' He took hold of her hand, looked over his shoulder and made sure that the room was empty. Then, with his demeanour changing, he held her hand firmly against the bed and saw the look of frustration and fury behind her gaze. 'You know you can't speak, but you need to stop worrying about Mason. You know I've taken care of him. He's in a very safe place...'

# 21

# DAISY

With the pain that had begun in her back getting worse, Daisy eased her car down the lane towards Pipistrelle. The terror of where the pain was coming from filled her mind with such angst she could barely drive, and with her fingernails digging into the leather of the steering wheel, she began to breathe faster as the pain accelerated.

'No, no, noooooo – what the hell's happening?' She swallowed hard. All she could think of was phoning her sister, and with an agonising twist in her stomach, she reached across the passenger seat for her bag.

During the latter part of the valuation, Daisy had felt the discomfort begin. A pain that had increased and, in the end, she'd made her apologies, cut the meeting short and with a grimaced smile, she'd given Mr and Mrs Baxter a promise that she'd do all she could to sell their home before scrambling for the car, where for a few moments she sat and gulped at the air.

'Sarah, I need... Sarah.' Puffing up her cheeks and blowing out slowly, Daisy realised quite quickly that Sarah was the only person she could speak to and no matter how much she wanted

Cole, he was the last person she'd call with the news that she was pregnant and that right at that moment, she was potentially losing that baby. It wouldn't feel right. There would be so many questions. All of which she wouldn't want to answer.

'Of course, you can call him, he's your husband... he cares, he...' She spat the words, and began the to and fro battle with her conscience. 'Sarah or Cole... Sarah or Cole?' She tried to decide who she wanted the most, who would be the best person to help her because, whether she liked it or not, she needed some help.

'My baby—' With every ounce of strength she had, Daisy clambered out of the car. 'If I could just get inside, I just know... I'll be fine. And then... then I'll call Sarah. She'll get me some help,' she said through pained, gritted teeth. This was not a version of herself she wanted anyone to see, not even Sarah, but she didn't have any choice, not if she was going to save this baby. It was a baby she hadn't realised she'd wanted, not until the moment she knew it was here, and now she felt terrified of what was to come, and with her hands held outward, she stumbled across the aggregate that Cole had laid and reached for the gate.

After practically crawling as far the door on her hands and her knees, Daisy stopped short. The door was open. It swung back and forth in the breeze, leaving her to feel scared and confused, and for a few seconds she shuffled backwards. Felt her back come into contact with the log store and she sat there on the cold ground taking short, sharp, sporadic breaths.

'Think... who could be here?' There was no car. No sign of a broken entry. No noise she could home in on, not even the sea. Even the seagulls had gone quiet, their normal 'keow' strangely silenced, and with a million different terrifying thoughts spinning around her mind all at once, the most prominent terror was the thought of losing her baby.

Shuffling across the path, Daisy could feel her heart pound. It boomed audibly in her chest and the fear inside her was palpable. She gasped at the air and as slowly as she could, she pulled herself towards the front door. All she wanted was to go inside. She wanted to call Sarah and then she wanted curl up on the floor and wait till she came, and with a fierce determination to hold on to the baby inside her, Daisy pulled herself forward and up the step on her hands and knees, and even though every part of her mind told her to run, she couldn't and instead, she tentatively crawled into the hallway.

Flitting her eyes left and right, she nervously looked into the lounge with its adjoining kitchen. With most of their possessions having been taken out of the house, the room looked untouched. It looked bare, and void of their normal clutter, just how she had left it. The sight gave her a sense of relief, but then the doubt kicked in. Maybe she had left the door open. Maybe she hadn't checked it in the same way she always had. Or maybe there was someone waiting inside, hoping to hurt her, and slowly, she held her breath, pulled herself around the corner, where she reached upward to turn on a light, as another fresh burst of pain surged through her.

'Is anyone there?' She pulled her phone out of her pocket. 'I'm phoning the police,' she shouted. But as far as she could see, there was no reason to call. The house was in silence and with a finger shakily over the screen on her phone, she clicked on Sarah's number.

'Hey, this is Sarah. I'm not around so leave me a message...'

'No, please God, answer your phone.' Hitting the screen to end the call, Daisy felt herself sob. She'd been desperate to speak to Sarah; she felt cheated by the sound of the voicemail and, in annoyance, she pushed the phone in her pocket, dragged herself to the bottom of the stairs and with a stubborn, determined effort, she pulled herself upward. But every step was an effort, and without knowing why she was taking the risk, she crawled unsteadily on her hands and knees until she reached the door of the room that just the day before had been her bedroom.

It was the room she'd always felt safe in, until now when nothing made sense. A dark red stain now covered her jeans and, with an agonising scream, she dragged herself into the en suite. Before she reached toilet, Daisy already knew that the baby was gone. That the stain that covered her jeans was a testament that the baby had been there at all, and with an explosion of tears erupting from her, she angrily pulled at her jeans as another wave of pain tore through her.

'Damn you... this is wrong, cruel... What did I do to deserve this?' she shouted to no one in particular, and after throwing her jeans into the shower cubicle, she left them there before she lay on the bathroom floor and allowed the grief to take over her body.

When Daisy woke up, she was surrounded by darkness. Finding the energy from somewhere, she crawled across the bedroom in blood-covered underwear until she sat cold and alone by the upstairs balcony door. From here, she could see that the stars had scattered themselves haphazardly across the skyline. The sun had long since set and the sky was now filled with a moon that lit up the room. Shivering relentlessly, she refused to move and she sat to simply take in a view she'd always loved, but the grief was too much and once again it surged through her body. Tears rolled down her face as guilt took the place of the sadness and then, once she'd cursed and growled at the world outside, she felt a small amount of relief.

'At least now I don't have to tell Cole...' she whispered. 'At least now I don't have to face his parents, or...' She sighed, felt another sob rise to her throat. 'But I do have to tell Sarah.' Thinking carefully, Sarah had realistically been the only person who knew, until Daisy's mind shot back to the message that Tom had sent.

*'I know that you're pregnant!'*

The message had confused her. He'd mentioned her baby but she had no idea how he'd known. Which infuriated her more. The fact that he knew at all was chilling and so, determinedly, with the intention of reading the message again, Daisy began to search for her phone, which she eventually found in the pocket of her jeans in the bathroom. Sitting with her back to the shower cubicle, Daisy immediately saw the raft of missed calls. Three from Sarah, two from Cole and six from Tom, along with multiple messages. The most prominent, a short, sharp message from Tom that had been sent earlier that day.

TOM

Bitch. You didn't take the mirror with you. I find that unbelievably ungrateful.

# 22

## SARAH

With her phone held in her hand, Sarah lay in a bath surrounded by candles. The smell of lavender came from an oil burner and, for just a short while, she breathed in deeply to relax her mood.

After the day she'd had, she'd needed a bath. The two separate downpours she'd been caught in that day had left every inch of her shivering with the cold to a point where she'd never thought it possible to get warm again. Stupidly, on the second occasion she'd left the umbrella behind that she'd taken from Cole's car following another heated exchange.

'I can't keep doing this...' Sarah said out loud as she twisted the tap with a toe and sighed as the hot water travelled slowly up the length of the bath. She shook her head, lifted her hands and tightened the messy bun that wobbled on the top of her head. She thought back to the conversation, and the ultimatum she'd given. 'Maybe you should leave. He wasn't too bothered when you said that you might.'

'Maybe it's for the best,' Cole had said as the rain had begun. 'Things are getting heated, Sarah. Up to now I've kept you out of it but—' He'd turned, looked her straight in the eye. 'You need to do what's right for yourself. While you can.'

'Cole!' she'd yelled. 'Your wife is pregnant, don't you think *you* need to do what's right too?'

Shivering relentlessly after Daisy had left the shop for the day, Sarah had run to her car and made her way back to her small, two-bedroom, end-terraced cottage. It wasn't as big or fancy as either of the houses her sister owned, but it had been their mother's and Sarah had happily moved in and made it her home.

Sitting up in the bath, Sarah flicked at the screen of her phone. She'd been messaging back and forth with Confident Sparky for the past half hour but suddenly remembered that, after missing a call from Daisy earlier, she still hadn't managed to get hold of her sister, even though she'd attempted on more than one occasion. Normally at the end of each valuation, Daisy would give the office a call and give a quick run-down of what she'd agreed. She'd email all the photographs she'd taken across to the office, where it was Sarah's job to drop them, fully labelled, on to the server. But today, after leaving work early and running through the rain, Sarah had missed the call, and now Daisy had taken to radio silence, which wasn't surprising because she'd been in a mood all day. Which was probably her hormones that were bouncing off of the walls and making her grumpy.

Sarah contemplated calling her again and checking in, but she stopped herself as another message flashed up on her screen, catching her attention.

It was at least the tenth message in as many minutes. Confident Sparky was ready to go, and Sarah was enjoying the way the banter between them had shot back and forth in fast succession. He sounded witty, charming, and undoubtedly confident, which was a refreshing change from the men who normally messaged. She'd always chosen looks over personality or banter. But that, she realised now, had been a mistake. Those kinds of men were always going to love themselves so much more than her. They were all full of their own self-importance and, more often than not, if she'd failed to respond immediately, she'd been ghosted or blocked. Confident Sparky was just a little more assertive. He didn't take no for an answer, nor did he seem to take offence at her warped sense of humour, and for the first time in years she felt just a little excited that finally she'd found someone who she could really connect with.

Confident Sparky: So, what are you up to tonight? A woman like you must have a date?

Executive Lady 1999: Definitely not a date night. I'm much too choosy. Besides, it's been a tough day. I'm currently laid in a bath, surrounded by candles, lavender and patchouli oil, warming my bones. *Smiley face*

Giggling, Sarah knew that if her message wasn't feeding him a line, then nothing would, and she watched and waited for a response to come. She moved to one side, carefully lifted the plug out with a toe and allowed just a little of the water to escape before turning the hot tap back on and closing her eyes with a deep, welcoming sigh as, once again, the heat began to swarm around each of her feet. It was the warmest she'd felt all day and after putting the phone down on the side of the bath, she picked up her wine glass, took a long slurp and smiled as her phone bleeped, and another message dropped in.

Confident Sparky: Pleased to hear that something is warming you up. It's a cold night. I'm about to drive back from Berwick. You don't fancy climbing out of that bath and inviting me round for a drink, do you? I could be there in twenty minutes!

Executive Lady 1999: You must drive fast. Takes me thirty!

Confident Sparky: Then I could be there in thirty. Is that a yes?

Sitting forward, Sarah swished the water around her body, and felt her heart begin to race with excitement. They'd only been chatting for the last half an hour, which wasn't long enough for her to invite him here. Messaging with a guy didn't normally mean that she'd meet him, but now he'd suggested it, she began to think of how nice it would be to see who he was.

Executive Lady 1999: Sorry. It's a no. You're not coming to my house. I don't know you. I don't even know your name??

Closing her eyes, Sarah pulled a breath in. Blowing hot and cold was her way of gaining more information. She'd long since learned that if she gave a little before pulling back, the detail would come because most men didn't like to think they'd lost the control, whereas others simply lost interest and disappeared. From her perspective it was better for them to show their true colours at this stage, rather than wait until they were six months down the line when she'd become emotionally invested.

Confident Sparky: So, if I tell you my name, do I get the invitation?

Feeling slightly annoyed with the conversation and with no intention of inviting him into her home, Sarah lay back, flicked some bubbles away from her face and turned her attention back to Daisy. Once again, she began to flick through her phone just in case Daisy had messaged, but after clicking in and out of various messaging platforms, Sarah pursed her lips. The radio silence was odd and almost unnatural. Even on days when they'd had an argument or when she went off grid to London, there would still be some kind of contact, which made Sarah suddenly worry and, once again, she clicked on Daisy's name and listened as the call rang out, then went straight to voicemail.

Disgruntled. Sarah went to throw the phone down on the floor and tried to think of all the reasons why her sister would have failed to call. Admittedly, she'd been pissed off that the appointment had been made in the first place; going to do a valuation on a Monday afternoon in the rain was never Daisy's idea of fun but Sarah had thought that the idea of going back to the bay would excite her, would give her an excuse to call at the house, and watch the sunset. Which would have been when Sarah had expected Daisy to call her, but she hadn't.

SARAH

> Hey hun, are you okay? How were Mr and Mrs Baxter? I missed your call. Worried. *Sad face emoji*

She clicked send and stared at her phone screen, willing Daisy to reply. Sighing, she looked across the bathroom to where her long blue towelling dressing gown hung on the back of the door in the shadows. It was thick and snug, and it was hung there as though it were waiting for her to pull it on and wrap it around her. The thought of leaving the house made her shudder – it was the last thing she wanted to do. The rain would have made the roads dangerous and icy, and she was snug and warm for the first time that day. But there was something about Confident Sparky and his insistent messages that drew her in. Even though she'd previously had no intention of leaving the house, she found herself climbing out of the bath, pulling the dressing gown around her and heading into the bedroom.

Executive Lady 1999: I'm not inviting you round. It's a school night.

Confident Sparky: You're still at school? Wow. Back off, sister.

Laughing, Sarah typed her response.

Executive Lady 1999: No, silly. It's just a turn of phrase. Haven't you heard it before?

Confident Sparky: So, you're not still at school. Phew!

Executive Lady 1999: Not a chance. But I do have to be up for work tomorrow.

Confident Sparky: Come on, one drink, one hour, anywhere you choose. *Smiley face*

With a nervous excitement, Sarah pulled open her wardrobe and automatically began to search through her clothes. Most of her dresses were too short or thin for this kind of weather. Her trouser suits, although smart and fitted and perfect for work, gave off the wrong impression for a first date. Eventually, she pulled out a long, pale blue denim shirt dress which she hadn't worn before and she thought, with her head tipped to one side, if she dressed it up with a pair of stilettos, it would be perfect to wear for a first outing.

Executive Lady 1999: Okay. Middle Inn. 8 p.m. One hour max.
I'll see you there. *Smiley face*

With an exciting first date about to happen, Sarah tapped at the phone and tried to call Daisy again.

'Where the hell are you, for God's sake?' Sarah shouted as she moved her phone from one screen to the next. A couple of years ago they'd installed an app called Life360 as a way of them seeing where the other was, and although Sarah didn't log into it often, it took her a while to find the app on her screen.

Initially, Sarah had thought the app was Daisy's way of keeping tabs on her movements. But an agreement had been made, and they'd both promised that the app would only be used in case of an emergency. And after two missed calls and no check in, Sarah considered her sister's disappearance as being just that.

Tapping into the app, Sarah hesitated before clicking into Daisy's profile. It was a small circle that showed her face, a marker in Budle Bay, with the words 'Daisy. At home since 3.45 p.m.' written beneath it. They were words that made Sarah smile, knowing that the app would still have Pipistrelle marked as Daisy's home. With a satisfied nod, Sarah relaxed. Daisy was safe and sound at the house, and she had a date to go on.

# 23

## TOM

Sitting beside his wife's bed, Tom stared down at his phone. Since waking up half an hour before, he'd been messaging Sarah. Right now, everything he was planning was quickly dropping into place.

Tonight, he would make Daisy regret that she'd ever pushed him aside. The thought that she was pregnant had infuriated him to the core. Especially when she'd once again chosen Cole over him. It was a cycle that had happened again and again. His mother, Daisy, then Grace. Well, in his eyes he'd taught Grace a valuable lesson: she'd lost her son, her mobility, and would soon lose her life. And now, it was a lesson that Daisy needed to learn. She too should know what loss felt like. She too should see what it was like when everything around her fell apart.

'Is all okay?' A soft voice came from behind him as a door opened, then closed and a nurse walked in. Her hand immediately rested against Grace's shoulder, her gaze constantly searching the room. 'It must be difficult for you to see her like this but don't be afraid, she isn't in pain.'

Standing up, Tom nodded with eyes full of fake tears. 'I hope not,' he whispered as he purposely leaned across Grace's bed and, in an act that deserved an Oscar, he dropped a soft, gentle kiss against her forehead, bit down on his lip, allowed it to quiver and then, as a final part of his act, he gave out a loud sob.

'I'm so sorry—' he said. 'It's just— it's just so hard to see her this way.'

'Seriously, it's fine.' The nurse's hand had moved from Grace to Tom; she rested it gently against his arm with compassion. 'My name's Ava,' she said with a smile. 'I'll be popping in and out tonight, caring for your wife, and I shouldn't really say this, but the morphine she's taking, it will help her to take her last journey.'

Hiding the excitement that shone out from his eyes, Tom moved to the opposite side of the bed and held up his phone. 'I'm just messaging her friends and letting them know what's happening,' he lied, but tempered a smile as another message from Sarah dropped on to his screen.

'Your wife, does she have any family?' The nurse lifted Grace's hand up from the bed, rested her fingers gently against her wrist and felt for a pulse. 'Sorry to ask but no one has been, apart from you.'

'There's no one,' he said with a shake of his head. 'My wife belonged to a commune. She went to live there after her parents had died, and when she met me, we moved to live close to Bamburgh.'

During the time since the accident, Grace had become pale and drawn. Her body had become emaciated, her eyes sunken and her cheek bones prominent. Part of him felt a sense of satisfaction that Grace had suffered. That she'd finally paid with her life for the death of his son. After all, it had been her fault. If she hadn't tried to snatch him away, she wouldn't have fallen. Mason wouldn't have died, and a huge part of Tom hoped that he'd never have the need to look at her face, not ever again.

He'd felt as though he'd been taking a test of endurance which had begun in the days leading up to the accident. He'd spent the night with Daisy, after which, even though she hadn't known, he'd felt sure that Grace had acted differently. He'd stupidly mentioned that Daisy had lived around the corner, which had sent Grace off on a tangent even though he'd explained that it had been a long time ago. One comment had led to the next and, following her outrage, Grace had been planning to leave him. She was going to go back to her commune, to a place where she'd easily disappear and where, even if he'd wanted to, he'd never be able to visit his son.

Which would have been fine, if it had been his decision, but it wasn't, and he'd watched through venomous eyes as Grace had hugged their son closely while hovering on the top step of the stairs. At the time, Tom had despised her. He'd chewed on the inside of his cheek until it bled while listening to his wife's persistent bleating.

'Your daddy loves Daisy, a woman who cast him aside, more than he loves us.' The words had cut into him, deep and cruel, and even though they were true, he'd hated the fact that Grace had known him so much better than he'd ever really known himself.

Hearing the rattle of the trolley outside, Tom bid Grace a silent goodbye just as another nurse walked in to give Grace another cocktail of drugs and, respectfully, he gave her what he'd hoped would look like a kind and melancholy smile, before he stealthily crept out of the room and into the long, daunting corridor.

Outside the room, Tom had immediately homed in on the

drugs trolley. It was standing there, right outside the door, unlocked, just as he'd hoped it would be, and after quickly checking that no one was watching, he pulled open one drawer after the other and quickly scanned the contents. It didn't take him long to find the box he wanted. A white box with a distinctive blue hexagon right under the word 'Rohypnol'. Trembling with anticipation, rather than fear, he opened the box, pulled out a single small strip of the tablets and surreptitiously he pushed them into a pocket with one hand while replacing the box and closing the trolley with the other.

Then he made his way back down the staircase, past the chairlift and listened to a house that was full of noise. Every cry for help was followed by the dreaded sound of the matron's voice. It was a voice he'd come to hate, and as he rounded the corner, he fully expected to see her there. For her to be stood, waiting for him, demanding that he go to her office for another meeting he just couldn't face and, rather than put himself through an uncomfortable ordeal, he pushed open the fire door with the full intent of sneaking out of the back of the building without being noticed. But as he did, a loud, piercing alarm went off in reception.

'Damn you...' he said out loud as he quickly pushed the door to a close behind him and scurried across a lawn that was still wet from the rain. The water soaked in through his shoes. The feeling made him jump from the grass and into the flower beds, leaving him standing in the shadow of a tree that was rough and gnarled, with branches that drooped heavily downward. It was all the shelter he needed and, as he stood there, he held his breath and watched as one light after the other was flicked on in the house. It was a sure sign that the carers were going from room to room, making sure that residents were safe, and that none had escaped. With a smug smile crossing his face, Tom laughed at how easily he'd made his escape and confidently he walked to his car, unchallenged.

Pulling open the car door, he climbed inside and breathed out a sigh of relief. Once again, he'd managed to avoid the awkward questions and hadn't had to face the demands for payment, or worse, listen to all the intimate details that Matron would divulge about his wife's condition.

It was more than obvious, to anyone who cared to look, that Grace was dying. Her body had finally given up, and he didn't need some jumped-up, overweight matron to tell him that Grace's time was about to end. He was just pleased that it was, that the waiting game was almost over, that his debts would be paid and that the battle of the bailiffs would be at an end.

Under the cover of darkness, Tom eased the car out of the car park before turning on his headlights. He laughed at his own audacity, took a final look over his shoulder and wondered if he'd ever have the need to come back. Whether he'd end up sitting by Grace's bedside, playing the doting husband while she took her last breath. Or whether he'd simply get a call in the night to say she was gone. He prayed for the latter.

Smirking, it occurred to Tom that no one suspected that Grace's fall had been anything more than a tragic accident. Tom had created an alibi for when the accident happened and since then, he'd been portrayed as nothing other than a kind, loving husband. One who'd sat by Grace's bedside and sobbed like a baby, always with a profound apology to the nurses for being so weak. His reasons were because he'd loved her so much. Flowers had always been brought. Something visual that would last for quite a few days following his visit, and every day without fail, he'd phoned and asked for an update but hadn't really listened to the answer.

He just couldn't wait for the act to be over. It wouldn't be long before Grace would be gone. The truth about what happened that night to her and to his son would die with her, with no family on either side to ask any questions.

When he thought back to that night, he remembered the way he'd brought on his act. The way he'd screamed her name and pretended he'd cared.

'She'd asked me to go for some milk... and... I did what she asked.' He'd said to the ambulance crew while shaking his head theatrically. 'I went to the post office because they sold lottery tickets and if I hadn't, she might not have fallen.' He'd paced up and down between the lounge and the kitchen while the ambulance crew worked on Grace. 'I thought... I thought that with a lottery ticket, our luck might change. But I got chatting to the man in the shop. I was asking him about the area; it's a long time since I lived here and I thought that things might have changed.' He'd pointed to the boxes that still needed unpacking. 'We've only just moved in, and we were laughing and I'd joked that if we won, I'd remember him. You know, if my numbers came in.' Tom had wiped his tears against the back of his hand, pulled his wallet out of his pocket and, with his alibi in mind, he'd produced the ticket. 'But it turns out that Grace had other plans. As soon as my back was turned, she'd packed a bag and... she must have fallen in her hurry to get down the stairs, which is where I just found her.'

What Tom failed to mention was a single word of the truth. Grace had stormed upstairs; she'd gone to the office where, stupidly, he'd left the images on his screen of his weekend in London. Maybe a part of him had wanted Grace to see and to know what he'd done. But with Mason in her arms, he'd watched incensed as she'd pivoted precariously on the top step.

'If you want to leave me, Grace, you go ahead. But you're not taking my son...' Tom hadn't even known why he'd said it. He hadn't wanted Mason. Not any more than he'd wanted Grace. But selfishly he'd made a grab for the baby and frantically Grace had pulled against him. In the blink of an eye, the accident had happened. Grace had fallen and their son's lifeless body was crushed and lying beneath her.

For a moment, he'd waited for his son to wail, for the persistent crying that normally came from him. 'Come on,' he'd whispered, 'just a murmur, or maybe a scream, you're good at screaming.' He'd hoped for any noise that would have told him that Mason was alive. But when it didn't come, Tom had panicked. He'd run back upstairs, paced back and forth at the top of the landing and, periodically, he'd glanced over the balustrade in the hope that the scene might have changed. 'It's murder. They'll charge me with murder, I'll... I'll go to prison...' he'd chuntered as his hands had gone up to his hair and he'd dragged at the roots.

With his eyes going upward towards the loft door, he'd quickly pulled down the ladder, climbed up and in an act that even he was ashamed of, he'd searched the loft for the small, blue cold box he'd bought for picnics, a box they still hadn't used, and eventually he found it under a pile of other things they didn't want or need. It was plastic and waterproof, with a lid that was secured each time the handle was moved from one side to the other, and in his opinion, the perfect size in which to hide Mason's teeny tiny, five-month-old body.

Finally, he'd stepped over Grace's broken, unconscious body. It was partially blocking the door, but with the movements of a contortionist, he squeezed his way past and, after heading down the path, he'd waved at the window and shouted goodbye, just in case someone saw him, and then, casually, with a smile on his face, he'd climbed into his car and set off on his mission to create the perfect alibi.

'I need an ambulance,' he'd screamed hysterically down the phone the moment he returned and forced open the door. 'I've just got home and my wife, she's fallen on the stairs. She's right behind the front door and, oh my God, she looks really bad. I'm not sure if she's dead...'

He'd looked up as he spoke and then frozen as he'd spotted the tiny security camera that he'd roughly installed just a week before. It had been his one attempt to look after his family in the knowledge that, if anyone ever broke in, they'd have looked upward, and their faces would have been caught on the camera.

But the camera he'd installed to protect Grace would now be his downfall for what he'd done and, as quickly as he could, he'd dismantled it, pushed the bare wires into the wall cavity, while hoping that Grace would die before the ambulance arrived.

Now, with a sense of anticipation racing through him, Tom drove back towards Bamburgh, with one eye on the clock. He'd stopped the car briefly to send Sarah another of his messages and had taken amusement from her gullible responses, although her cheeky sense of humour had made him smile. It was a good distraction while a part of him had been waiting for his phone to ring, for someone from Seacroft Park to call him and to sympathetically tell him that Grace's ordeal was over.

Pulling up in the layby above Budle Bay, Tom slouched in his seat, surrounded by darkness. From his vantage point, he could see Daisy's house. It too stood in darkness, with just a small outside light that showed him that her car was parked on the driveway. Staring at the house, he searched the windows with a piercing gaze. He looked for the smallest amount of movement, the slightest flicker of light and, for a brief moment, he considered going back to the house. At least then, he could tell her how he felt and for once, it would be in person and not on a message. He was angry and confused that, once again, she wanted Cole more than him. Especially after the night in London, where with just a little encouragement, she'd fallen into his bed with ease. He fingered the strip of tablets that sat in his pocket and laughed. It wasn't the first time he'd used the drug and he smiled sardonically as he thought of the small chunk he'd dropped into Daisy's drink to make her wanton, needy and unbelievably passionate. It had made Daisy want him, which was why he'd bought her the mirror. He'd wanted her to have a memory of London, something tangible that she could look at and each time she saw her reflection, she'd be able to imagine him there, standing right beside her. But now he was furious, she'd left the mirror behind, which had been an insult, especially when the rest of the house had been cleared and a part of him felt the need to teach her a lesson.

A ping that came from his phone brought him back to the present and, with a quick glance down, he spotted the message from Sarah.

Executive Lady 1999: Getting ready and just wanted to be sure that you're still up for tonight?

Laughing, Tom shifted his gaze back to the house. He knew that Daisy was there. That she'd turned out the lights and that, right now, she was probably sat wondering what he'd do next, and with meeting Sarah in mind, Tom remembered the promise he'd once made to himself, the message he'd sent to Daisy: '*I will prove what he's up to and I will find a way to be a part of your life.*'

With the way Daisy had abandoned him and the humiliation he'd felt after being dismissed by Cole, Tom closed his eyes and flicked though his memory of contacts. Somewhere he must know someone who could dish the dirt on Cole, someone who hated him just as much as Tom did and would give up all the knowledge they knew to see him go down. Then, Tom began to laugh wildly as he realised that the person who could give him the answers was Sarah, and with the tablets held in his hand, he knew just the way he could get them.

# 24

DAISY

With the moon shining through the balcony doors, Daisy's eyes
slowly flickered as she took in the familiar surroundings. After
reading Tom's second message, she'd simply curled up in a ball
and let exhaustion take her. But now, with her body shaking
relentlessly with the cold, the significance of what the message
had said hit her.

She remembered being sat in the en suite, reading the
message over and over, and the way her body had totally recoiled.
The thought that he'd been here, in this house, bothered her
more than she'd thought. After all, Tom was a man she'd loved.
Correction: he was the boy she'd loved. The rest, the time they'd
shared in London, had been nothing more than unfinished business, which she'd played a part in, but still she didn't understand
why she had. It had all been too easy: the excitement, the passion,
the drifting in and out of the moment. And then, the next morning, she'd felt so many regrets and had made it clear to Tom that,
once she left London, the dalliance was over and that from that
moment she'd go back to her husband and being Mrs Bailey. And

the fact that Tom had pushed his way into her personal life in more ways than one was something she hadn't expected.

With hands that were shaking with cold, Daisy turned on to her back and, with her head tipped to one side, she looked over the bay. She desperately wished that the message had been a figment of her imagination. But a deep trembling in the pit of her stomach made her heart rate accelerate and she tried to remember whether or not his words could have been true, and whether the mirror in the hallway had been hung where she'd left it. But the minutes after arriving back at the house had blurred; it was a memory she wanted to forget and, with doubt creeping into her mind, she picked up the phone and re-read the message.

TOM

Bitch. You didn't take the mirror with you. I find that unbelievably ungrateful.

With the door having been open, Daisy knew that Tom must have been inside. There was no other way he could have seen the mirror. Not where it was hung. 'Which means, he could still be here,' she whispered with a distinct audible tremor as her eyes became fixed on the landing.

A part of her knew she should move. She should get up and check the whole house. But her energy had gone, and her motivation to protect what was hers, now that she'd lost her baby, had left her. Right now, she didn't care if there was an intruder, especially if that intruder were Tom. Deep down, she didn't honestly believe that he'd hurt her. Not intentionally. Not with the history they'd shared.

# 25

## DAISY

After finally making her way down the stairs, Daisy cautiously switched on a light and leaned against the front door where she immediately saw that the mirror Tom had brought her was missing. Following the message she'd received earlier that day, she was more than confident that Tom had been in this house and that for some reason that only Tom knew, he'd taken the mirror.

Staring at the spot where the mirror had been, she felt a sense of sadness. This was not the way things should have ended. They'd had their weekend in London, their unfinished business had been taken care of and yet he'd felt the need to take things further and infiltrate her world in a way she hadn't expected. First with the job at Bailey Construction and now this, and instinctively, Daisy pulled her hands in and out of tight threatening fists and felt ready to fight.

Rolling her gaze around the hallway, she realised that she'd never been afraid of this house until now. It had always been a property that had surrounded her with a hug, but now she felt invaded. It was as though the walls, which had once felt warm and familiar, were holding their breath. They were listening, watching and waiting for the next thing to happen. Something she instinctively felt afraid of.

Trembling, she almost dared herself to move forward. But the fear overwhelmed her, and just for a minute she slid with her back to the door and sat on the doormat.

Watching the clock tick forward, Daisy waited for her energy to build. She hadn't felt so weak in years, and with every ounce of strength she could find she crawled into the downstairs bedroom to dig through the boxes she'd placed there, and after rummaging around she found a bright pink hoodie, some tracksuit bottoms and a pair of trainers, which she hastily pulled on and breathed out a sigh of relief as warmth slowly began to creep back into her body.

Now dressed and feeling less vulnerable, Daisy picked up a poker that had been standing by the living room fire. Systematically, she walked from room to room and checked that each one was empty and that nothing else was missing. Which wasn't a difficult task, since most of the clutter was gone and the only things that had been left behind were the big furniture items and the boxes that were stacked in the bedroom, and so, eventually, Daisy concluded that only the mirror was missing.

'That's fine, absolutely fine, Tom. You take the damned mirror...' She growled the words while protectively holding on to her stomach. 'With the mirror and the baby both gone, you... you need to be gone too.' As the words left her mouth, she almost hoped that Tom was still here, because she wanted someone to blame for her losing the baby, and with her phone in her hand she vehemently tapped out a message.

DAISY

> How dare you come into my home and why take the mirror? It's hardly your style.

Watching, Daisy saw the telltale dots that covered the screen. An indication that Tom was typing. With her heart in her mouth, she read his response.

TOM

Because I could, and by the end of the night, it won't be the only thing I'll have taken.

With his phone in his hand, Tom tapped it against his leg as he walked past the pub window. Looking inside he could see that, although it was still quite early, it already looked crowded.

Groups of people were sitting around tables; some were leaning in so close that their heads were almost touching. Others sat in relative silence, pushing food around their plates and staring intently at phones and devices. One woman who sat on a bar stool was obviously used to being the centre of attention and she sang out loud to the music that came from a juke box, much to the disgust of an elderly gentleman who sat beside her in his overcoat and dusty flat cap. He held a newspaper in his hands and periodically stretched his arms out wide and rattled the paper in her direction.

Somewhere in the background, through an open window, he could hear a man shouting out questions. Each question was quickly followed by jeers. Others occasionally looked up from phones and threw a disgusted look in the general direction of anyone around who'd dared to disturb them.

'Must be quiz night...' Tom whispered as he pushed one of his hands deeper into his pockets, puffed his cheeks up and slowly blew out. A white mist left his lips and, with thoughts of the last time he'd been standing here outside this pub, he wished for a cup of that same hot chocolate that he'd held in his hands and sipped slowly while he'd looked for Daisy. He had a modicum of regret that the night had turned out like it had, and even though he was still annoyed that she'd left the mirror behind, he wished for the chance to be standing there, waiting for Daisy again, rather than Sarah.

'What are you thinking?' he grumbled into the darkness and felt himself jump each time a car drove past. 'Do you think this is a good idea? Because if you do, you must be downright crazy, stupid or just fucking both... This will have no good outcome. You know that, don't you?'

Tom considered his options. Right now, Confident Sparky could still disappear. All he'd have to do was climb in his car and leave before Sarah arrived. If he deleted his profile this would all end, right here, right now. Men ghosted Sarah all the time, she'd already said so. One minute they were interested and the next they were gone. Why shouldn't he be any different?

Besides, wasn't it better to for him to disappear now than to go through with his ridiculous plan? And what was his plan? Start a relationship that wouldn't and couldn't go anywhere? Use Sarah to get back at Daisy or Cole? Because that would be stupid. Daisy and Sarah were sisters. They were close. More than close, and even if he could bring himself to form a relationship with Sarah, the first time they ended up in the same room as Daisy, he might as well light the touchpaper because things would definitely blow up. The whole room would erupt and, as normal, he'd be the one in the wrong, on the outside looking back in.

With his hand still firmly in his pocket, Tom rolled the pieces of broken tablet between his two fingers. They were rough, chalky and completely different in size. The tablet had been cut haphazardly into three unequal parts, which hadn't been the plan. He just hadn't wanted to give her a whole tablet at once. Not till he saw what effect it had. He only wanted her to have as much as she needed until she started talking and then, after he'd got the information he needed, he'd leave.

'First, you just need to know if the baby is yours, because if it is...' Tom closed his eyes. He could still imagine the sound of Mason's cry. A high-pitched wail that had demanded attention until the day when it had abruptly stopped, and his lifeless body had lain there, beneath the bitch who'd killed him. It had been her fault: the accident, the fall, and the taunting that had come moments before it.

'If he'd been Daisy's, you'd have been besotted...'

They were the words Grace had said, just moments before she'd threatened to leave, and he had to admit, that she was right. He would have felt differently if the baby were Daisy's, but now he was gone, and Tom wanted nothing more than to be a part of the life of a baby that he and Daisy created.

'Go home,' he suddenly growled. 'Just forget all about the stupid meet-up with the equally stupid sister and leave the damned past behind you. Leave Daisy behind you.'

As he said the words, he could feel his heart constrict. He wanted nothing more than to make a family with Daisy, for that family to have already been formed, and the thought that she might never make love to him again was destroying his mind.

Looking down at his watch, he tried to concentrate on the breaths that were going in and out of his lungs. His mind was crammed with a list of all the jobs that he still needed to do. The wiring still needed sorting. The hole in the wall needed refilling and painting over. Putting a new camera back in its place was out of the question. To do that, he'd have to spend money that he just didn't have. He was just grateful he'd had the time to move the camera, to stop anyone from asking questions. As far as the odd neighbour who'd asked was concerned, Mason had been taken back to the commune and, in his mother's absence, he was being looked after by his extended family. The lie would give him the time and the chance to bury his son, and until Grace died and the money came through, he still had to find a new job in order to fend off the bailiffs. And on top of that, he still had to play the doting husband, until Grace was gone.

Peering through the window, Tom focused on a large conservatory. It was a pub he remembered well and knew that, if he were to go through with his plan, this was the room he should aim for, especially if the quiz had ended.

If he were lucky, he'd find a quiet corner, order some food and enjoy it. It's what he deserved, especially after the day he'd had. He cringed at the thought that he'd have no choice but to play the gentleman and pay for Sarah's food too. Another debt to add to all of the others, which was another reason he hadn't been going out on dates. Dates were expensive and, without a job, the small amount of savings they'd had had been depleted.

'Which is another reason you should leave, right now, before she arrives.' Tom growled out loud before giving out an audible sigh. For a moment, he tapped his phone against his leg, paced back and forth and lifted a hand to his head. It was spinning with a million different thoughts, hundreds of scenarios playing all at once, and with a loud, angry groan, he realised that none of the scenarios worked in his favour.

Pulling his car keys out of his pocket, Tom took a step forward towards his car, which he'd been fortunate enough to park right outside the pub's door, but the sound of footsteps on the pavement stopped him, and he looked up to see Sarah walking towards him.

# 27

## SARAH

Rounding the corner to walk on to Front Street, Sarah spotted the Christmas tree Daisy had mentioned and smiled. It stood at least twenty feet high, with myriad lights twinkling in the darkness, as the odd tiny speckle of snow floated past.

'Okay, so that is pretty,' Sarah said as she walked. She was quite aware that everyone around her knew about her dislike for Christmas but, if she were totally honest, she didn't really hate it at all. What she did hate was the way that people decorated their homes in an overzealous way, the tree that clearly should be living outside and the false smiles that came alongside the gifts that no one could afford but still they felt obliged to buy. But this tree that stood on the green looked good. It was bright and it was cheerful and tonight, it matched her mood, which buzzed with the excitement that only a new date would bring.

Taking each step with care, Sarah walked as confidently as she could in her new tan shoes; they were high and strappy and the heel was rubbing against her skin. She felt sure that any time soon, she'd have a blister the size of a house. Now just a few hundred yards into her walk, she wished that she'd taken a leaf out of her sister's book, who, since her trip to London and the disaster she'd had with a pair of stilettos, had traded her heels for a pair of comfortable wedges or pumps.

Thinking of Daisy, Sarah lifted her phone out of her bag and hit the call button for what felt like the hundredth time that day. She still hadn't managed to get in touch, and if nothing else, Sarah wanted Daisy to know where she was going and who she was meeting. Sarah had already decided that the evening wouldn't be a late one. She had every intention of being home before ten and in her own bed, but she suspected that she might not be alone. It had been a long time since she'd had a first-date hook-up. For her to do that, they had to be special, and from what she could already tell, Confident Sparky had something about him that she felt sure she would like.

But annoyingly, the call once again went to Daisy's voicemail...

'Come on, Daisy, for God's sake, your voicemail has been on for the past four hours now. I can see you're at Pipistrelle; I checked the app you insisted we had so, come on, who the hell doesn't check their phone for this long... Call me, but if I don't answer, I'm out on a date. Meeting Confident Sparky at Middle Inn, and if he plays his cards right, he's probably going to be one hell of a lucky old man.' Sarah laughed at her own joke and tried to remember if age had been a part of the discussion. On his photo, which admittedly was a little distant, he did look like he had a good physique. He looked slim and muscular, and his sense of humour didn't come across as being old or stuffy. She quickly flicked back through the messages they'd already exchanged.

'Nope, no age...' she moaned, with indifference. The truth was, she didn't care how old Confident Sparky was. She was way beyond being judgemental about someone's age or even their looks, and she had to admit that she always felt a lot happier with someone who had the ability to make her laugh than someone who didn't. In her humble opinion, a guy needed a sense of humour. One that she could relate to, and if that great humour came with great sex, then that was a bonus.

'Sarah...' A distant but familiar voice broke through her thoughts. 'What the hell. It can't be, can it? Is that really you?'

Looking up, Sarah gasped. She'd walked much further, and a lot more quickly, than she'd thought, and as she looked around herself in shock, she found herself staring at the man who had spoken.

'Tom?' she whispered, her eyes opening wide as she looked up and down at the boy she'd once known as a brother. One memory after the other came at her in quick succession, just about all of them good, apart from the fact that when he and Daisy had split, Tom hadn't even come over to say a goodbye. 'What... oh wow, what are you doing here? I...'

Apprehensively, she looked over her shoulder at a pavement that was empty. On the grass verge that stood between her and the road, there was just a single dog walker with a German shepherd tied to a lead. There was still no sign of her date and, uneasily, Sarah glanced at the time. Then, as Tom opened his arms, she surrendered herself into the hug that he offered.

'How are you? I mean... it's been so long.' She smiled and spotted the glint of amusement that crossed his face, before he nervously looked down at the pavement and traced the edge of the grass with the toe of his boot. For a moment, she remembered the friendship they'd shared and the times he'd spent at her house when they'd sat and chatted for hours about everything and nothing. In the days when he'd been dating Daisy, he'd turned into the best brother she could have ever wished for, and on more than one occasion, he'd even taken her to school on the back of his motorbike, a ride that, during the summer, she'd loved and she could easily remember the days when she'd purposely missed the school bus just to go for a ride.

But things had changed overnight. He and Daisy had called it a day. It had been a brutal ending to what Sarah had considered the perfect relationship. But the end had been her sister's decision. It was no longer the life Daisy wanted. She'd made a decision to make a life with Cole and, whether her family agreed or not, Tom had no choice but to walk away. He left everything and everyone behind him – including her family.

'I'm so pleased you came...' Tom muttered as his cheeks flooded with colour and, with a nervous laugh, he took a deep breath. 'I didn't think you'd turn up to meet a guy called Confident Sparky, who right now doesn't feel that confident.' His voice wobbled, his shoulders sagged and the sparkle in his eyes suddenly dimmed. 'Especially now you know that Confident Sparky is me.'

'Wait a minute.' Sarah blinked repeatedly, her hand went up to her mouth as though it were trying to stop herself from speaking and, while completely confused, she looked over Tom's shoulder, half expecting the real Confident Sparky to be standing right behind him and for the Tom she knew to break into laughter. But when nothing happened, Sarah furrowed her brow, indignantly. 'Okay, so...' She paused. The last thing she wanted was to make a statement that would make her sound stupid. 'You're Confident Sparky?'

'I'm sorry...' Tom laughed with embarrassment. 'You must be completely disappointed that I'm your blind date...' He paused, pulled in a breath. 'If I'm completely honest I didn't recognise you. Not on your picture...' He took a step backwards, and she noticed the way he ran his gaze up and down her. 'Because, wow, you've really grown up since the last time I saw you.'

Shaking her head incredulously, Sarah needed something to

do with her hands. Nervously, she checked her phone for calls. She felt completely stupid that she'd left Daisy a voicemail telling her that Confident Sparky was about to get lucky, because the moment she'd found out that her date was Tom, Sarah realised just how unimaginable her lucky night would turn out to be.

'Look' – she pointed over her shoulder towards the car park – 'maybe I should go... I don't want to, you know, waste your evening.' Anxiously, Sarah looked everywhere but at him.

*And this is why,* she thought, *you should always be sceptical about the men on the site who had a blurred or distant picture.*

'Hey,' Tom said as his hand reached up and, fondly, with a smile, he dropped it on to her shoulder and squeezed. 'Come on, you're not wasting my night and, look, we're here now. So, no pressure.' He glanced towards the pub where the laughter and music were still blaring out from inside. 'We're just two old friends, popping into a bar for a drink.' He laughed, playfully. 'What do you say? We do have a lot of catching up to do, and besides, one drink won't hurt anyone, will it?'

'Right...' Rubbing his hands together, Tom realised how cold they'd been. On top of that, he was nervous. He was out with Daisy's sister, thinking unimaginable things while surrounded by so many people who were all bumping shoulders and wrestling for a position to stand at the bar. 'What are you having?' he asked her as casually as he could, with a smile. 'And order something real because I seem to think that when I knew you before, you'd have been much too young to drink real alcohol.'

Laughing, Sarah sidled up beside him. She'd taken her coat off and hung it up on the rack. She seemed to have lost the initial disappointment that he'd seen on her face, which had been helped by the fact that she'd spoken to at least three different people since arriving, most of whom had greeted her with a kiss and a hug and Tom concluded that as well as being well known in the area, she'd definitely relaxed.

'Go on then, I'll have a gin and tonic.' She laughed. 'But only one, I'm driving.' She lifted her car keys up in the air, rattled them jovially and gave him an appreciative smile, which was followed by a cheeky wink. 'Make it heavy on the tonic, and plenty of ice.'

Watching her walk through the bar, Tom noticed the looks that other men gave her. Every man in the bar would have enjoyed an evening with Sarah, and he felt himself smile proudly. For once, the other men were envious of him. Every one of them wanted to be in his shoes. It was a feeling he'd only ever had when he'd walked out with Daisy during the night they'd spent together in London.

Glancing over his shoulder in her direction, Tom waited to be served and looked for the table that Sarah had chosen. It was the table furthest away from the bar and right next to the back doors, where beyond them was the beer garden, surrounded by long strings of bright Christmas lights.

Nonchalantly, he watched the way Sarah picked up a menu. She glanced at the list but then, as though she'd quickly got bored, she tossed it across the table, flicked her hair back with one hand and, with eyes that were searching for him, she gave him what looked like a genuine smile. It was enough for Tom to feel assured that making his move was the right thing to do and if Sarah was adamant that she was only having one drink, he knew that his chance would be limited; with sleight of hand, he dropped one piece of tablet into her drink, and with a smug, self-righteous smile, he picked up a stirrer.

Pulling in a deep but furious breath, Daisy turned off the road, on to the unadopted lane and, even though every single sinew inside her still ached, she squeezed the accelerator to make the car go faster. For once she didn't care how much pain she was in, or about the potholes that littered the lane, and the last thing she wanted to worry about was the deep, water-filled ditches that were full of cold, stagnant water. Not tonight. Tonight, all she cared about was Sarah and the message she'd sent about Tom.

> **SARAH**
>
> Daisy don't phone me back. I've just nipped to the loo to send this message. You'll never guess what, Confident Sparky is Tom. He's acting a bit weird, saying all sorts of odd things. But don't worry, in about ten minutes I'm going to make an excuse and I'm going to head to The Willows. Meet me there. xx
>
> PS: Might stay at yours tonight and use that gym in the morning. xx

Reading the message over and over, Daisy had ignored Sarah's words, hit the call button repeatedly and, with the aggravation seeping out of her pores, she'd listened to the monotonous sound of Sarah's voicemail that played on a loop.

She thought back to the message Sarah had left about the app and, after pulling over to one side of the road, she quickly logged in and, with relief, she saw that Sarah had already left the pub and seemed to be heading out of Bamburgh. It was enough to make Daisy relax and, feeling relieved, she closed the app down.

'If you've told her anything about London, about us, I swear to God...' Daisy yelled as she peered out of the windscreen. The thought that Tom would tell Sarah their secrets drove her insane, and with one eye on the clock, she ploughed the car forward, taking each of the corners at speed with a determination to get to The Willows first, just in case.

Hitting the brakes, Daisy began to regret the short cut she'd taken. She'd felt sure that this would be an easier route, but the road was treacherous and waterlogged and she found herself anxiously watching the skeletal trees and bushes that shrouded each side of the road.

With a gasp, Daisy ducked and caught her breath as brown, muddy water sprayed up to hit the windscreen. It was like a tidal wave hitting the glass and she squeezed the brakes some more and watched the way her wipers flew into action. Her heartbeat accelerated as she turned off the track and spotted the bright, flashing amber lights of the crossing ahead. The train tracks were blocking her route, and she was forced to come to a complete stop behind a row of tractors that were covered in fairy lights, all of which flashed randomly.

'Urgh. Do you know what, Sarah is right. I have no idea what the excitement is about flashing lights and fake bloody trees.' Daisy slumped back in her seat, dramatically. She thought back to the conversation she'd had with Olena about putting a tree up in the hallway and now, even though she loathed everything about her mother-in-law, she hoped that Teresa would take on the task of dressing the house and have a tree put up in her absence.

Sitting there with no choice but to wait, Daisy rested a hand against her stomach where the cramps pulsated. A low, subdued pain remained, and she felt a tear drop on to her cheek for the baby she'd lost. It was something she didn't want to think about right now; she had to think about her sister. All she really wanted was to do was go straight back to Pipistrelle and curl up beneath her duvet until the pain of loss went away. Selfishly, she thought about turning the car around and heading back to the house, but she couldn't. Sarah needed her, and no matter what, she was going to be there.

# 30

## DAISY

Squeezing her brakes uneasily with the toe of her trainer, Daisy navigated the lane that led to The Willows. It was long and icy, and with the sky full of snow that looked ready to fall heavily, Daisy slowed the car down and kept her eyes firmly fixed on the lane as she turned into the corner.

It was a house she hated, but tonight she needed to get there. She needed to see Sarah, to know she was safe and, once she did, Daisy knew that she had no choice but to sit down with her sister and tell her the truth. It's something she should have done before, and now she silently berated herself for everything that had happened. She should never have agreed to the meet-up in London. She should have shut that conversation down before it began and under no circumstance should she have given him her number. All of this alone would have been her biggest mistake since she'd married Cole, but then she took her night in London a huge step further. The night had become hazy, full of magic and, even on a cold winter night, she'd felt a heat burning inside her, and without thought for her marriage, she'd allowed herself to get caught up in the moment. Which had, in her eyes, been unforgivable and now, after the day she'd had and the threats Tom had made, she knew without a doubt that it was the right time to talk to her husband.

Turning into the lane that led to the house, Daisy furrowed her brow with confusion. The lane that was normally lit by flood lights was in darkness. The gate was ajar and, with her fingers still gripping the wheel and the indicator still clicking to show the amber light flashing repeatedly, her mind accelerated from zero to a hundred miles an hour as a million different scenarios flashed into her thoughts.

'Maybe there's a power cut...' Daisy swallowed hard and pushed a hand through hair that felt grimy, unkempt and desperately in need of brushing. 'Maybe no one is home.' She reached for her phone and, for a few seconds, she considered phoning Cole but then, in the beam of her headlights, she spotted a black SUV through the gates. It was big and dark and parked next to Cole's. The number plate was impossible to read from where she sat and even though she didn't recognise the vehicle, she now felt sure that Cole was at home. That, power cut or not, someone was here.

With the moon shrouded by a sky that was thickening more and more with snow by the minute, Daisy held her breath before attempting to climb out of the car. She already knew that with the weather they'd had, the path underfoot would be icy and, with a firm stare, she wished for the gates to open for the car. But they didn't, which meant that making a dramatic entrance was going to be out of the question.

Leaning back in her seat, Daisy held on to her stomach. The cramps were still there. Not as bad as they'd been, but still coming back in disgruntled waves and for a moment, she considered walking straight into the house but the thought of a stranger standing in the hallway wasn't appealing. Not when she looked as she did, with her hair unbrushed and her face stained with the tears that had been falling for hours.

'Come on, Cole... Are you in there?' she whispered. 'Are you at home and, if you are, who the hell are you with?' Trembling with the cold and exhaustion, Daisy's mind went into overdrive, and she tried not to think about all the nights Cole had stayed here, apparently alone.

'Damn it, Sarah, where the hell are you...?' Daisy mumbled as she cracked open the window, just a fraction, and she listened to the unbearable silence. She desperately wanted to hear the commotion that she normally complained of. She wanted to watch Sarah swoop in like a hurricane and, most of all, she wished that Sarah's headlights would appear on the lane right behind her and for her to cause a diversion while Daisy got into the house and up to the bedroom.

Climbing out of the car, Daisy tentatively took a step forward. As she'd imagined, the ground had turned icy, which wasn't helped by the aggregate beneath her feet, which was both sharp and uneven.

With only the light from the headlights to guide her, Daisy inched as slowly as she could to where one of the gates stood slightly open. It towered above her but with every step, her trepidation grew worse. Her stomach turned with anxiety and her fingers trembled as she reached for the keypad and began to press all the numbers that Cole had told her but the gates didn't move and, once again, she searched the lane behind her, all the time looking for the sign of her sister's headlights approaching.

'Cole...' she uttered, 'Cole, are you there...?' With her steps slowly faltering, Daisy pushed open the gate with her hand and felt a sense of relief when it swung slowly open. But as she did, her mouth went dry. The silence she'd previously hated was now filled with noise. A loud ear-splitting and explosive crack filled the air. A sound quickly followed by a door being opened and slammed at speed and then, from somewhere inside, she heard the unmistakable sound of Teresa screaming.

'You can't do this...' Teresa's voice suddenly shrieked out from the direction of the office. 'I don't care what you were told, we don't have that kind of money and you just can't do this, it's...'

'Mum, stay inside. Go back to Dad, make sure he's okay...' Cole shouted in a voice that was loud but with an obvious tremble. 'And you, you need to get off me, you moron. I swear to God, if you've hurt him, or anyone else in my family, I will make you pay...'

Another bang was followed by a loud, piercing scream that came from Teresa. It was a sound that made Daisy catch her breath, and frantically, her hands shaking with a terror that was exploding deep within her, she pulled her phone out of her pocket, and while launching herself back towards the car, she stabbed at the screen with a finger.

'Police. I need the police. I'm sorry, I don't know what's happening,' she said to the operator, 'but I just got home and...' Her mind had gone blank and for a moment she lost her ability to speak. 'I... I... I think there's a robbery. It's taking place at my house, and I heard...' She tried to think, tried to make some sense of the sudden burst of sound she'd heard. 'I think it was a gun.'

'Miss,' the operator urged, 'I need you to stay on the phone but please, I need you to find somewhere safe to hide and then, if you can speak without being heard, I need for you to tell me what's happening.'

'Are the police coming?'

'Yes, I've despatched a firearms unit and I've picked up your location from your phone, so please don't worry, they're coming right to you.'

With her body slouched in the passenger seat, Daisy rolled

down the window and, with the phone still pressed to her ear, she watched and she waited, and after a few seconds she began to have doubts. What if she'd imagined the sound of the gun? What if armed police were about to descend, and she'd be charged with wasting their time?

'Move it, right now...' A deep Scottish voice suddenly rang out, and Daisy choked back a sob as the tall, muscular frame of a man strode out from the trees. He was wearing a hoodie that had been pulled up to cover his head – unlike Cole, who was dressed in nothing more than a pair of jeans and a thin cotton shirt, and Daisy felt herself gasp in horror as she saw her husband drop to his knees and cower right in front of the stranger.

From inside, she heard another high-pitched scream from Teresa. It was a noise that made Daisy's blood run cold with anguish knowing that screaming was not normally Teresa's way, and that for her to act in this way, she must be in imminent danger.

Remembering the call she'd made, Daisy turned her attention back to the phone. 'We have an intruder, he has a gun and he's beating my husband...' Daisy knew that the words were a lie, that she hadn't actually seen a gun, but she had heard one and the threat had been there and right now, right at that moment, she was prepared to do and say anything to stop what was happening and save the lives of her family.

'I can hear screaming. Someone must be hurt, and there's a man, he's trying to kill my husband and... and his parents. They're in the house too.' Daisy paused, and with every ounce of energy left in her body, she hit the accelerator and held her breath as the car sped forward. 'Please,' she yelled, 'I'm going in, and I really need you to come.'

## 31

### SARAH

Thrashing from side to side, Sarah felt an intense pain behind her eyes the moment she tried to open them.

'How much did I drink?' She blinked repeatedly as a hundred strange images circumnavigated her mind. Her subconscious told her that she was no longer asleep, but she felt so distant and lethargic that it was also difficult to believe that she'd woken at all.

Bright, geometric shapes began to jump up from the bed. They spun around in the air before flying violently towards her. Ducking beneath the duvet, Sarah lay there trembling. The fear inside her grew by the second and with her breath held tightly, she opened one eye just a fraction at first, and peeped over the top of the duvet to see a bright red circle turn into a hoop, which hooked itself over her head and slid down her body to leave her to feeling trapped and restricted, and for a good few minutes she found herself struggling with a duvet that had wrapped itself around her.

As the images slowly dispersed, they were replaced by bright flashing lights. In the distance, she could hear a strange tapping.

It was a noise she wanted to make stop so that she could go back to sleep. Her mouth was so dry, her throat raged with an unnatural heat, and as she tried to shout out for someone to help her, the words she wanted to say came out in nothing more than a husky whisper.

Fighting to keep her eyes open, Sarah tried to move her legs from one side of the bed to the other, but her legs felt like lead. She was oddly disorientated; she could barely move but her bladder was screaming out to be emptied. As she lay there, with sweat forming on her skin and a panic raging in her mind, she knew she had to get up. She had to make it to the bathroom, and with her breaths coming thick and fast she succumbed to the inbuilt terror that tore right through her.

Lifting her head, just a fraction, she quickly worked out that she was in a room she hadn't been in before, but the door was open and there was a light coming from the room next door, which meant that she wasn't a prisoner. But it did mean that someone else was there, in the next room.

Screwing her eyes up as tight as she could, Sarah couldn't understand where she was and, impatiently, she furrowed her brow, pressed her fingers over her eyes and tried to recollect her evening. She'd gone on a date and... Tom. Tom had been there and, somewhere in the back of her mind, she felt sure that Tom had mentioned having a wife and a child. Which was bizarre. If Tom had got married and had a child, surely someone would have told Daisy and, in return, Daisy would have told her.

Slithering helplessly off the bed and on to the floor, Sarah stared at the carpet. It was scattered with clothes that had obviously been left where they'd been dropped, and initially she found them amusing. Until she realised that her body was naked and that the shoes with multiple straps and the torn long denim dress were the ones she'd worn. With her mind spinning with fear, she pulled at the duvet and wrapped it around her and shuffled towards the door, where, sleepily, she looked across the landing to where Tom sat at a desk. He was slouched in front of a screen, fully engrossed.

Looking over her shoulder and back at the bed, Sarah didn't know whether she should run or hide, but her body didn't feel capable of moving. Her strength had gone, her mouth felt dry and, anxiously, she lifted her tongue to the roof of her mouth and tried to pull the moisture from somewhere. Instinctively, she began to swallow repeatedly and, once again, she thought of the alcohol. The small amount she'd drunk, and after deliberating for what felt like a very long time, she concluded that this feeling, this lethargy, couldn't possibly be just the drink, which was when she began to focus on the hallucinations that she clearly remembered.

'You... you were drugged,' she whispered under her breath. 'He drugged you...'

With tears filling her eyes, Sarah began to dig her fingers into the carpet, and with every ounce of strength she had left in her body, she began to drag herself to one side of the bed where she hid behind it and curled up into a tight defensive ball. It was all she could do before the nausea returned, the trembling began, the floor moved beneath her and the tears rolled down her cheeks without effort as her body gave in and she drifted back into a deep, troubled sleep.

# 32

## DAISY

'Oh my God. What the hell?' Screaming the words as loud as she could, Daisy hit the brakes, and without stopping to turn off the engine or close the car's door, she leapt out and on to feet that were moving so much faster than her body wanted to go, but then stopped in her tracks. She could hear Teresa's high-pitched voice screaming from inside the office. It was more than obvious that something bad had happened and even though Cole was trying to escape his clutches and get to his mother, the man's strength was too much for him and, without effort, he pulled at Cole's shirt until it had been twisted tightly at the collar, making Cole go bright red in the face and barely able to breathe.

'If you don't give me what I want, you're a dead man, have you got that?' the man snarled. His gaze was cold and lacking emotion. The hands that were gripping Cole by the throat were big enough to dig a trench in the road.

'Please.' Holding an arm out towards him, Daisy tried to calm the situation and even though Teresa's yells had now gone oddly silent, she could see the fear that bulged from her husband's eyes.

The way he kept trying to scramble back in his mother's direction and the way that, each time he did, the man's grip grew tighter and how the material that had once been a part of Cole's shirt had now been wrapped around his neck like a long fabric noose. His face had become a vivid shade of red, his eyes were wide and unbelievably terrified. A situation that was made worse every time the man yanked the material tighter and then laughed uncontrollably as Cole fell and stumbled towards him.

'Get off him. Please. For the love of God, I'm begging you, leave him alone... He can't breathe, can't you see he can't breathe?' Throwing herself forward, Daisy began to claw at the man who stood a good foot taller than Cole. As her fingers curled into fists, she felt them bounce relentlessly against his solid and impenetrable muscles, making every blow feel as though she'd hit a brick wall, and Daisy felt tears fall down her face in fear and frustration. After throwing her best punch and getting nowhere, her energy failed. Miserably, she realised that this was a fight she was never going to win. The hulk of a man was much too strong and fired up with adrenaline. She slid to the ground, dropped her hands by her sides, and with the gravel piercing her skin like a hundred needles she considered picking up the stones and throwing them at him, in the hope that it would give Cole an opportunity to escape from his grasp.

'Please, I'm begging you. Whatever happened. Whatever you want, this... this isn't the answer. Is it?' Daisy paused, ran her fingers through the sharp shards of aggregate. 'Let me speak to him,' she begged, 'I can convince him to give you whatever you want and all you have to do is give me a few minutes.' She spoke at speed, looked into the man's eyes. Knowing that the police were heading their way, she kept considering the idea of throwing the stones, but Cole was so close and could easily be hurt.

Throwing Cole to the ground, the man ran a hand across his

firm, square jawline and laughed, hysterically. 'What's it like, Cole, getting the little wife to come and save you?' His face was full of amusement and, as though toying with Cole, he once again grabbed at the scruff of his shirt and gave him a yank. 'But she won't save you, will she, Cole? Just like your daddy didn't save you either,' he growled in a deep, Scottish accent. 'You thought you were being clever, didn't you?' He paused, snarled. 'Well, we got tipped off tonight. A reliable source, he tells me that you were trying to rip off the boss man and that's why he's sent me over. He wants me to find out if it's true.'

'Kai, look I'm sorry, I don't know who said that but...' Cole's hands went straight to his neck, his fingers traced the place where the lengths of material had cut into his throat. 'You have to understand, none of this happened on purpose, things went wrong... it wasn't my fault and... she's right, this isn't the answer.' Crawling on his knees, Cole swiped the blood from his face with his hand, 'I'll give you what you want... all of it. I'll give it to you. I'll give it you right now... you just need to...' It was a feeble attempt at negotiation and as though Kai sensed that Cole had been allowed to breathe for just a little too long, he grabbed at his shirt, twisted the material around in his hand and, with a loud, riotous laugh, he lifted Cole off his feet and propelled his body heavily forward.

'I don't need you to do anything. Don't you get that?' Kai spat. 'The boss, he wants your body in a bag, and if I don't take you back in one, he'll be wanting mine. So, do you want to lay a bet on how this is going to end?' The words were growled through teeth that were clenched together, while he lifted his top lip to one side and sneered.

Another tug of Cole's shirt was followed by an agonising scream that made Daisy bite down on her lip. Her whole body trembled, her stomach was twisting itself in knots and, with her mouth turning dry, the acid that had been burning her throat threated to rise and expel itself from her. On her hands and knees, and with the stones piercing her skin as she crawled, she did all she could to get to her husband, who had lain on the ground, like a wounded animal waiting to die.

'Come on, you have to stop now, you've proved your damn point...' she yelled, as she looked over his shoulder and into the trees that shrouded the property. A part of her wanted to know that Teresa was okay, and even though Daisy had lived in the Bailey shadow, she still didn't want them all to be hurt and so, uneasily, she began to scour the treeline. For a moment, Daisy thought she spotted some movement. Maybe a fox or a rabbit. But the more closely she looked, she felt sure she'd spotted something much bigger, something that looked more like a man, crouching and crawling around the bushes and, right now, she didn't know if they were friend or foe. She just hoped that the police would arrive and that the movement wasn't from friends of Kai who were sat, waiting to pounce.

'Daisy, please...' Cole held a hand up towards her and, with eyes that became fixed with hers, he shook his head hastily. 'I'm so sorry,' he murmured. 'I didn't mean for all this...' His threw his head backwards, and with eyes that were full of remorse, he stared at the house that towered before them. 'It was supposed to be just one deal... a way to provide a fresh start, for the both of us...'

'Heart-warming as that might sound, I've heard enough of the fucking confession.' Kai spat the words out with venom and he leaned in, with his face and lips almost touching with Cole's, as he bellowed his orders. 'I want what he owes the boss... and you,' he shouted towards Daisy, 'you shouldn't have come here.' His arms bulged out from beneath the jet-black hoodie and Daisy held her breath, cowered and braced herself for the punch she thought might come. But all she could hear was Cole, the agonising yelps as he clawed his way across the ground towards her. Moving into the light given off by the headlights, Daisy felt a horrified gasp leave her throat as she searched Cole's face. Blood seeped out of wounds to each side of his head and bruises were forming around both of his eyes. He had a deep gash across the top of his eyebrow, and a dark shadow had formed on his cheek-bone and splatters of blood fell from his mouth.

'It's going to be all right,' Daisy whispered as hot, scalding tears rushed to her eyes. Seeing Cole hurt was more than her heart wanted to take, and with a rush of emotions she stared into his eyes, almost pleading for answers. 'Cole, I really don't know what's happening here, but you just have to hold on, I've...' She kept one eye on where Kai paced as she spoke. 'I've phoned the police,' she mumbled, 'they're on their way, they're coming, they'll be here any minute... and then, they'll sort everything out.' She forced a hopeful smile, but recoiled the moment Cole turned and snapped.

'Why, Daisy? Why the hell did you do that?' Lifting his hand to his face, Cole covered his eyes and let out a long, mournful wail that cut straight through her. 'The police can't help me and, right now, all they're going to do is make things worse.'

'Cole?' Daisy was hurt and completely confused. She had no idea how the police could make things worse, or why he'd snapped, and automatically her fingers reached out towards him. She waited for him to take hold of her hand in his, for him to wind his fingers around hers in the same way he always had, and for him to hold her close until the memory of this night disappeared. 'Please... I don't understand. They're coming; they're going to save you...'

'Who the hell is going to save you? The damned police?' Kai's voice was loud and furious, and, terrified, Daisy tried to shrink into the aggregate. 'You shouldn't have done that.' As he yelled, a part of her wanted to bury herself beneath the gravel but she couldn't move, not quickly enough. Without warning he took a fast step towards her, the back of his hand connected with the side of her face and the pain seared through her. Automatically, her hands went to protect her stomach and with all the air practically leaving her lungs, she hit the hard, unforgiving ground, as she tried to scream but couldn't.

'Please, I'll do anything you want, but please... don't hurt her,' Cole suddenly yelled. He frantically clawed at the loose stones, his fingers closing around the shards in a futile attempt to close the divide that still stood between them. 'And Daisy, I need you to listen,' he said as, once again, Kai grabbed his shirt and pulled him back towards him. 'Daisy...' He paused, sobbed out loud and pressed his lips firmly between his teeth making the blood seep from them a little more than it already did. 'I'm going to sort this out. Kai and I...' He averted his gaze and then he looked up at the house. 'We're going to go inside, and I don't really know what's going to happen, but you can't follow us.' Cole's eyes connected with hers for just a second and he gave her a look of love, of sorrow and mostly of regret. 'You have... you have to promise me that you'll stay right here... and that you'll look after our baby. I've got a feeling you're going to have to look after it... for the both of us, do you understand me?'

'How, how do you know?' she whispered while nodding. The last thing Daisy ever wanted was for Cole to find himself at the mercy of a man who could easily crush him or tear him apart without breaking a sweat, but, somehow, she still needed to give Cole some hope and couldn't bring herself to tell him that the baby was gone. For the first time in years, Daisy saw the years of their marriage flash past her in a kaleidoscope full of images. A marriage she'd almost ended with a one-night stand, and now it was all going to end in this way.

Slumping to the ground in a tight, curled-up ball, Daisy held on to her body and, with her eyes fixed on Cole's, she felt momentarily connected by an invisible thread. But then she closed her eyes, and bit down on her lip as Kai dragged her terrified husband behind him in the direction of the house.

# 33

## SARAH

The sound of a door closing downstairs jolted Sarah back to the present.

She heard a bang, the turn of a key. A noise that made her jump nervously, and for a second she stared fearfully out of the room and into the hallway, where she managed to stare at a wall without the bright neon lights floating towards her.

Thoughtfully, she ran her fingers across the strange bedding, and it quickly occurred to her that it wasn't the first time she'd woken up in someone else's bed. The difference this time was that the bed belonged to Tom, which made her feel anxious inside.

'You don't even know where he lives, do you?' Sarah questioned herself and twisted the bedding as tightly as she could around her fingers. 'You're a damned disgrace and you ought to know better.' Wiping the tears away from her eyes, Sarah listened as carefully as she could to the sounds of the house. Outside, there was an inexplicable thud. A noise that was sudden and sharp and followed by another, and another. Each time it happened, she felt her whole body jump with the fear of not knowing what it might be, and uneasily, while shivering relentlessly, she curled her knees upward, picked up a pillow and wrapped her arms around them, as she rocked herself back and forth in a self-given hug.

With the pillow still in her arms, Sarah tugged at a duvet that felt thin, grimy and had a smell that was more than unpleasant. But it was all she had, and as she had earlier, she used it to cover her body, as the sound of her own heartbeat pulsated heavily in one side of her neck.

Dragging the duvet behind her, Sarah gingerly wove her way through the random items that littered the floor beneath both of her knees, and after reaching the corner, she began to shudder with a sense of confusion and, unintentionally, she felt herself drifting back in and out of a sleep that had an overwhelming power. Moments of clarity were interchanged with moments of vagueness. Each tiny memory was like the piece of a jigsaw being dropped into place, and Sarah knew deep inside her that the only way she'd work out what had happened would be if she could join the pieces together and turn the broken jigsaw back into a fully formed picture.

'Where the hell am I?' she mouthed as the tears scalded her face. She fought to stay awake and, instinctively, she swiped at the tears that had dripped down to her chin. As she did, the floor began to move beneath her. She felt as though it would tip and she'd fall, and she held on to the bed and stood up on legs that wobbled unsteadily. 'I need to get out of here,' she muttered, 'but first, I need some clothes and, most of all, I need my phone, I need to phone Daisy.'

With that thought in her mind, Sarah slumped heavily against the wall, and as she did, she noticed that the noise outside had got louder, and with the inability to do anything sensible, she cautiously tugged at the dark patterned curtain and allowed herself to peep through a small but adequate opening.

'Wait... that's my...' Confused, she lifted a hand up to the window and, without any thought that she might be seen, she pressed her nose to the pane. The view from the back of the house was one she'd seen at least a hundred times before. 'If I just...' She tipped her head to one side, but her legs felt more than unstable, and she almost toppled over.

'I can see it...' she stammered, 'I can see my house, and that's... that's my...' She was going to say that she could see her garden, but after the night she'd had, she couldn't be sure of anything. The hallucinations had scared her, but with a wish to prove that her vision was real, she whipped open the curtain more widely, and with her heart fluttering at speed, Sarah blinked as hard as she could and tried to think about what Tom had told her.

'He'd just moved in... that's right, that's what he said.' She smiled to herself in a congratulatory manner; her memory was returning, and the deep sense of confusion she'd had was beginning to dissipate. 'He's lived here for the past three months,' she recalled, 'after buying the house to live in with his wife and his baby.'

Furrowing her brow, Sarah wondered where his wife and baby were now. It was a question that had no answer. She felt sure that if his wife had been here, she'd have seen her, and with her eyes screwed up as tightly as she could, Sarah tried to think of what else had happened to bring her into this house. She went through her day, and then her evening and, slowly, she began to put the pieces of the jigsaw back into place. She thought about Tom. The bar, the drinks... and then she lifted her fingers up to her bruised, swollen lips. 'I need to know what happened, I need...' Leaning forward, Sarah once again pressed her face against the window. The sound was now coming more frequently. A loud, monotonous thud that drove her insane, and with eyes that searched relentlessly, Sarah eventually spotted Tom, stood beneath a tree with a spade in his hands.

Jumping backwards, Sarah gasped for breath. It wasn't a time when most would be gardening and no one in their right mind would want or need to dig a hole when the temperature was somewhere close to zero. Puzzled and confused, Sarah began to pace back and forth, but each time she approached the window, curiosity took over and, with the curtain to shield her, she felt perplexed as she watched the way Tom stopped, rested against his spade and, with a face that showed no emotion, he stared aimlessly at a bright blue cool box that stood by his feet.

Raking her hands through her hair, Sarah fell to her knees and, frantically, she rummaged around on the floor. 'He's going to kill you,' she mouthed, nervously. 'He's... he's digging a grave... He's going to kill you. He must want to get back at Daisy.' Rubbing her eyes, Sarah felt the need to sleep wash over her. 'Oh my God, and I'm so tired, I feel...' She leaned against the bed, bewildered by the thought that she might want to sleep when her life was in danger. The realisation hit her and, without trying to stop it, a loud sob emerged from her throat. 'He drugged you, and now... now he has to get rid of you.' She lifted her fingers up to her head and, once again, she pulled at her hair. 'But why... why would he? This is Tom, this is the same Tom I've known for most of my life, this is Daisy's Tom. The man she'd loved until...'

It was then that she remembered the venomous way Tom had spoken about Cole. He'd talked about loss and humiliation. The way he'd been fired, in front of the others, and finally he'd raged on about bringing him down, about how he'd always loved Daisy and how Sarah must know of a way to help him. Under the influence of drugs and the romantic notion of how things might have turned out between Tom and her sister, Sarah had spilled the beans without thought. She'd told him all about the way Cole had moved some drugs. A single shipment of aggregate that was delivered abroad. But then, the people he'd worked for had tightened the screws. The single shipment had turned into a few and no matter how many times Sarah had tried to talk him out of doing any more, Cole had been in too deep. It had started out as a quick way of making some money, and now Sarah had told the one person who hated him the most how he'd reneged on the deal and how many millions he'd stashed in a safe.

Suddenly, Sarah felt a pressure press down on her shoulders. It was as though someone had stood on her chest, and she was unable to breathe, to function or make a rational decision. Single-handedly, she'd put Cole in danger and, with that, her whole family could be at risk, including her, which was something she'd never knowingly have done.

Saying that, a lot had happened, and just a few hours before, she'd never have believed that Tom would have drugged her, but now it was more than obvious that he had and apprehensively, she scrambled across the cold, littered floor until she found her dress lying at the foot of the bed, discarded.

Looking down, Sarah fumbled for buttons that were no longer there and she stopped to stare at the damage. She tried to comprehend the force that would have been used to tear them open. It was something else she couldn't remember happening, but right now she didn't care. All she cared about was leaving and going home. Once there, she could get some help. She could try and piece the jigsaw of her evening together and, most of all, she could phone Daisy and let her know what she'd done.

Inching along the landing that was shrouded in darkness, Sarah spotted the room where she remembered that Tom had been sitting. There was a small shaft of light coming from beneath the door, and with her eyes squeezed to a close she saw a small flash of memory come back. She'd been in that room. Tom had taken her in there. He'd been laughing, her bag and phone had been placed on a desk and... 'He kissed me.' Lifting a hand to her mouth, Sarah gasped in horror. Tom had kissed her and, what's more, she'd allowed him to do it.

Horrified at the thought, Sarah pushed the door open. She felt sure that this room was where her phone would be, and after scouring the desk that was surrounded by rubbish, she homed in on a gaming controller that had been tossed to one side, and a pair of baby's pale blue dungarees hung over the back of the chair and, for a moment, Sarah simply stared at the small yellow duck that had been carefully embroidered on them.

'There was a baby,' she whispered, 'I saw a baby.' Her eyes flashed across the screen as she remembered the image she'd seen there, along with the flash of fear that had crossed Tom's face as he'd realised the computer was still on and how, hurriedly, he'd leaned across her to switch the screen off. But then, she thought of another memory. One when she'd watched him slouch over the desk, with those very same images flashing past on his monitor.

It was something she simply couldn't think about. Not right now. Right now, all she wanted was her phone, and after spotting where it stood right next to the computer, alongside her keys, she felt triumphant. A smile crossed her lips and, with a sharp look over her shoulder, she reached across the desk to pick them up, but gasped in horror as she caught the mouse with her wrist and watched uneasily as the screen jumped back into life, and without being able to tear herself away, she sat down and watched the way Grace had fallen and exactly how their baby had died.

# 34

## TOM

Pulling in deep breaths, Tom listened to the sound of the sea crashing against the harbour wall in the distance. It was only on a night like tonight, when the town had fallen to sleep, that he could he hear it at all, and with his gaze fixed on a snow-filled sky, he knew that any moment now, the weather would turn and that, without a doubt, the snow would fall. If it did, like he suspected it would, it would cover the ground for at least a few days, maybe longer, and if that happened, he'd lose every chance he had to bury his son before the bailiffs came back and began the process of sifting through every one of his belongings, while looking for things they might want to sell.

He looked down at the small patch of land he was attempting to dig and with the enormity of what he knew he needed to do, he swallowed repeatedly. His heart became constricted and tight with pain at the thought of burying his boy. It was the last thing he'd ever thought he might do. But Grace had killed him and the thought that he'd end up taking the blame and going to prison had been too much and, instead, he'd taken this route of self-preservation.

'It's your mother's fault,' Tom whispered to the box where his son's fetid remains were still hidden. 'You need to blame her. She was going to take you away and make you live in a commune, and Mason, my boy, there wasn't a chance I was letting that happen...' He paused, stifled a sob and squeezed his eyes shut as he thought about Grace lying in that bed, slowly dying. 'It won't be much longer before she's gone and then you, my boy, you will get justice. She'll pay for what she did to you and to me and then, after what I've just done to Cole, I'll get the chance to start again, and this time it will be a life with Daisy in it and...' He leaned forward, lay a hand on the box. 'It's a secret, but Daisy, she's pregnant and I... well, I'm going to be a daddy and this time, it's going to be different...' With the temperature dropping below zero, Tom took in a short, sharp breath of self-satisfaction. He wiped his hot, sweaty hands down the side of his jeans and picked up the spade before thrusting it as hard as he could back into the ground. The ground was hard and unforgiving. Each time his spade hit the hard soil, Tom felt the shudder and shock of the impact vibrate right though him, but he couldn't stop. He had to carry on and worked frantically while the adrenaline flowed, and with an anger that burned through his hands and into the spade, he pondered over the chain of events that had brought him to this moment.

'You're a goddamned failure,' he growled out loudly as he stopped digging and looked up at the house. 'You fail at everything. You were a failed fiancé, you were the one Daisy didn't want. The one she pushed to one side, and then you became a failed husband, and a failed father.' He suddenly struck out at the blue cool box, watched in horror as the spade went through the outer plastic coating. 'You didn't love Grace. She was never enough for you, and you didn't protect Mason, not in life, just like you didn't protect him in death. You can't even bury him without messing it up.' Yanking the spade away from the box, Tom felt himself gasp as small slithers of insulation poked out from within. It was a sight that made him retch repeatedly, and with his eyes fixed on the box, he watched and waited, knowing that at any moment, his son's remains could seep out.

Tom dropped the spade on the ground. 'And tonight, you excelled yourself, didn't you? You can now add being a failed lover to your ever-growing repertoire.' Kicking the spade with force, Tom knew that he should never have brought Sarah back to this house. It had been a mistake. All he'd done the whole time he'd been with her was think about Daisy. The memory of London had filled his mind and, for a short while, he'd become lost in the moment, and it had been Daisy he'd been kissing not Sarah. He could easily imagine his fingers moving across her soft, delicate skin and he could hear the words she whispered and moaned every time he'd touched her. She'd been giving, almost wanton, and with no effort at all she'd opened herself to him, and even though he'd laced her with drugs, it had been what he'd wanted, until he'd realised that it was Sarah that lay beneath him, not Daisy, and without warning, his erection had failed. He'd been left lank and useless, and he'd thrown his body back against the pillows, pathetically.

Kicking out, Tom cursed out loud as his foot once again connected with the spade. 'Why the hell did you bring her here? You'd already got the information you needed, she'd sung like a bird, and you'd already made the damn call, so what more did you think would happen apart from the fact you ended up looking so stupid?'

'I went to work for her husband,' Tom had revealed to Sarah, 'and on the first day after I'd put in a full shift, the bastard got rid of me and do you know what makes it worse? I've had bailiffs banging on the door and I really needed that job.' It had been a line he'd given her while they'd been sitting in the pub and, for effect, he'd patted his pockets. 'I don't have a pot to piss in right now.' It had been a way of gaining some sympathy, in the hope that Sarah would empathise, that she might buy them a drink and, while he'd waited, he'd stared into the depths of his glass, with his shoulders slouched dramatically forward.

It had only taken Sarah a moment to reach for his hand, for her to squeeze it supportively. 'Cole's under a lot of pressure right now, Tom. Please don't hate him.' She'd spoken slowly, and had leaned against him and pressed a soft, tender kiss against his cheek. 'You have to understand, Cole's a bit mixed up, and Daisy, well, she's his world and now they have a baby on the way, and things are going to change, which means that Cole needs to sort himself out and start playing life just a little bit safer.'

'Safer?' he'd questioned lightly. He knew that Sarah had said more than she'd intended, and before long, she'd told him all about the way Cole did business. The drugs he'd shipped beneath mountains of aggregate and how he'd ripped off the dealer for a cool two million.

'Oh my God, Tom, I'm sorry, I shouldn't have said that...' Sarah had giggled, childishly. Another trait of the drug. 'Cole's a good man, honestly he is.' She'd looked down at the floor and pushed her bottom lip out. 'He's just... he's...'

'Hey, come on,' Tom had responded with a sympathetic smile, and with his tongue pressed firmly into his cheek, he'd pulled his credit card out of his pocket, tapped it gently against Sarah's glass. 'Let's stick another drink on the plastic and worry about paying for it later.'

'No, here...' She'd reached into her bag, and after just a little rummaging around inside, pulled out a twenty-pound note and flashed him a smile. 'I insist... It's my turn and do you know what, the car can stay in the car park tonight, I'll have another gin and tonic and, this time, let's turn it around and go heavy on the gin.'

After another drink laced with Rohypnol, Tom had sat back and listened to the way Sarah spilled all of the beans without effort. 'He's up to his neck in it. The dealer, Buster Cunningham, he isn't one to mess with and Cole has ripped him off big style.' She nodded in an over-enthusiastic way and Tom could tell by the way she'd leaned against him that it was almost time for them to leave. 'I met up with Cole at the cemetery on Saturday and I begged him to stop, to get rid of the heat. I've told him that he has to play the game straight now, because he has to... he's about to become a father.'

Bringing himself back to the present, Tom took a step back, picked up the spade and continued to dig until he felt sure that the hole was big enough. That he'd created a place for his boy to rest, and without showing any remorse, he picked up the box and nonchalantly placed it in the hole just as his phone pinged in his pocket, and while pushing at the earth with his feet, Tom pulled out his phone and read the message.

UNKNOWN NUMBER

By midnight, Cole Bailey will have been taken out of the game. The boss will have his money back and, as agreed, you will be a half a million richer.

It was a message that Tom had expected. The earlier call he'd made to a few friends that he knew made sure that word got to Buster, and more importantly that he knew where the information had come from. Finally, Tom had stitched Cole up like a kipper and now, all he had to do was bide his time before making a move and claiming his prize. Being richer, he'd have more to offer, and he'd already proved that Daisy had wanted him, he just had to make sure that she believed it.

# 35

## DAISY

'Kai, listen... Aaaaaah stop, please, where are we going?' Cole screamed out. 'You have to stop, you have to listen to me, I'll give you everything I have... just...'

'Stop whimpering,' Kai yelled back as they went up the steps that led to the house. 'You wanted to play the big game and now, you and I... we're gonna go and take a bit of a swim.' The hysterical menacing laughter once again began as Kai moved so quickly that Cole's footing became constantly lost. 'We're going to play a game,' Kai continued. 'We're going to sit on the bottom of the pool and we're going to see whose bubbles stop first.'

Shaking with fear, Daisy wanted to scream but she couldn't. Her throat had filled with acid. She gagged repeatedly and felt paralysed as the tears streamed down her face. A darkness attempted to take over her mind and with a determination she didn't know she had, she forced her eyes open to witness what she felt sure would be the last memory she'd ever have of her husband.

Falling on to her stomach, Daisy slowly pulled herself back towards the car. Its engine was still running, and she knew that if she could only get to the car, she could get to her phone... and do what? Hope that this time the police would come. That when they did, she could ask Olena to make a nice pot of tea?

The sudden thought of Olena and Borys made Daisy twist on the spot. They were normally here, and according to Cole, they rarely went out. So where were they?

'Help... Borys, help me...' Daisy suddenly screamed in a voice that would have easily shattered glass. From nowhere, the adrenaline took over and with every shred of energy she had left in her body, she dragged herself into the car, slammed the door and, still blinded by tears, went to hit the accelerator. But from nowhere she was surrounded by blue flashing lights and not just one police car, but three, maybe four.

The relief was immense and suddenly she was surrounded by noise. Somewhere in the distance she could hear someone shouting. A number of boots hit the gravel seemingly all at once, and a place that just a few days ago she'd thought silent to the point that she couldn't even hear the birds sing was now a hive of activity that made her wish for the silence.

Without warning, the car door opened. 'Okay, I've got her, she's in here,' a voice shouted, above the sound of others. 'Daisy Bailey?' the voice questioned more softly. 'Do you think you could get out of the car for me, Daisy? We have a few questions we need to ask you.'

'I can't... I...' Daisy attempted to move one of her feet and then the other but couldn't. Her whole body had collapsed into a world of its own, and while wrapping her arms tightly around herself, she rocked back and forth as the relief of seeing the police swept through her.

'Actually, can I get some help over here?' the officer commanded. 'Quickly...'

Through her tears, Daisy could see that the officer was slim, almost svelte, and dressed in a simple pair of jeans and a navy-blue jacket, and during the few moments that it took for the paramedics to respond, she took hold of Daisy's hand and rested her fingers carefully against Daisy's pulse.

'Please...' Daisy pleaded, 'I don't know anything... I...' She closed her eyes and felt herself drift in and out of consciousness to the point where she had no recollection that the paramedics had arrived. Somehow, they'd lifted her out of the car, where the movement brought her back to the present and Daisy opened her eyes to see a flutter of snowflakes falling from the sky and drifting towards her.

'Hi there, it's Daisy, isn't it? Daisy, I'm Lindsey, I'm a paramedic and I'm here to help you, and this is my colleague, she's called Maria.' She smiled, and searched Daisy's eyes with her own.

'I think I've had a miscarriage. My baby... I've already lost it,' Daisy said as she slumped to the ground and the two paramedics immediately lifted her up to sit on a gurney.

'There you go, that's better than the ground, isn't it?' Lindsey said with a questioning smile. 'Why don't you have a lie down, while I take a quick look at you?' With a hand on Daisy's shoulder, Lindsey paused, waited and leaned in a little closer. 'I'd like to nip you into the hospital, just for a quick check-up. Would that be okay?' She tapped at a small portable monitor, and scanned the screen before looking up.

'No. I'm sorry but... I don't want to go...' With the emotion choking her voice, Daisy turned to looked away and at the driveway that had quickly become covered with a dusting of snow. There was nothing she could do for her baby, not any more. But Sarah was different and, right now, her sister was out there and she needed her help. 'My sister, she should have been here by now and she could be in trouble, I... I have to go and I have to find her.'

Squinting, Daisy lifted an arm, shielded her eyes from the blue flashing lights and looked into the distance, where she anxiously searched for Cole. She was both angry and relieved at the same time. Anxious for his safety, but furious that he'd brought so much trouble home to their door. Blinking repeatedly, Daisy moved her head from side to side as she hastily ran her gaze across each of the vehicles. Multiple police cars were parked next to a van, and three different ambulances had pulled in behind.

Spotting Cole sitting in the back of an ambulance, wrapped in a silver tinfoil banket to warm him back up, Daisy felt her breathing relax. Cole was alive. Daisy wanted to lift a hand, make some kind of connection, but she spotted the handcuffs that were there to restrain him. A sure sign that Cole had done something wrong. That whatever it was would change the way they lived and, for a moment, she wasn't sure who she'd married. The words 'tipped off' and 'rip off the boss man' stuck in her mind and told her that Cole's secrets were much bigger than hers and, if she were honest, no matter what he'd done, a part of her would always love him, just like a part of her had always loved Tom. A hand went to her stomach, to the life that had lived there, and she nodded a sorrowful acceptance.

'You can't do this; I won't let you arrest me.' Teresa's voice shrieked out from behind the trees as power was returned and the lights came on both inside and outside the house.

From where she lay Daisy could see that Teresa looked dishevelled. Her face was streaked with tears, the knees of her white trousers were covered in grime and her T-shirt was splattered with something that Daisy presumed might be blood.

'I'm not a criminal, and my husband, he needs me...' Teresa suddenly seemed to take in the enormity of the situation. She looked from Daisy, laying helpless on a gurney, to Cole, who sat with his shoulders slumped and a look of despair crossing his face.

'Let my son go, immediately.' Pushing her shoulders back, Teresa pointed a long, finger at Kai, who was already sitting in the back of a police van. 'He's the damn criminal, not me or my son... so you can take these stupid cuffs off us both, this minute.'

Her yells went unheard, and with a wry smile, Daisy wondered how, if she were guilty of a crime, a woman like Teresa would fare in jail. How she'd cope with living in an establishment where the fridge wasn't perfectly laid out in the way she commanded, and a place where the food might not be out of date but would certainly be cooked by another, whose hygiene might not meet the exacting standards she'd always fully expected. Whatever happened, it was more than obvious that both Cole and his parents were guilty of something and, whether she liked it or not, Teresa might have to get used to someone else dishing out both the food and the orders.

'Daisy. I really do think we should pop to the hospital,' Lindsey whispered in a soft and caring voice that eased its way into Daisy's thoughts, 'and get you checked out.'

Shaking her head dismissively, Daisy began to unclip the restraints that had somehow been fastened across her on the gurney. Going into a hospital and being poked around with was the last thing she wanted. Instead, she wanted to know what was happening. She needed to know what had led to this moment, and in a vain attempt to catch her husband's eye for one last time, she sat up and twisted around to look across the driveway where nothing felt real; her whole world had suddenly become surreal. She felt as though she'd landed in a different universe and watched almost bemused as Teresa was forcibly led towards one of the police cars – which under the circumstances wasn't at all strange, but the fact that Borys was the one who had hold of her arm and led her towards it, definitely was.

'Okay, Mrs Bailey, you are under arrest, which means that, whether you want to or not, you are going to be taking a seat in the back of my car.' He uttered the words in a soft Scottish accent that rang out almost musically in a song-like pattern. The Ukrainian accent was gone and with a look of smug satisfaction, he pulled open one of the car doors and stooped until he'd firmly pushed Teresa inside, before slamming the door behind her.

Turning, he pushed his shoulders back and, with quick glance in Daisy's direction, he strode to where Olena stood, and with his hand held out, he shook hers firmly and gave her a smile. 'Good job, detective.' He rested a hand against her shoulder in a congratulatory manner. 'It took us a while, but thanks to the tip-off tonight, we eventually got there.'

'We did do a good job, didn't we?' She returned his smile and, sympathetically, she looked across at where Daisy now stood.

Slowly, Daisy pieced the puzzle together. Both Borys and Olena had been undercover, which fully explained the way Olena was always in the room, watching and listening to all that was said, and Borys's reasons for making out that his sister needed to live here. For a while, Daisy looked at them and as she climbed into her car, she heard Olena say, 'It's her I feel sorry for. She didn't have a damn clue what the husband was up to, did she?'

# 36

## SARAH

Looking from the monitor to the staircase and then back again, Sarah felt the air drain out of her body as she scrambled helplessly to click the mouse and turn the video off. She couldn't let Tom know what she'd seen, not when she knew how easily he'd hurt both his wife and his son, two people he'd been supposed to love.

'If he'd hurt her and his son, he sure as hell wouldn't think twice about hurting you...' She gasped, pulling the air back into her body, and tried to calm her heart rate, which was currently racing. She had to think logically but couldn't ignore the fact that Tom was dangerous. He'd happily allowed Grace to lay there; her injuries had been exacerbated by Tom's failure to help, which in Sarah's opinion was indefensible, and now she had no choice but to climb down the same stairs that Grace had fallen down, to reach the front door.

'He pushed her...' she whispered as her mind worked feverishly to look for a weapon. She needed something she could use to defend herself should she need it, and even though the desk was covered in carnage, there was nothing she'd consider useful.

Hastily, she pulled open a drawer and, with her eyes widening in disbelief, she reached out in slow motion as she spotted the small, clear packet. It was just two inches wide and inside were the drugs she felt sure he'd fed her.

'You bastard,' she growled, 'you did drug me...' She picked up the clear packet and, with her breaths coming short and sharp, she stared at the drugs before quickly pushing them into the pocket of the dress, along with a short metal ruler that, if needed, she could use as a weapon.

Sitting on the edge of the chair, Sarah turned the ruler over and over between her fingers and, once again, she stared at the staircase. 'He laughed,' she said through clenched teeth. 'He laughed as she fell and...' With her eyebrows knitted together, she could still visualise the way Tom had grabbed at his son's limp, lifeless body. How he'd cradled him for just a few seconds, and how he'd dispassionately stepped over his wife. He'd left her there, hurt and injured, while he'd walked up the stairs. At first, Sarah had thought he'd been going for help, that he had a phone in the office, but instead, he'd casually walked back down again, carrying the same blue box that she'd spotted outside, right next to the hole where Tom had been digging.

'Sweet mother of God,' Sarah said as she jumped up from her seat and held on to the architrave. 'That's where his son is. He's burying his son...' With her mind skipping from one thing to the next, she realised that the thought of running down the stairs was almost too much. That with her mind still mixed up by the drugs in her system, a part of her didn't care what happened to her and all she really wanted to do was to curl up and into a ball and fall back to sleep.

But a noise downstairs alerted her. A door had been opened and closed, and if she wanted this nightmare to be over, she had no choice but to run for the door.

'Yes, this is Tom Burgess.' Tom held the phone to his ear, but as he did, he dropped the spade and reached for the coal bunker that stood right beside him. He hadn't thought seeing the words 'Seacroft Park' appearing on his screen would come as a shock, but for some reason, it had, and a deep, involuntary tremble had begun deep within him.

'Mr Burgess, I'm afraid to tell you that your wife, she just passed away.' The soft voice at the other end of the phone spoke slowly, with control and a modicum of empathy. They were the words he'd wanted to hear but even though Tom thought he'd prepared himself for this moment, now it had come, he felt scared. The sweat that had been forming on his brow had suddenly turned to ice. The trembling had turned into a shake, which had now taken over his body and shook him in a wild and uncontrollable manner.

Staring upward, and toward a snow-filled sky that would have normally been filled with stars, he felt a moment's remorse. Grace was finally gone, and with his face contorted with emotion, he stepped into the house while trying to listen to what the carer said, although in truth, the words seemed to float straight past him and, like a song that had been played on repeat, he no longer listened.

'If it's any consolation, Mr Burgess, Grace wasn't in pain. She just quietly slipped away in her sleep.' The voice sounded much too young to make a call of this nature, and for a few seconds Tom wondered if he were reading the words from a script. 'I'm afraid the paramedics have been, Mr Burgess; they did try to revive your wife but unfortunately, they couldn't.' He stopped speaking, waited sympathetically for Tom to cut in, but when he didn't, the young man continued. 'If you'd like to see her, Mr Burgess, we can make her presentable.'

'No,' Tom quickly yelped. 'I don't. I don't want to see her, not now, not like that...' He moved to the sink, turned on the tap and tried to conjure up the emotion he thought he ought to be feeling. A part of him thought that he should be sobbing at the pain of losing a loved one. Whereas in reality, it was all he could do to stop himself from cheering. Grace had gone and, very soon, Cole would be gone too. Which made music he wanted to dance to. Their deaths were going to make him rich. He'd have more money than he'd know what to do with and, because of that, he'd be easily able to hold off the bailiffs.

'Mr Burgess, are you sure?'

'Yes, I'm positive,' he muttered, 'I saw her earlier, and even though I did think it was close, it's still... it's still a bit of a shock and...' He swallowed hard and moved slowly through the kitchen and into the living room, where he immediately felt the draft from the front door that stood open. 'I'm so sorry,' he barked, 'but this is all a bit much and I have to go.'

He quickly ended the call, moved to the door and, with the snow still dusting the pavement outside, he homed in on the shape of the tiny footprints that led to his gate and beyond. Footprints leading away from his house that could only be Sarah, who was obviously heading back home, and with the fury of yet another failure building up inside him, he stared at his phone. He had to get to Daisy before Sarah did, and jabbing hurriedly at his screen, he typed his home address and quickly followed it with a short, succinct message.

TOM

Life or Death. Please, come quickly. xx

# 38

## DAISY

Sitting in her car, Daisy puffed up her cheeks, blew out a breath and reached for her bag. The fact that Sarah still hadn't arrived was worrying. When she had checked the tracking app, Sarah had already left the pub and had been on her way. With a sense of dread suddenly overtaking her, Daisy thought about all the water-filled ditches along the lanes that Sarah would have driven down. Not to mention the fact that Tom had been acting so weirdly. Which was the understatement of the year: he'd broken into her house, he'd stolen her mirror and then he'd pretended to be someone else in order that he might date her sister. Like everything else tonight, nothing made sense and, ominously, Daisy clicked on the tracking app again and sighed with relief.

Sarah was home, most probably tucked up in her bed, fast asleep. Daisy realised that tonight at least one of her prayers had been answered. Until the moment she saw the message pop up on her screen.

TOM

Life or Death. Please, come quickly. xx

As she read Tom's message and saw the address he had written, she immediately registered which house it was and how close it was to Sarah's. It was a property that had been recently sold. Another agent had taken the sale and, being just a few hundred yards away from the house their mother had owned, Daisy had felt resentful over the lost commission.

And now, it was the second time that Tom had pulled the life-or-death card in less than a week. The second time he'd fully expected her to run to his aid. But this time, she wasn't as desperate to see him. This time, she felt nothing. Too much had happened, and she felt numb and detached and simply couldn't deal with Tom's issues, not any more.

'You've gone too far,' Daisy whispered to the phone. 'You involved my sister – you involved Sarah – which was a big mistake.'

Leaning back, Daisy felt tears spring to her eyes again. For once, she had to put herself first, she had to find a way to get through all of the commotion that was happening around her and find a way to move forward, although, right now, she had no idea how she would do that.

The one thing she was sure of was that this house, The Willows, wasn't going to be her home. What she did care about was Pipistrelle. The house by the beach with the glorious sunsets. It was her sanctuary, and even though Tom had been there, she wasn't going to stop herself from sheltering within it and watching the waves roll in on the shore.

Looking up, Daisy caught Lindsey's eye and gave her a smile.

'If you're sure you don't need us, Daisy' – she smiled and began to secure the back door of one of the ambulances – 'we'll head back, but hey' – she nodded towards where the police still stood in force – 'do you need to use a phone or anything, before we go?'

Daisy held her phone up in the air. 'It's okay, I've got this. I'm going to give my sister a call...' As if timed to perfection, her phone vibrated, and Sarah's name flashed up on the screen. 'And right on cue, there she is...' Daisy said with a smile as Lindsey climbed into her cab.

'Sarah... thank God, I was just about to call you,' she said as she answered the phone to hear the torrent of words that came from her sister, with nothing left out, along with the sound of her sobbing hysterically.

# 39

## TOM

Pacing up and down the living room, Tom continually looked from his phone to the door. Sarah had left and a part of him was pleased. At least now, there wouldn't be an awkward goodbye. He'd be spared from making the apology he'd been expecting to make for his lack of performance, a blessing that had come in disguise. Now, he could honestly tell Daisy that nothing had happened, that he was devoted to her and that, as Grace had rightly said, no other woman would ever compare.

Checking his phone again, he realised how late it had got, and he stood on the step and glared at each of the houses that stood opposite his, with their small, darkened windows. He hadn't had the chance to meet many of the neighbours already, too much had happened, and Tom wondered if any of the people were watching and whether they knew anything about him at all.

Laughing out loud, Tom realised how none of them would know how easily he'd just buried his son. He'd done it with no ceremony, no priest and no holy ground. And for just a moment, he wondered if that had been his loneliest hour. Or whether Grace's death would cause him more problems. It was a death that would now need a post-mortem, which in itself would bring more questions, and he presumed that because of that, the police would come, that he'd hear their sirens cut into the night – or would he? Would they arrive all guns blazing, or would they come under stealth, quiet and foreboding like an animal, creeping up on its prey?

Holding a hand to his chest, Tom felt his heartbeat quicken, and with his breath held tight, he smiled warmly as he watched Daisy's car come around the corner.

'Tom, what the hell happened, are you okay, what's wrong?'

Watching the way Daisy jumped out of the car, he held out his arms and pulled her towards him.

'I got your message,' she said. 'I came as soon as I could.'

Pressing his body into the curvature of hers, he pulled her in as tightly as he could and with his face buried in the nape of her neck, Tom closed his eyes and took in a deep breath.

'I really needed you,' he said as he sobbed, deep and throatily. 'I can't believe that you came.' Stroking her hair, Tom began to twist it playfully between his fingers. It was something he'd often done in the past, a memory of yesteryear, and with his shoulders heaving sporadically, he felt the grief well up inside him.

'Hey, you should have known I'd come,' Daisy whispered as she took his hand in hers and he watched the way her fingers became intermingled with his. 'I was in the shower when you messaged,' she said, 'but don't worry, I'm here now.' Pausing, she caught his eye, smiled lovingly and eased him back into the house and towards the settee. 'Why don't you tell me what happened and...' She looked over her shoulder, into the kitchen. 'I'm going to make us some tea. It's what people do, isn't it. You know,' she said awkwardly, 'when someone's sad or upset, they make the other some tea.'

'Look, I'm sorry, the kitchen...' Tom jumped up from his seat, began to apologise. 'It's a total mess and I'm going to sort it all out but...' He sat back down and then shuffled to the edge of the settee where he began to pick nervously at the threadbare fabric with his fingers. 'My wife.' He paused, swallowed hard as he quickly realised what he was about to tell her. 'Grace, she died tonight, and I didn't know what I should do...'

As he said the words, he watched the way Daisy froze on the spot. But then, thoughtfully, she picked up the kettle, dropped it into place and flicked on the switch.

'There, that shouldn't be long. Now, do you want to tell me about your wife?' she finally questioned. 'I didn't know that you had one.'

Nervously, Tom walked up behind her and turned her to face him. 'I know, I'm sorry, I should have told you.' Pulling Daisy into his arms, he rocked her gently against him. 'I did mean to tell you, but the accident happened, it happened right after I got back from London, and Grace, I had no choice but for her to live in care. She was at Seacroft Park in one of their upstairs rooms. It was awful. A long, dark corridor that smelt like death. There were barely any windows, but if I'm honest' – he paused, tipped her face towards his – 'it was all she needed. When she went in, we knew she was dying and, ever since, I've known this day would come, I just didn't know when.'

With his arms locked around her like a vice, Tom realised that for once in his life someone had put him first. Daisy had turned up when he needed her the most and with his eyes closed and the tears still streaming down his face, he reached for her, tilted her mouth up to meet his and carefully, as though he were kissing her for the very first time, Tom grazed her mouth with his. 'I didn't know who else to call and...' A loud sob left his lips. 'And I really didn't want to be all alone.'

# 40

# DAISY

Standing in Tom's kitchen, Daisy leaned into the kiss. It was something she'd done at least a thousand times before and for her, she'd always found it easy to kiss Tom without thinking. But today, even though there was a smell in this house that she couldn't identify, she had an agenda, and Daisy had every intention of giving Tom her Oscar-winning performance.

It was a performance that was going to be hard because, in reality, all she felt was a mixture of hatred and repulsion rising up within her. The call she'd had from Sarah had been nothing more than a torrent of words. Filled with expletives. A hysterical recital of all that had happened, with nothing left out. A call that had left Daisy screaming with fury, and after the day and night she'd already lived through, this extra event almost tipped her over the edge of a cliff – and it would have, if only she had one to fall from. Instead, she'd rushed to Sarah's side, knowing that she was hurt, drugged and alone, and with the ferocity growing inside her by the second, nothing else had mattered apart from getting to her sister and making sure she was safe.

After jumping into her car, and taking on board all that Sarah had said, she'd ended the call and had taken a moment to decompress before driving away. Which was when she'd heard a police radio blast out from behind her.

'Yeah, we have three in custody, one deceased. Did anyone call that private ambulance?'

Spinning around in her seat, Daisy had gasped out loud as the officer had given her a sorrowful look, before quickly bowing his head. 'I'm so sorry,' he'd whispered as he turned the radio down to a point where only he could hear it and then, as the van-style ambulance pulled in through the gates, she had seen Cole crumble as another officer told him the news that his father was dead.

Numb with shock and trepidation that this night couldn't possibly get any worse, Daisy had given Cole a final look before she'd driven to Sarah's, and with a determined plan to end this whole messy charade, she'd jumped into a shower, and with the tears streaming down her face, she'd washed away the blood that had still covered her body. As the water had trickled down her back, for what felt like hours, she'd tried to understand how she'd possibly loved two men who, in reality, she hadn't really known. With her heart breaking in two for the life she thought she'd had, she'd wrapped her body in soft white towels and taken the time to dry her body and hair, then after raiding Sarah's wardrobe, she'd lain down with her sister, who was already sleeping, and with her arms wrapped tightly around her, she'd held on to her as though she were the most precious cargo she'd ever carried.

'He'll never hurt you again,' Daisy had promised, profusely. 'I swear to you, no one will ever hurt you again.' It was all she could say but Daisy meant every word, and as Sarah slept her deep, drug-induced sleep, Daisy had retrieved the small packet of pills that Sarah had mentioned and pushed them into her pocket.

Closing her eyes in despair, Daisy now took in the carnage

surrounding her in Tom's kitchen, and for a moment, she could still remember the boy that he'd been. The young, cheeky, innocent teenager who'd doted on every word that she'd said, and with a twinge of regret that things had ended between them in the way that they had, she could no longer imagine a life where Tom would be in it. He wasn't the man she'd thought he would be and her whole body was sickened by the way he spoke of his wife, about the way he'd put her in a room without a window because, in his opinion, a woman who was dying hadn't needed a view.

'Look, why don't you sit down, and I'll make us a nice cup of tea?' She turned away from him, rinsed out two mugs and after fumbling around in the disorganised cupboards she couldn't help but wonder what Teresa would think to this kitchen. The plates were all dirty and piled up on top of others. Food was still smeared across them. Mugs had been used and thrown into the sink, and the water they were in was covered with a thick slick of grease, which immediately made her mind flash back to that night in London and the way she'd been repulsed by the water she'd stood in when she'd climbed out of the taxi. Even that had been cleaner than the water that stood in Tom's sink and, with her face fixed with a permanently glazed look, she made the tea, and with a cautious smile, she passed the mug to him.

# 41

## DAISY

'Where've you been? I woke up and... you were gone.' Sarah was sitting by the fireplace, with hair that had become tussled and roughly tied up in a knot on the top of her head. In place of the dress she'd previously worn, she now wore a pair of navy-blue cotton pyjamas that made her look much younger. Soft lighting lit the room, and the smell of lavender and patchouli oil filled Daisy's senses as she noticed the candle that stood on the fireplace.

'Do you want to tell me where that came from?' Sarah looked at the mirror that Daisy held in her hands and watched with uncertainty as she rested it against the wall, by the door. 'Why is that here?'

'Settle down, Mother,' Daisy joked as she kicked off her shoes and furtively pushed them under the shoe stand with her foot before walking into a living room that was warm and welcoming. Aiming for the corner of the settee, close to the fireplace, Daisy stared into the flames that were licking the back of the stove in colours of orange and blue. A large log lay at their centre, and it already glowed with bright red embers, which told her that Sarah had been up for a while.

'I went to Tom's,' Daisy finally said with a cynical smile. 'His wife died. He messaged me and he asked me to go around, so I did, and while I was there, I retrieved my mirror.'

'Tom had your mirror?'

'He did. He'd broken into my house and stolen it and I wanted it back.' Stretching, Daisy pushed off her coat, leaned forward and, with her fingers, she began to massage some heat back into her toes. 'Tom bought it for me, but that didn't give him the right to steal it back.'

'Wait a minute, do you want to rewind? You went around there, and you did what?' Sarah yelped, her eyes flicking from Daisy to the mirror and back again. 'After what I told you on the phone, you actually went around there? Are you absolutely frigging crazy? Because I'm beginning to wonder.'

Thoughtfully, Daisy reached into her pocket, opened the door on the burner and tossed the packet of pills into the flames. 'I thought I'd help him take a nap,' she said. 'Let him see how it feels.'

'You didn't?' Sarah lifted a hand to her mouth and gasped with laughter. 'Oh my God, Daisy, he's not gonna know what hit him, not if he sees all those things spinning around him, like I did. Jesus Christ, they were evil personified.'

Standing up, Daisy took Sarah's hand in her own, and she held it tightly.

'After what you told me, he has to pay for what he did to his wife and his son. But first, he needs to be taught a big lesson for what he did to you. He needs to know how it feels to be out of control. For someone else to make that decision for him.' She smiled, but this time the smile didn't quite reach her eyes. 'I want to hate him, Sarah, but I can't. So in the morning, I'm going to let you phone the police. I want you to tell them exactly what you saw on that video, but until then...'

With tears pricking her eyes, Daisy knew what she'd done was wrong. That no matter what the reason, drugs were never the answer, and she stood up, walked into the kitchen and picked up the kettle.

'I'm going to make us a drink...' She was going to say that she'd make a nice cup of tea, just like she had at Tom's house, although this time she had no intention of adding the extras.

Pulling the mugs out of the cupboard, Daisy deliberately turned off the light and homed in on where Tom's house stood in the distance with one of the upstairs windows lit up with a bright amber light.

Squinting, Daisy opened the back door and stepped outside. She needed the air, and in her bare feet, she slowly walked around the side of the house on the path. For once, it was nice to walk on something smooth rather than aggregate. The happenings of the day had left her body fuelled with fire and disbelief, and angrily she walked toward the front gate where she stood and watched as the small flakes of snow began to flutter past her.

It was a moment of joy and clarity. 'Everything's changed,' she whispered out loud. 'It's all changed in a way I'd have never imagined.' She blinked repeatedly as she stepped from foot to foot, with the cold seeping in. She was surrounded by the quiet and the darkness, and if she listened really carefully, she could hear the sound of the sea crashing against the shore in the distance. A sound only disturbed by the engine of a single car that turned the corner. And the sight of Tom driving the car made her legs weaken.

# 42

## DAISY

Standing in Pipistrelle's kitchen, Daisy lifted each box on to the worktop in turn. She rummaged through the contents, lifting out the items one by one, and with a thoughtful smile, she placed them back in the drawers where they'd originally come from.

All of the things that they'd taken to The Willows were lost. The investigation would be ongoing for a long time, and even if she could have gone to retrieve her things, she wasn't sure she would have. Instead, she hung the ugly clock Sarah had once bought back up on the wall. The pots and pans were put back in the cupboards, and with a cautious smile, Daisy pulled open the fridge and threw the contents of a small bag of shopping inside without caring which shelf they were on, or whether the fish went next to the vegetables. From now, this was her kitchen, it was her house and no matter who she met in the future, she was adamant that no one was ever going to change that.

Heading back down the corridor to the downstairs bedroom, Daisy smiled as she walked past Sarah at the bottom of the stairs. The night before, they'd decided that Sarah should move in and that sometime later, once they'd both unpacked, they'd sit down with a bottle of wine, and they'd make a nice meal. It was what they deserved and, even though so much had been lost, they felt the need to raise a glass to what they had left.

'Hey,' Sarah sang out as she hit the bottom step with her feet. 'Look what I found.' She lifted the small Echo speaker up in the air and, comically, she headed straight for the kitchen where she plugged it in and gave it an instruction.

'Alexa, tell me something about Bamburgh.'

Daisy laughed. It was a silly request, but one they'd often said in the past, and with her hand on the kettle, she listened as Alexa went through a list of interesting facts.

'Bamburgh Castle is one of the most important archaeological sites in the world.

'It has a museum that houses a collection of extraordinary finds...

'A local Bamburgh man, whose vehicle was involved in a head-on collision last night, has been named as Thomas Burgess. He's been taken to Alnwick Infirmary where he remains in a critical condition...'

# 43

## DAISY

'Tom, are... are you in there?'

With hesitation, Daisy tapped on the door before she walked into the brightly lit room, and immediately saw the hospital bed, with its sterile, pure white sheets. Tentatively, she walked to the window, to where the sight of urban streets stood to one side of her view, open countryside to the other. From here, she couldn't see the waves crashing against the shore, or the seagulls flying above her in the sky, searching for food, and with her breaths being dragged in and out of her body at speed, she pushed at the frame and opened the window. It was all she could do to rid her nostrils of the strong smell of antiseptic, the heavy scent of guilt that clung to her daily.

'I got a call from your doctor. He said you'd spoken, that you'd uttered the words "life or death".' She choked back the tears as she spoke, but they were not tears of sympathy. She was standing in a room that was clean and functional. The adjustable bed with its hard metal rails stood square and central and an uncomfortable visitor's chair stood beside it, with no cushioning for comfort, and already she could feel the numbness that she knew she would get if she sat there for more than an hour.

'Your doctor,' she whimpered, 'I just saw him. He asked me to sign this.' She pulled the paperwork out of her bag – a large, white envelope that didn't look out of place in the room – and without looking directly at him, she dropped it on the table before him. 'It's a power of attorney?' she said in question. 'A document that apparently means that I can control your health and your finances.' She nodded, pressed her lips tightly together, and with the acid rising up in her throat, she gave the paperwork another gentle push. 'I just don't understand, Tom. Why the hell would you want me to do that?'

Pacing for what felt like forever, Daisy listened to the rise and fall of his chest. To the breathing that came from the man that she'd loved, and after a long conversation with Tom's doctor, she knew how quickly his time would come. How soon his injuries would take him. Without a doubt, she felt responsible for the fact that he was here, like this, with so many injuries, and for a few moments she stared at the floor, took short sharp breaths and couldn't find the courage to look directly at him. Yes, she felt guilty but she also felt hatred. Especially when she thought about what he'd done to ruin her family.

Because of his greed and his jealousy, Tom had caused Cole's downfall. Not that he hadn't deserved it; he had. The police had already been making a case; both Borys and Olena had been undercover and watching every move they made. But Tom's call had been the blow that had caused her life to implode. Cole had been arrested and placed on remand. He'd lost everything and, with that, so had she. Her husband was still waiting for a trial date and his mother, Teresa, as an accessory, had been given a similar fate. According to the law, they were both deemed to be too dangerous for release, and according to Cole's solicitor, the evidence against them had been more than damning.

Along with Sarah, Daisy had moved back into her house. To the home she'd wanted to go back to above anything else. But everything had changed. Sarah wasn't the same. Since the night she'd been drugged, she'd had constant nightmares. She'd spent hours screaming out in her sleep, and Daisy spent most of her nights doing all she could to show her some comfort. Which in itself was something she hoped that time would heal. But the house was different. It no longer felt like the sanctuary she'd craved, and even though she'd done all she could to turn it back into a home, she could no longer sit there and watch the sunset with a melancholy gaze. The magic had been lost, at least for now.

And now, just a few weeks later and much to Sarah's annoyance, Daisy had dropped everything and rushed to Tom's side. For a few uncomfortable seconds, she walked to his bedside and moved her fingers slowly across the pale freckled skin that covered the back of Tom's hand. His skin was thin and almost transparent, and with memories of the life they'd once had flashing before her, she could feel the emotion threatening to rise in her throat. She tried to focus on why she'd come here and thought of her sister, who Tom had drugged and practically kidnapped. It was an act she could never forgive him for, and out of revenge, she'd taken matters into her own stupid hands. She'd fed him the same formidable drugs. An act she'd always regret. Two wrongs didn't make a right. But in her defence, she couldn't possibly have foreseen the events that had followed.

And now, with her lips pressed tightly together, Daisy could feel the way the acid rose in her throat. Nervously, she looked from Tom to the door and she considered walking away, but then she thought about the last time he'd sent her a life-or-death message. The night when Tom's poor, defenceless wife had died and a night when he'd taken his son into the garden and buried him in a patch of cold, unconsecrated ground. All totally unforgivable.

Taking hold of his hand, with her whole body shaking with fear, Daisy tried to remember the good times they'd shared. The fun they'd had, the laughter and the passion that had passed between them and how, somewhere in the middle of it all, they'd created a child of their own. A baby that they'd also managed to lose, and with thoughts of how her life might have turned out, Daisy began to grieve for what she'd lost. But then with the realisation of what she was doing, and as though his hands were as hot as lava, she dropped them and took a giant step backward.

Snatching at the documents, Daisy moved back to the window and closed her eyes. For a moment she felt claustrophobic, and with her mind spinning with a million different confusing thoughts, she pressed her face into the small space between the frame and the sill and, desperate for air, she breathed in deeply.

'Daisy,' Tom whispered, his voice deep and throaty. 'Please.' He gave her a distinct nod of his head. 'Please, look after me.'

Twelve years ago, she'd have probably done what he asked; she'd have sat here, held his hand and she'd have told him she cared. But now, she couldn't. No matter how much history they'd shared, it was all a long time ago, and with a stride that was now bold and confident, she lifted her head in the air and walked straight to the door, to complete her escape.

'Daisy, don't go. You promised, if it were life or death, you'd be here and... I need you to look after me.' There was a faint whimper to his voice that almost broke her. For a split-second she considered a change of heart, but too much had happened since that one-night stand they'd shared.

'Tom, it isn't for me to do that, I—' She wanted to admit to him what she'd done, how she'd fed him the drugs and how, if it hadn't been for her actions, none of this would have happened. But she couldn't and with tears scalding her face, she kept her gaze on the door, the finger plate and the stainless-steel handle that she was desperate to hold.

'I didn't drink it.'

'What?'

'The tea... I didn't...' he said breathlessly. 'I didn't drink it and... it wasn't your fault.'

Confused, Daisy closed her eyes. Finally, the truth had come out and deep inside her, the relief had been lifted off of her shoulders. The pressure had gone, and the guilt had gone with it, but the hatred remained. Tom had drugged her sister. Which left her with only one question.

'The drugs,' she probed. 'Is that what you did to me too? In London, you drugged me?'

Waiting, Daisy saw the immediate look of guilt cross his face. The look of betrayal and a truth she knew that he'd never admit. But the look told her all, and instead of waiting for him to make up an answer, Daisy lifted her hand, held it up and palm forward. 'Don't. Please don't lie and please don't make up any excuses; it won't change any of this, or what happened, will it?'

Choking back the tears, Daisy rested a hand on the door handle and pressed it down firmly. Everything she'd thought about that night had been nothing more than a lie. The one-night stand that had thrown her life into chaos had caused her to question every single part of a life that hadn't been perfect, but it had been a life she had wanted. A life she'd chosen. But being unfaithful had changed everything and the guilt of it had torn her apart.

'At least I know the truth. I know that you drugged me. I know that I didn't fall into your bed by choice and that because I didn't come running back, you went after my sister, and for that alone, I would have never forgiven you.' She paused, thoughtfully, and furrowed her brow. 'And I'm sorry that I tried to take my revenge, that I made myself as bad as you were, but at the time you deserved it.'

'I didn't mean to hurt you—' He took in a sharp breath and Daisy saw the tormented look that filled his eyes, and the desperation that sat there. 'I just wanted to love you.'

'Don't you dare, Tom. Please don't go there because, do you know what? You're going to get your wish, and I'm going to do what you asked me to do.'

'You'll look after me?'

It was a simple question that got a simple nod for an answer, and for a good few minutes she stared up at the ceiling. Tom had asked her to take care of him, he'd asked his doctor to put the paperwork in place, and with a single tear dropping down her cheek, Daisy lowered her eyes as she turned and took a step back towards him.

'Tom, give me a few minutes.' She lifted the envelope up in the air. 'This, this is the paperwork you asked me to sign, and do you know what?' Without warning her legs began to fail her, the floor was moving beneath her feet, and with all of her effort, she moved backwards and, gripping the handle for support, she leaned heavily against the hospital door in the hope that Tom hadn't noticed. 'I'm going to sign it.'

Turning, Daisy moved her gaze to the window where the darkness had begun to pull in. Dusk was upon them and the bright lights of the town beyond had begun to come on, giving them the most beautiful view, and for a moment Daisy remembered the window she'd stared out of in Tom's kitchen and the conversation they'd had on the night his wife had died. She could still hear the venomous way he'd spoken. The cold and brutal way he'd reacted, and Daisy had wondered if she'd ever really known him at all. And now she looked at him with a gaze that could have easily penetrated steel, and with her eyes narrowing with hatred, Daisy took in a long, deep breath.

'Once I've signed it, Tom,' she continued, 'I'm going to do what I've promised and I'm going to make a quick phone call.' She nodded by way of affirmation and smiled selflessly. 'I'm going to call Seacroft Park because, do you know what, Tom, I remember you once telling me, they have some nice upstairs rooms...'

\* \* \*

## MORE FROM L.H. STACEY

The next breathlessly gripping psychological thriller from L.H. Stacey is available to order now here:
https://mybook.to/StaceyNewBackAd

# ACKNOWLEDGEMENTS

This was a story I really wanted to tell, and it all began after I went to a house where the occupants seemed to have everything they could ever want. This house was grand in scale, probably had more bedrooms than anyone could ever sleep in. There were polished marble floors, a wine cellar that was sunk into the hallway floor, a pool table that had probably never been used, a swimming pool that was kept at temperature just in case and a glass-fronted garage that housed at least twenty cars, most of which would never be driven, but they were on show for all of their friends and family to see.

It was probably the most beautiful house I've ever seen, certainly the most luxurious. But then, I began thinking. If I had the chance, would I really want to live there? Would I want to live in a house in the middle of nowhere? Would I feel safe if I were in it alone? And would I use all of its facilities (well maybe I would if I didn't work for a living) but seriously, I couldn't imagine a life in those shoes because I couldn't work out whether or not the occupants were really happy. Yes, they had every single thing they needed... but did they have the life they wanted? Or did they wish for something simpler, somewhere cosier, somewhere more like a home than a castle?

I think in life we always wonder what it's like to live the high life, but realistically, after the initial excitement wore off... My question to you is: would you really want it?

While writing this story, I lost my wonderful sister-in-law Jayne, who this book is dedicated to. Following her diagnosis, she truly showed us all what bravery and courage looked like. We miss her daily, minute by minute, but she was very much a lady who got things done and she fully expected others to do the same. So, I wrote this book for her during a time when I found writing at its most difficult. Jayne was one of my biggest supporters, she was the first person to tell me to go for my dreams. She'd always championed my work and had proudly told everyone she met about my stories, and I wanted to take this opportunity to thank her for the support she gave me.

I'd also like to acknowledge Sarah Kingsnorth, who won a competition to be named in this story. Sarah is one of the administration team of the Facebook group The Friendly Book Community. She, along with Hazel, Marie, Louise and Jessica, have unwaveringly supported the author community with their constant book chat, recommendations and reviews and I'd like to thank you all for what you do – you're all amazing and it was so good to meet some of you this year at our annual afternoon tea in York.

From day one I've had the best support from our blogger community, ladies who quickly became friends and supporters.

So, a big thank you goes to:

Babs Wilkie https://bookescapes.home.blog

Anne Williams https://beinganne.com

Vikki Wakeham https://littlemissbooklover87.wordpress.com

And last but not least, to the TikTok duo, mother and daughter team, Sarah and Emily of @therookiebookies. They make the most amazing videos and not only are they very supportive, but they're also very funny and a pleasure to watch.

Take a look at their blogs, reviews and TikToks; every one of these ladies is 100% amazing.

To friends, AnneMarie Brear, Rachel Dove, Jane Lacey Crane, Victoria Howard, Jane Lovering, Chrissie Bradshaw, Kathy Kilner and Milly Johnson... I have no idea how I'd get the books written without your constant advice.

Also, to friend and author Michael Fowler for the constant information he gives me on all things to do with police procedural. Check out his books, they're all amazing. And to paramedic friend Lindsey Ann Cant, who gave me some advice on procedures when attending a medical emergency.

As always, I'd like to thank my hero at home, husband, Haydn, for all that he does. If it wasn't for your constant support, your love and the hours you spend looking after both myself and our amazing puppy, Barney, I couldn't create these books.

Huge thanks go to my amazing editor, Emily Ruston, who is always supportive. During this year, she's been unbelievably patient with me and has given me all the time I've needed to write this story, which at times I wasn't sure I could finish. Also to fellow copyeditor, Debra Newhouse and proofreader, Helen Woodhouse, who have both worked tirelessly to make this book the best it can be.

I also feel incredibly fortunate to work with my publisher, Boldwood Books. Everyone in the team at Boldwood is amazing. They all work incredibly hard, and I feel more than privileged to work with you all. xx Thank you xx

And finally, to you – to my reader.

Without you, I'd have no reason to write, so I'd like to personally thank you for buying this book. I really hope you love Daisy's story, along with that of her sister, Sarah, and her former fiancé, Tom, all of which play the main characters. I think you'll find that they have quite a story to tell, with a few twists that I'm hoping you won't spot coming.

Like all authors, I'd love to know what you thought to this

story, and I'd be more than delighted if you could possibly take a few moments to leave a review.

Much love

Lynda x

# ABOUT THE AUTHOR

**L. H. Stacey** is the bestselling psychological suspense author of over seven novels. Alongside her writing she is a full-time sales director for an office furniture company and has been a nurse, an emergency first response instructor and a PADI Staff Instructor. She lives near Doncaster with her husband.

Download your exclusive bonus content from L.H. Stacey here:

Visit L.H. Stacey's website: https://lyndastacey2912.wordpress.com/

Follow L.H. Stacey on social media:

f facebook.com/LHStaceyauthor

X x.com/Lyndastacey

O instagram.com/lynda.stacey

BB bookbub.com/authors/lynda-stacey

# ABOUT THE AUTHOR

# ALSO BY L.H. STACEY

# Boldwood

Boldwood Books is an award-winning fiction publishing company seeking out the best stories from around the world.

**Find out more at www.boldwoodbooks.com**

Join our reader community for brilliant books, competitions and offers!

**Follow us**
**@BoldwoodBooks**
**@TheBoldBookClub**

**Sign up to our weekly deals newsletter**

https://bit.ly/BoldwoodBNewsletter